WILDFIRE GRIFFIN

FIRE & RESCUE SHIFTERS: WILDFIRE BOOK 1

ZOE CHANT

CHAPTER 1

The bolt of lightning came, without warning, out of a clear blue sky, straight into the heart of a dry, dead pine. With a sound like a cannon, the towering tree blew apart in a cloud of flaming splinters.

That's impossible.

For a long moment, Edith simply stared down at the thin plume of smoke rising from the distant trunk. She'd been outside cleaning the windows of her fire lookout tower, and had happened to be glancing straight at that part of the forest at the moment of impact. Even with the after-image of the dazzling flash still dancing on her retinas, she couldn't believe what she'd witnessed.

She knew the weather in these mountains better than the rhythms of her own body. There wasn't a cloud in the vast Montana sky; not a hint of electric ozone in the air. The lightning bolt had simply materialized out of nowhere, as though the poor tree had suddenly offended some petulant god.

Heart hammering, she dashed back inside her tiny dwelling. The tower's firefinder stood on a plinth in the precise middle of the room —a circular map, with a mechanism for triangulating the precise location of any fire visible outside the windows.

She hunched over the device, swinging the viewfinder around until it was precisely lined up with the smoke rising outside the window. Locking the angle, she triple-checked the reading before walking her fingers across the firefinder's map to the coordinates where the fire must be.

Only a mile away. Edith relaxed a little. Her fire tower was smack in the middle of nowhere, miles from any popular hiking trails. There wouldn't be any campers in the affected part of the forest. No one would be at risk.

No one, she belatedly realized, except her.

"It's okay," Edith said out loud. She always fell into the habit of talking to herself during the long, lonely months of fire season. "Everything's still wet from spring. Even if it does catch, it won't burn fast."

Nonetheless, one hand started tapping nervously against her thigh. She focused on the familiar rhythm, using it to shut out the rising clamor of anxiety. With her other hand, she fumbled for the radio.

She had to wait for five agonizing minutes, repeating her call sign over and over, before someone responded. "Base here, Officer Warren on duty. Edith, this had better be important."

The deviation from protocol threw her. Words jammed in her throat. Of course it was important—why would she call if it wasn't?

Warren muttered a curse as she sat in frozen confusion. "Edith, I don't have time for you today. *Some* of us have actual work to do."

Warren had never bothered to hide his opinion of manned fire lookout towers—archaic, primitive systems that served no purpose in today's modern world of satellite surveillance and reconnaissance drones. She'd once overheard him refer to her as "that charity case in Tower Thirteen."

Edith took a deep breath, forcing her chin up. She *wasn't* a charity case. The work she did was real, not some made-up position thinly disguising a government handout for people who couldn't cope with regular jobs.

"I've got eyes on rising smoke near Tower Thirteen, Base." With effort, she managed to keep her voice smooth and calm. "A lightning strike. The exact coordinates are—"

"Lightning?" he interrupted her. "Are you kidding me? This is a hell of a time to suddenly start trying out practical jokes, Edith."

Her shoulders tightened at the barely-restrained irritation in his voice, obvious even to her. She'd never known how to defuse his simmering hostility at the best of times. Her free hand beat harder, faster, trying to push back panic.

"Negative, Base," she said, hoping that formality would magically make him believe her. "I personally witnessed the lightning strike the snag. The fire is well on its way to becoming established."

She heard computer keys tapping. "Edith, meteorology shows nothing but sunny skies in your area. Lightning is only formed by thunderclouds. There aren't any clouds near you. Are you sure you aren't looking at some mist?"

He sounded like he was talking to a five-year-old. Edith gritted her teeth. She was tiresomely familiar with that particular condescending tone. She was autistic, not incompetent.

"Base, I'm a qualified firefighter. I know smoke when I see it. The wildfire is small at the moment, but we need to get a team out here before it becomes a problem."

Edith prayed that he *had* a team to send. It was only early June, a week before the official start of fire season. Most of the smoke-jumpers and wilderness firefighters would still be scattered across America, at home with their families or relaxing on vacation. *She might hate every minute of off-season, and return to her remote outpost as early as she was allowed, but she knew she was an anomaly.*

Let's hope someone else started work early too.

Warren blew out his breath as though she had personally started the fire just to annoy him. "It costs money to deploy firefighters, you know. I'm going to need additional confirmation before I dispatch anyone. Hold on."

If it had been any other fire watcher, Edith suspected he would already have been scrambling a plane of smokejumpers. The nervous twitching of her hand spread through her body and down her leg. She

3

stared out the window, the toe of her workboot drumming against the worn wooden floorboards. The wind was definitely blowing the plume of smoke straight in her direction.

The phone crackled against her ear. "It's your lucky day. I've got a hotshot out of Thunder Mountain who's willing to swing by and take a look. He says he can get his squad to you within the hour."

Edith blinked. "That fast?"

That couldn't be right. Hotshots were ground crew—they didn't parachute in like smokejumpers did. Either the hotshot had just happened to decide to picnic right on her doorstep, or he was being wildly optimistic about how fast he could reach her.

"That's what he says. Apparently they just happened to be camping in your area. Sit tight until he arrives to assess the situation." A sigh gusted out of the phone. "And don't call again unless you're actually on fire, understand? We're busy setting up the new drone system, and I don't have time for your interruptions."

The phone went dead before she could answer. Biting her lip, she glanced out the window at the smoke. Was it thicker than it had been two minutes ago?

"It'll be okay," she whispered under her breath. "It's not dry enough to burn fast. There's plenty of time."

As if in answer, a *second* bolt of lightning struck out of nowhere, followed immediately by a deafening crack of thunder. Edith stifled a shriek, reflexively covering her head as a tree blew apart barely a hundred yards away. A swirl of burning leaves pinged like gunshots off the tower's wide windows, even though her lookout platform was twenty feet off the ground.

Edith cautiously raised her head, peeking over the edge of the window. From her vantage point in the tower, she had an excellent view of the nearest lightning-struck tree. The dead snag was burning fiercely, but fortunately it wasn't close enough to any other trees for the fire to spread through the canopy. Instead, it was crawling through the undergrowth, chewing up fallen branches and shrubs.

She started to reach for the phone, but stopped. Warren had been

4

very clear. And even if she did disobey his order and call anyway…he probably wouldn't believe her.

She was on her own.

"You're always on your own. This is no different." She pressed the heels of her hands to her forehead, trying to squeeze her thoughts into focus. "You can do this. Remember. Air, fuel, heat."

She'd learned about the fire triangle years ago, when she'd still been chasing impossible dreams. Just recalling those words it now brought back a torrent of acute sensory memories—the chafe of her uniform collar, the taste of campfire smoke, gnawing shame and black loneliness.

She flinched, but there was no time to dwell on old hurts now. Pushing back the unwanted emotions, she focused on her training. The classroom, muggy and filled with sweating bodies; the teeth-clenching screech of chalk over blackboard as the instructor sketched trees, flames, lines…

Air, fuel, heat. Those were the three things a fire needed to burn. To put one out, you had to remove one of them. The fire was already too big to smother by any means at her disposal, so she couldn't remove the air. She didn't have a convenient fire engine to hose down the fire to remove the heat.

The only thing she could take away was the fuel.

Her forestry tools were neatly arrayed on hooks by the door. She grabbed her axe and shovel, the well-worn handles familiar and comforting in her sweaty hands.

The instant she stepped outside, bitter smoke slapped her in the face. Coughing, she raced down the rickety stairs as fast as she dared.

Her tower was built on the top of the ridgeline, the thick wooden pillars sunk deep into solid rock. She fervently blessed whoever had picked the site; the stony outcrop made a natural break in the forest, so there weren't any mature trees within thirty feet. But there were still tough grasses and wiry bushes growing in the thin soil. A few scattered patches were already smoldering where burning leaves had landed.

Remove the air.

Dropping her axe, she beat out the small fires with the flat of her shovel before they had a chance to spread any further. She dumped dirt onto the smoking patches to make sure they wouldn't relight as soon as her back was turned. These tiny blazing patches were just scouts, thrown out by the main body of the fire. She could hear the hungry crackle getting closer. It would eat her alive before she could smother even a tiny fraction of it.

Remove the fuel.

She sank her shovel into the rocky soil. Tough matted roots resisted the blade, but she drove through them with the strength of sheer desperation. Turning the soil over, she dug again, and again, and again. With every thrust of her shovel, she extended the shallow trench. Creating a line.

Not just a line—a fireline.

Fire couldn't jump across bare earth. Even the fiercest flames could be stopped by a wide enough break. And for a small blaze, you only needed a few feet...

Sweat stuck her shirt to her back. She dug frantically, switching to the axe to hack at the tougher roots. She wished she had a proper Pulaski, a kind of hybrid half-hoe, half-axe tool that would have made short work of the hard ground. But that was specialist equipment, only carried by real firefighters.

She did the best she could with what she had, scraping with the side of her shovel to make sure she hadn't left any bits of plant that the fire could use as fuel. Her shoulders and arms burned from the repetitive movements.

Cut, dig, scrape. White light flashed with a deafening *crack*, but Edith didn't glance up. No time to worry about further lightning strikes now, no attention to spare for the growing orange glow flickering through the trees.

Cut, dig, scrape. Everything else fell away. No thoughts in her head, no sense of self. In all the world, there was just the shovel, the axe, and the ever-growing fireline. Cut, dig, scrape. Dig, cut-

An agonized scream split the air.

Edith very nearly thrust her shovel through her own foot. Her hyperfocus shredded like tissue paper. The whole world came roaring back, flooding into her eyes and ears and nose. Flickering light and hissing crackle and bitter smoke blurred into a sensory tsunami that swept away breath and sense. The terrified shriek voiced her own confusion and panic so perfectly that for a dizzying moment she thought that *she* was the source of the sound.

Black spots danced in front of her eyes. Edith sucked in a great, gasping breath. The screams continued on, growing higher pitched and more desperate.

She grabbed onto that panicked cry like clutching a lifeline, focusing on it through the swirling chaos. Someone was in trouble. Someone needed help.

"I'm coming!" she shouted as loudly as she could. "Hold on!"

Casting the shovel aside, she plunged into the forest. Immediately billows of smoke surrounded her, thrusting bitter fingers down her throat. Coughing, she pulled her shirt up over her mouth as best she could as she ran.

Orange light glowed balefully through the thick, choking clouds. Flames ran like water between the tree trunks, gobbling up the under-brush. Most of the flames were only knee-high, but here and there patches leapt higher, the fire greedily feasting on old, dry fallen branches.

Edith shied away as a sudden gust of wind fanned the fire, making it roar up higher. A tangle of brambles went up like a firework, spattering her with sparks. The scream came again, very close now.

"Where are you?" Straining to see through the stinging smoke, Edith caught a glimpse of movement through the flames. "Follow my voice, I'll get you to safety!"

Another swirling flurry of wind swept through the tree trunks. For a moment, the smoke parted like curtains drawing back.

Not a person—a snowshoe hare, trapped in a closing ring of fire. It dashed in tight, spinning dashes, all the while shrieking that thin, panicked cry. Edith had never heard an animal make such a human sound.

She couldn't let the poor bunny burn. Holding her breath, she leaped as high as she could over the hissing flames. Heat scorched her ankles, but she landed safely on the other side.

The hare froze, staring at her. Fire reflected in its wide, black eyes.

There wasn't time to be gentle. Fast as a snake, Edith grabbed the animal. She wasn't sure whether it recognized she was trying to help, or was just paralyzed by terror, but in any event it hung limp in her arms, as docile as if it was stuffed. The hummingbird-fast thrum of its heart beat against her own chest.

Wind whipped smoke into her eyes. The fire roared as if angry to have been cheated of its prey. She plunged through them, hunched over the hare to shield it from the fierce heat. Then she was running, faster than she ever had in her life, back toward the safety of her tower.

The fire pursued her. The wind howled, abruptly storm-gale strong, fanning the wildfire's wrath. Flames snapped at Edith's heels like a pack of hunting dogs.

She broke from the forest barely ahead of the rising inferno. Still clutching the hare, she hurdled her fireline. It seemed a ludicrous defense now, no more protection than a line drawn in the dirt by a kid with a stick. The fire roared toward it like the tide sweeping down on a sandcastle—

And stopped.

Shaking, sweat-stained, Edith watched the fire like a hawk, every muscle tense. Though the flames spread like—well, like wildfire— through the dry scrubby grass on the far side of her line, the narrow trench held it from going any further. The wind tried to whip the flames onward, but the embers fell futilely onto the bare earth. No matter how the fire strained, it couldn't reach her.

Just as she started to breath easier, a hammer-blow of wind hit her. Caught off-guard, she staggered, disoriented by the sudden screaming gale. Vicious, swirling gusts clawed at her from every direction, nearly tearing the hare from her grasp. It was as if she'd been caught in the downwash from a helicopter.

Edith squinted upward through the smoke—but there was nothing there. Yet though her eyes searched the sky futilely, her every other sense screamed at her that *something* was hovering over her.

Something vast.

Something *angry*.

An ancient, instinctive terror gripped her. The wind was full of the sound of monstrous wings. She broke and ran, scurrying like a mouse before a hawk.

She raced up the stairs to her tower so fast her feet barely touched the wooden treads. And then she was inside, dropping the hare in her haste to slam the door shut behind her, sliding the bolts home.

Wind howled around the tower, rattling the windows. Some storm-tossed piece of debris struck one of the wide glass panes with enough force to leave a star-shaped crack. Heart in her mouth, she tore around the room, fastening all the interior storm shutters.

Her hands beat against her thighs with agitation. She clenched her fists, trying to get a grip on herself. It was just her hypersensitivity that made the wind sound like vast claws scraping at the shingled roof. Just her atypical brain wiring, generating invisible monsters out of the storm of sensory overload. There wasn't really anything out there, trying to get in—

A blinding flash of white light made her shriek, dropping to the floor and covering her head with her hands. The wooden support pillars groaned as the sturdy platform lurched sickeningly.

Lightning, Edith realized, her ears ringing. It must have been a direct strike on the tower, but fortunately the lightning rod on the roof seemed to have done its job, earthing the strike safely. Nonetheless, her hair snapped with static, and sparks showered from the radio equipment. No chance of calling for help now...even if anyone would have believed her.

Edith squeezed her eyes tight shut, clamping her hands over her ears and rocking back and forth. *Just a storm. Just a thunderstorm. Not a monster. Monsters aren't real...*

Something soft and wet brushed against the back of her hand. Edith screamed, recoiling so hard she fell flat on her butt. The hare leaped away from her flailing arms, dashing back to the far side of the room. It fixed her with black button eyes, quivering.

"Oh," Edith gasped. "Sorry."

Somehow, it was easier to be brave when there was someone to be brave for—even if it was just an animal. She took a gulping breath, trying to get herself back under control. Her entire body felt as though it was filled with bees, but she made herself hold still. She didn't want to terrify the poor creature any further.

"It's okay," she said, voice shaking. "It's just a storm. Everything's going to be okay."

The hare's shivering stilled. One ear slowly cocked forward, followed by the other. Its tiny tongue darted out, licking at its muzzle. Tentatively, it crept forward, never taking its eyes off her.

"That's it," Edith said, focusing on the animal in a desperate attempt to ignore the storm screaming all around. "It's okay, little guy. We're safe here."

A strange red light glittered deep in its eyes, like reflected flames. Its lips wrinkled back, exposing teeth as sharp as chisels. It was a peculiarly predatory gesture. If she hadn't known better, she would have called it a snarl.

Then it leaped for her throat.

CHAPTER 2

*R*ory MacCormick stared out the windscreen of the hotshot crew truck at the thick plume of smoke billowing from the crest of the mountain.

In the incident description, the dispatcher had made it sound like some hysterical firewatcher had mistaken morning mist for smoke. From the man's weary, annoyed tone, he clearly hadn't thought it could be anything serious.

"I am going to call that stuck-up, self-important, incompetent excuse of a dispatcher," Rory growled, "and make him eat his own radio."

"No idle threat, coming from you," Blaise murmured. She kept her eyes on the road, handling the twisting mountain track with smooth skill. "Looks like we'll be getting some action rather sooner than anticipated."

Rory grimaced. He glanced in the rear view mirror at the rest of the squad. Callum was studying the rising smoke with his usual cool, unreadable detachment. No worries there; Cal was a veteran fire-fighter, even if most of his experience had been on an engine crew rather than out here in the wilderness.

Joe and Wystan were another matter. The two rookies pressed

against the other window, broad shoulders wedged against each other as they stared in open fascination at the orange glow glimmering through the trees. It was the first time either of them had seen a real wildfire.

Rory looked back at Blaise, pitching his voice low. "How fast is it spreading?"

Her brown eyes went abstracted for a moment, looking at something that only she could see. Her lips compressed into a thin, worried line. "Faster than it should, given the conditions. I don't like it."

Rory didn't have Blaise's special talents, but he felt the same way. Years fighting wildfires across America had taught him to listen to his instincts, and right now every one of them was screaming at him. It should have been too wet, too early in the season, for the forest to catch so easily. Something wasn't right.

He drummed his fingertips on the dash, staring unhappily at the smoke column. It was noticeably thicker than it had been just a few minutes ago.

It was too risky. If he'd had the entire Thunder Mountain Hotshot crew with him, he wouldn't have hesitated to go in…but he only had his own squad. And nearly half of his firefighters were untested, rookies. He couldn't put his friends in danger.

"We're not equipped for this." Rory reached for the satellite phone on the dashboard. "I'm going to call the control center. See if there's anyone else in the area."

"There isn't," Callum said with calm certainty.

Joe sang a few short, staccato notes that sounded like a snatch of Vivaldi and was actually a particularly vile curse in sea dragon language. He switched back to English. "You sure there's no one else we can foist this on, Cal?"

Callum gave him a flat stare, not bothering to dignify the question with an answer. Pegasus shifters had the power to locate people, and Cal was more sensitive than most. If he said there wasn't anyone around, there really wasn't.

Joe slumped down in his seat, crossing his arms. "We're not even meant to be on the clock yet. This was supposed to be our last farewell to freedom, before we spend an entire summer choking on our own sweat. Can't we have one weekend of beer and bonding without something spontaneously igniting?"

"You're the one who wanted this particular mountain for our camping trip," Wystan observed mildly. "You were very insistent, as I recall."

"Yeah, well," Joe muttered, sinking even lower. "That's me. Fate's bitch."

"Well, fortunately we're here." Blaise shifted up a gear, flooring the accelerator. "And we're the only crew that's here, so we're going to have to handle it. We may not have fought a live fire together before, but we've trained for this."

"Right." Wystan leaned forward, bracing himself between the two front seats as the truck bounced over the rutted road. "Trust us, Rory. This is what you recruited us to do, after all."

Rory blew out his breath. "I don't like taking you all into an unknown situation."

Blaise's hands tightened on the steering wheel, knuckles whitening. "Let's not tiptoe around it. You mean you don't like taking *me* into an unknown situation."

An uncomfortable silence fell. Joe opened his mouth, then shut it again. Wystan made a vague, embarrassed gesture that could have signaled either agreement or denial. Callum was still studiously ignoring the rest of them, focused only on the distant fire.

"No, I don't like it." Rory didn't try to hide his honest concern. "This could be a big one, Blaise. You going to be all right?"

"If I'm not," she said tightly, never taking her eyes off the road, "I'll tell you."

He'd known her long enough to know it would be futile to argue. Blaise was even more stubborn than her father. All Rory could do was privately vow to keep an eye on her.

Anyway, he still had his last team member to check up on. Rory opened his mind, feeling down the pack bond.

Fenrir? he sent telepathically. *You keeping up?*

Birdcat the one not keeping up. Fenrir's mental tone was faint. Rory had an impression of panting breath and burning muscles, the hell-hound stretching himself to his full speed. *Metal man-box is slow. Am running ahead of the pack, scouting out the prey.*

"Rory." Callum's terse voice broke Rory's concentration. The pegasus shifter was staring at the smoke column with even more intensity, his auburn eyebrows drawn down. "Look."

Rory narrowed his eyes, focusing. Even when he wasn't shifted, his vision was far better than an ordinary human's; the distant smudge resolved into pin-sharp detail. He could make out a tall, narrow structure built on the very top of the ridge, a little distance from the edge of the forest. He didn't think the building was on fire itself yet, but thick black curtains of smoke curled around it.

Something about the way the smoke was moving struck him as odd. Even though it was a still, calm day down where they were, the top of the mountain seemed to be whipped by a storm. The smoke eddied in tight swirls, as though buffeted by cyclone winds.

For a split second, he saw something moving through the smog.

A dark, jagged shape…like the edge of a vast wing.

"Something's up there," Callum said.

Rory's eyes burned. He didn't dare blink. "I see it."

"Oh, come on," Joe said. "You can't possibly see anything at this distance. It would have to be the size of a dragon."

"No." Callum's emotionless voice was even flatter than normal. "Bigger."

"Stop the car," Rory said to Blaise.

They'd grown up together; she knew exactly what he was thinking, and *he* knew exactly how much she didn't like it. "Rory, don't be an idiot."

Rory was already unbuckling his seat belt. "All of you, stay here," he said, simultaneously sending the words telepathically so that Fenrir would hear too. "Don't come any closer until I give the all clear."

"Are you out of your mind?" Joe said. He struggled to free himself from his own harness, elbowing the other two in the ribs. "Of course we're coming with you. Wys, you go with Rory. I'll ride Cal."

Callum did not look thrilled by this prospect.

"No," Rory said firmly. "This isn't up for debate. I'm going alone."

"Rory, you can't," Wystan said, catching his arm. "Think. You hammered that point into us yourself, during training. Basic protocol, right? No one *ever* goes in alone. This is no different to a regular fire situation."

"We're a team, Rory." Blaise hadn't slowed down at all. "We stick together."

Pack hunts with the alpha, Fenrir put in. *Otherwise no pack. Just lone wolves running in the same direction.*

Rory clenched his jaw in frustration. He didn't have *time* for arguments or explanations. He hated having to do this, but his squad left him no choice.

"I said, *stop the car.*" Alpha power filled the command.

The truck fishtailed as Blaise involuntarily stomped on the brake. Yelped curses came from the back seat.

Even before the car slewed to a halt, Rory was opening the door. He leaned down to haul his gear out from under his seat. He was glad he was already wearing his turn outs—the fire resistant fabric wouldn't do much to stop anything paranormal, but it would protect him from the wildfire itself.

"*Stay here,*" he ordered, still using the alpha voice. "*Don't move.*"

All four of them froze in position. A telepathic whine came down the pack bond. None of them could speak, held by his command, but their eyes betrayed their furious resentment.

Rory bit down on an apology. Instead, he jumped down from the truck. He'd soothe his squad's ruffled feathers—and fur—later.

Right now, he had to protect them. Whether they liked it or not.

Even at this distance, he could smell the smoke from the wildfire. Adrenaline surged through him at the familiar, bitter taste.

Turning his face to the sky, he gave himself up to his griffin.

His beast surged up from his soul, eager as ever to be released. Golden fur wrapped round him, his body shifting smoothly into his other form. With a single leap, he launched himself into the air.

Acrid smoke blew into his beak. His transparent second eyelids— just like an eagle's—flicked automatically across to protect his sensitive eyes. He searched through the dark haze surrounding the lookout tower.

There!

He could make out strange, bright flickers in the swirling smog, like sparks of electricity crawling through a thundercloud. They illuminated a black-on-black shape, a darker shadow in the midst of the smoke. A winged silhouette, far larger than Rory's own size.

It hovered like a vast bird of prey over a small figure on the ground. It was hard to tell from this distance, but Rory thought it was a woman, running hunched over as though carrying something.

From the way she never glanced up at the looming monster, he suspected that she couldn't see it. Many supernatural creatures—including himself—were invisible to normal human sight. But some deep instinct must have told her that she was in danger. She was sprinting flat-out for the safety of the lookout tower, as pitch-black talons spread above her.

His griffin roared in his soul, filling him with instinctive need to protect and defend. A fierce shriek of challenge burst from his beak despite the choking smoke. Folding his wings, he arrowed toward the half-seen creature, every talon extended.

The shadowy shape rolled in mid-air, evading his attack. Rory had a brief, confused glimpse of jagged wings, midnight claws, a blank white eye burning with captive lightning—and then he was past it, plunging down through thinning cloud.

He snapped his wings open, barely managing to pull up before he hit the flat roof of the lookout tower. The tips of his golden pinions brushed against shingles as he turned to attack again.

The world went white.

RORY!

His squad's frantic telepathic shout blasted through his mind as a hammer-blow of searing hot air knocked him across the sky. He tumbled beak over tail, completely disorientated. Only his cat-like reflexes kept him airborne at all.

With a twist that left his spine aching, he managed to right himself, a good fifty feet from the tower. Rising thermals from the smoldering ground fire steadied his wings. His ears rang as though he'd been walloped by a brick. His entire team yammered in his mind, a chaos of concern.

I'M FINE, he roared back. *Stay out of this!*

Sparks still snapped from the bent lightning rod rising from one corner of the lookout tower roof. It had saved his life, attracting the bolt that would otherwise have hit him dead-on. The churning clouds above the structure had gone black and dull, no longer seething with building electricity.

A chance!

This was his moment to strike, before the monster could summon the lightning again. Rory had no idea what sort of creature his unknown adversary might be, but he would bet his tail feathers that it needed time to build up a charge.

Of course, if he was wrong, his tail feathers would *literally* be toast.

He powered back toward the tower, cutting through the smoke like a knife. But his lion body and eagle wings were built for strength, not speed. Though he strained every muscle, his adversary was faster.

The smoke-shrouded creature spread its wings to full extent, shadowing the mountain. The massive pinions swept down with a sound like a thunderclap. Rory had to fight against a gust of wind as the creature shot upward.

What was that? Wystan exclaimed telepathically, echoed by a territorial snarl from Fenrir.

I have no idea. Rory slowed to a glide, watching the vast silhouette arc across the sky, trailing storm clouds. *But whatever it was, at least it's thought better about sticking around.*

In the space of a few breaths, the unnatural winds around the lookout tower quieted. In their absence, the forest fire calmed as well. Thick plumes of smoke still rose from smoldering undergrowth, but at least the wind was no longer whipping flames into a frenzy and tossing embers about like confetti. A lot of the forest floor was already burned to black, all available fuel consumed by the abnormally fast blaze.

Reluctantly, Rory turned his attention away from his retreating opponent and onto the more immediate problem. Balancing on the breeze, he scanned the forest with a practiced eye, assessing the situation. To his relief, the flames hadn't yet reached the tower.

In fact, they *couldn't* reach it.

His beak dropped open in surprise. A fireline protected the structure. It was hastily dug and a bit narrow, but effective. If he hadn't known better, he would have thought that one of his own crew had cut it.

He opened his mind to his squad as he swooped down. *It's safe. You can all come up here now.*

How very kind of you, boss. Rory winced at Blaise's acid tone. She was clearly smarting from his use of the alpha voice on her. *What's the situation?*

Under control. He landed to inspect the fireline more closely. The flames on the far side were dying away, blocked from reaching any further fuel.

Even though the lookout tower didn't seem to be in any immediate risk from the fire, Rory still had a sense of unease. Instinct screamed that there was something wrong here.

He glanced up at the lookout tower. He'd seen the fire watcher run into it at the start of the brief fight, but there was no sign of activity now. All the storm shutters were closed.

His griffin clawed at his soul. *Danger! Hurry!*

The platform was too narrow for his griffin form. Shifting back into human form, he took the stairs up to the platform two at a time. As a mythic shifter, his gear came with him when he transformed—which was handy, since if he'd turned up on the fire watcher's porch buck-naked, he would have had some explaining to do.

Just as he got to the top, a muffled shriek came from behind the closed door.

He didn't hesitate. The door might have been designed to be bear-proof, but it definitely wasn't shifter-proof. His first charge smashed it off its hinges. He kicked apart the shattered remains, stepping over the threshold.

The inside of the tower was as dark as a tomb. Rory squinted, his sensitive eyes struggling to adjust to the sudden change. "Hello? Are you-?"

And that was as far as he got, before a furry missile hit him square in the chest.

He barely managed to get his arm up in time to protect his throat. Razor-sharp teeth sank deep into the sleeve of his protective jacket.

Too startled even to shift, Rory leaped backward. Catching his heel on the splintered wreckage of the door, he stumbled, put a foot down onto thin air, and had a long, drawn out second to fully appreciate how much this was going to suck.

He fell down the stairs.

All of them.

With a snarling, slavering *thing* trying to savage him, Rory couldn't do anything to arrest his bruising descent. The best he could manage was a semi-controlled slide, careening down the switchback stairs like a human toboggan. His attacker rode him down the entire way, emitting muffled screeches around its mouthful of jacket.

Everything still under control, boss? Blaise inquired.

No! he managed to get out, as he crashed down the last few feet. *Under attack!*

Seriously? At least Blaise had been jolted out of her snit. *By what?*

Still flat on his back, Rory managed to haul the rabid creature away from his throat long enough to get a glimpse at it. *A rabbit!*

The mental silence was deafening.

Confirm that? Blaise said after a moment.

Yes, I damn well confirm it! It was very definitely a rabbit, albeit one apparently sent straight from hell. Its back legs kicked his abdomen with the force of a pair of jackhammers.

Birdcat needs assistance with this *prey?* Fenrir said, with only a hint of snideness.

For a moment, Rory was strongly tempted to say no. He was never going to hear the end of this.

Would you please, he gritted out, as the bunny did its level best to chew through his safety gear, *be so kind as to get this thing off me?*

A burst of delighted barking erupted nearby. The rabbit froze on Rory's chest, cocking its ears. It released his sleeve at last, gifting him with a last parting kick to the balls as it bounded off. With a flash of white tail, it streaked away.

Fenrir trotted up, ears pricked and tongue lolling out in a doggy smirk. *If that was an alpha challenge, Birdcat just lost.*

Rory groaned, allowing his head to fall back with a thump. Every inch of his body hurt. "To be fair, the stairs did most of the damage."

"Don't try to move! I'll be right there!"

It was the voice of an angel, floating down from high in the sky. A pair of battered workboots clattered down the stairs, upside-down from his perspective. Fenrir let out a low, rumbling growl, rising to straddle his chest protectively.

"No," the woman told the hellhound, very firmly. "He needs help. Let me see."

Without a trace of fear or hesitation, she shoved Fenrir's muzzle aside. The hellhound's snarl tapered off into a bemused whine. Fenrir backed off, giving way to the woman.

She knelt next to Rory, her hands hovering just over his body as though she was afraid to touch him. The sun made a halo around her head, backlighting her so that he couldn't make out her face. But just the line of her neck, the slant of her shoulders, even the cute curves of her ears…he was instantly gripped by the firm conviction that she was the most beautiful woman he'd ever seen.

Rory blinked. *Do I have a concussion?*

"You probably have a concussion," the woman said, echoing his thought. "How far did you fall? When I saw you lying at the bottom of the stairs, I thought you were dead. Oh, the fire! I have to get you away—but you might have broken something—I shouldn't move you —but the fire!"

"I'm fine," Rory said, despite all evidence to the contrary. He put a touch of alpha power into his voice, warm and reassuring. "No need to panic. We're safe from the fire here. Everything's going to be fine."

He'd only meant to soothe her, but to his surprise the attempt backfired. She jerked, her shoulders stiffening.

"I'm not panicking," she said. "I just...don't know what to do first."

"How about helping me up?" This time, he was careful not to use his power. Trying a friendly smile, he held out one hand.

She flinched again, as though he'd offered her a live spider. For some reason, that small, quickly stifled movement felt like she'd punched him in the gut. He didn't want her to recoil from him. He wanted her to lean into his touch, greedily demand his caresses, naked skin pressing against skin...

Right. He definitely had a concussion.

He would have dropped his hand, but he honestly wasn't sure whether he *could* get up without assistance.

Just as he was about to ask Fenrir to help haul him up, the woman's back straightened. Taking a deep breath as though steeling herself, she grabbed hold of his wrist with both hands.

Even through his fire resistant gloves, he could feel the heat of her touch. A strange thrill crackled through him like lightning, wiping away the aches of his bruises.

Only for a moment, though. He couldn't help grimacing as she tugged him to his feet.

"Anything broken?" she asked anxiously.

"Just my pride." He rubbed his hip, wincing. "And I think my dignity is permanently sprained."

"Um...do you mean you aren't hurt?" The woman sounded uncertain.

"I'll live." He glanced at her wryly, still investigating his bruises. "Though I can't say this has been the best day of my life."

He saw her properly for the first time.

"Oh," he said, staring into the eyes of his one true mate. "Wait."

CHAPTER 3

*E*dith froze, transfixed. Normally meeting people's eyes felt itchy, like ants crawling on her skin.

But *his* eyes…

It was like stepping out of an air-conditioned building into a hammer-blow of midsummer heat. His golden gaze fell on her soft as sunlight, but penetrated to the marrow of her bones. Every inch of her craved more. She was a plant finally breaching an icy blanket of snow and stretching, yearning, for the sun. She wanted to strip off every stitch of clothing and bask in that dizzying warmth.

She was staring at him.

And she'd forgotten to count hippopotamuses.

Edith wrenched her eyes away, mortification sweeping over her. Normally she was scrupulously careful to maintain eye contact for three seconds—counting *one-hippopotamus-two-hippopotamus-three-hippopotamus*—before looking away and counting again. It was just as unacceptable to stare at people as to never meet their eyes.

No one seemed to have taught the firefighter that social rule. Even with her own gaze fixed on his battered boots, she could still feel the force of his amber-gold eyes like a spotlight on her.

"Oh," he said again, his voice dropping to a deep, husky rumble that echoed through her bones. "Yes."

One-hippopotamus-two-hippopotamus-three-hippopotamus.

Ingrained habit tugged her head up again, although she felt like a deer turning toward an onrushing truck. She tracked slowly up his body, unable to help lingering even though she knew it was rude. Baggy, shapeless Nomex pants, equipment belt slung low over his hips. A heavy protective jacket in the same fire-resistant material, the original bright yellow color faded to dirty beige with ingrained soot. Turn outs made anyone look bulky, but he filled out the uniform in a way that left no doubt that there was a *lot* of muscle under there. Even bruised and battered, he exuded power.

She had to look up to see his face—she was by no means short, but he was still a good four inches taller than her. She didn't dare make eye contact again, in case she never broke free, so she focused on his mouth instead. He had a strong, square jaw dusted with tawny stubble. With his build, and the dirt and sweat streaking his face, he should have appeared rough and dangerous.

But that rugged face was split by the widest grin Edith had ever seen. For all his unmistakable masculine strength, he looked like a kid who had just discovered it was Christmas and Halloween and the first day of summer vacation, all at the same time.

Edith was pretty certain that this was not an appropriate reaction to falling down twenty feet of stairs.

More likely, she was completely misinterpreting his expression. Even though his whole face shouted pure, unalloyed delight to *her*, doubtless she was missing some obvious-to-everyone-else twist of the lip or eyebrow which turned *This is the best day ever* into *I am in hideous pain.* After all, he'd literally just *said* that this wasn't his best day ever.

Listen to his words, not his face, Edith decided. She'd long since learned that was the best course when trying to interact with people.

"We need to get you medical attention," she said. "Can you walk? Here, lean on me."

He didn't move. His smile stretched even wider. He was still staring at her with total, unnerving attention, but he didn't seem to be taking in a word she was saying.

"You're everything I ever dreamed," he said. "And more."

Edith blinked at him, thrown as much by his accent as the non-sequitur. He definitely wasn't American. The way he rolled his *r*s was as rich and heady as hot whiskey.

The tips of her fingers tingled, making her aware that she was still holding his wrist. Blushing, she tried to let go, but he twisted around, catching her hand again. His gloved fingers tightened around hers.

"What's your name?" he asked.

It was a perfectly normal question, she told herself. This was a perfectly normal conversation. Why was her tongue stuck to the roof of her mouth?

"E-Edith," she managed to get out. "What's yours?"

He let out his breath in a sigh that was practically a purr. "Edith."

This seemed unlikely.

"No, *I'm* Edith," she said, taking care to enunciate clearly. "Edith Stone. And you are?"

"Yours." He shook himself, seeming to come back to his senses a little. "I mean, Rory. I'm Rory MacCormick."

Edith was beginning to suspect that this was not, in fact, a perfectly normal conversation. She was also starting to wonder just how hard he'd hit his head.

"Nice to meet you, Rory." She glanced around for help. "Where's the rest of your team?"

He made a vague gesture in the direction of the dog...if it *was* a dog. Now that Edith had a chance to examine it properly, she wasn't entirely sure. It looked more like an unholy cross between a grizzly bear and a wolf. It had shaggy, jet-black fur, upright pointed ears, and startlingly bright eyes—copper-orange with crimson flecks.

It wore a reflective yellow harness with THUNDER MOUNTAIN HOTSHOTS emblazoned on the side, along with a logo of a mountain peak crowned with two lightning bolts. Edith had never heard of a dog trained to support wildland firefighters before, but she couldn't imagine a crew taking a mascot to an actual fire. It had to be some kind of service animal. From the size of those powerful jaws, she wouldn't have been surprised to learn that it fetched and carried whole trees.

The dog's heavy head cocked to one side. Its muzzle moved back and forth between Edith and Rory, rather like a spectator at a tennis match. Catching her eye, it held her gaze for a moment, then turned to pointedly look in the direction of the smoldering ground fire. One ear tilted back at her.

Don't know what's going on here, she could almost hear it saying. *But isn't that more important?*

"Right," Edith said, turning back to Rory. He was *still* grinning at her. "We need to get out of here, and get you proper medical treatment. Where's, um, the rest of your team? And your transport? You can't have just dropped from the sky."

He opened his mouth, paused, and shut it again. He rubbed at the back of his neck, his gaze sliding away from her at last. "Ah. Well. Actually."

Whatever he'd been about to say was interrupted by the appearance of a truck, kicking up clouds of dust as it screamed up the dirt track that led to her lookout tower. The chunky, ungainly vehicle looked rather like the love-child of a tank and a school bus. It was bright yellow, just like the dog's harness, and had the same logo painted on the side: THUNDER MOUNTAIN HOTSHOTS.

The truck pulled up at the base of the tower. Four figures piled out, running up in a confusion of overlapping voices. Edith flinched, caught in a storm of yellow uniforms and unfamiliar faces, unable to process the sudden arrivals.

"Hey. Hey!" Rory held up his hands, quieting the babble. "I'm fine. Start unloading the gear. I'll be with you in a moment."

"Not until I've checked you out," one of the men said firmly. His short, white-blond hair momentarily confused Edith into thinking he had to be old, but his handsome face was young and unlined. "What happened?"

"Yes, tell us," said a towering black man, grinning. "In great and excruciating detail, so that we recount the glorious tale again and again. A rabbit, I believe you said?"

Rory shot him a glare before turning to one of the remaining firefighters. "Blaise, take this comedian and put him to work, okay? We need to get this fire safely ringed."

The short, curvy woman nodded. She had burnished hazelnut skin and tight-curled hair, cropped close to her elegant head. Edith envied her air of calm confidence. "On it, boss. Cal, Joe, with me. Wystan, don't let Rory do anything stupid. Again."

"Not sure how I'm supposed to do that, short of knocking him out and sitting on him," the white-haired man remarked wryly as the other firefighters headed back to the truck. He glanced over at Edith, his graceful hands busy taking Rory's pulse. "Hello, by the way."

Edith knew that she was supposed to reply, but she was still reeling from the sudden onslaught of strangers. Words lay like stones on her tongue.

She struggled to spit one out. "H-hi."

"Edith, this is Wystan," Rory said. "And this is Fenrir."

Edith spent a second looking around for another firefighter before realizing that Rory meant the dog. It caught her eye, and its thick, plumed tail thumped against the ground in a lazy wag.

"Wys, Fen, this is Edith Stone," Rory continued, as if it wasn't at all odd to be formally introducing someone to a dog. "She's—"

He cut himself off, for no reason that Edith could discern. His mouth stretched in that broad, slightly silly grin again. "That is, she's the fire watcher here."

Wystan flung her a distracted smile, still busy checking Rory's injuries. From his swift, sure movements, he was obviously a trained paramedic. "Nice to meet you, Edith. Who else is here?"

"No one," Edith said, uncertain why he was asking. "Just me."

Wystan's eyebrows rose. "You cut the fireline at the base of the hill all by yourself?"

Edith nodded, making herself meet his eyes for a moment. "Is it okay? I didn't have any proper tools, or much time."

"I'm only a trainee, so I'm not a real judge of these things." Despite

Wystan's soft, polite tone, his voice reminded Edith somewhat of a movie villain. That gave her the clue to place his accent—British, from England. "But it looked good to me."

"It's more than good," Rory said, beaming as if he'd dug the line himself. She still couldn't pin down those exotic *rs*. "We're safe here, with that line holding the head back. I checked it—properly anchored, well judged, and a nice clean cut. Superb work, especially for one person under extreme pressure."

The praise kindled an answering warmth under her breastbone. It was a strange, foreign sensation, like a glowing bubble expanding from her heart. She hadn't felt anything like it for so long, it took her a moment to identify the emotion.

Pride.

"What crew did you work with?" Rory continued, turning to her. "You must have professional experience to cut line like that."

The bubble popped.

"Not really. Just…just a little training." She changed the topic with the grace of an elephant on stilts. "What happened to the hare?"

"You mean the deceptively fuzzy spawn of Satan that was lurking in your lookout tower?" Rory waved a hand in the direction of the unburned forest. "It ran off after it knocked me down the stairs. Is it your pet? Callum could track it down for you."

And now she was all confused again. "I thought the dog was called Fenrir."

"He means Fenrir," Wystan said. He pinned Rory with a mean-ingful—though indecipherable—stare. "Don't you, Rory?"

"Ah, yes." Rory rubbed the back of his neck again. "Sorry, still a bit dazed. From, uh, falling down the stairs."

"Clearly," Wystan murmured. The dog let out a deep *woof*, as though agreeing.

"Well, anyway, the hare wasn't my pet," Edith said. "It was a wild animal. I rescued it from the fire."

"I hope it was more grateful to you than it was to me," Rory said, one tawny eyebrow quirking up.

"Actually, it attacked me too. It let me pick it up and take it inside, but then it suddenly went for me without warning." Edith gingerly probed at her neck. "It was trying to tear out my throat when you arrived and scared it off."

A low rumbling noise made her jump. She thought for a moment the dog was snarling—but the sound came from Rory. His hands flexed like claws. "It hurt you?"

She took a step back, caught off-guard by his abrupt intensity. She wasn't *afraid* of him, exactly, but there was still something disconcerting about being close to so much focused power. It was like standing right next to a raging bonfire—contained, tamed, but definitely not *safe*.

Fenrir let out a high, quizzical whine. His black nose nudged Rory's clenched fist.

Rory took a deep breath, his golden eyes closing for a moment. His shoulders relaxed again. "Nothing," he said, as though answering an unspoken question. "Explain later."

Edith usually felt as though she was missing half of any conversation, as though everyone else was tuned into a radio station she couldn't hear. This one, however, was more like trying to follow a TV show playing in another room, where she could only catch every other word.

Rory pinned her with that unnerving sunlight stare again. "*Did* it hurt you?"

Her searching fingers found something sticky on the side of her neck, under the collar of her shirt. She became aware of a dull, throbbing pain, under the brighter jangle of sensory discomfort. "I think it bit me."

Rory moved so fast she didn't have time to react. Suddenly he was right up in her personal space, the heat of his body battering her skin, his spice-sweat-smoke scent overwhelming her senses. His sheer *presence* squashed her flat, like a mouse pinned by a lion's paw. She froze, unable to even breathe.

He froze too, as if her paralysis was contagious. The tips of his gloves brushed her collar, not quite touching her neck.

"*Rory.*" Wystan's hand closed on the other man's shoulder, dragging him back. "Don't just lunge at the poor woman. I'm terribly sorry for my colleague's appalling manners, Edith. May I take a look at your injury? I'm…a paramedic, of sorts."

Edith sucked in a shaky breath. Every inch of her skin felt simultaneously on fire and frozen. She managed to jerk her head in a nod.

Moving as though trying not to spook a feral cat, Wystan approached her. He lifted a hand—and jerked it back as another low growl came from Rory's direction.

"Sorry. Sorry." Rory pinched the bridge of his nose, scrunching his face up. "Don't pay any attention to me. Go ahead."

Wystan threw Rory another of those strange looks, but complied. His bare fingers were cool and impersonal against Edith's skin. His presence didn't light up her nerves in the same way that Rory's had; his closeness was simply uncomfortable. She forced herself to hold still for the brief examination.

"Not a bite. Just some shallow scratches from its claws." Wystan shrugged off his pack, rummaging in one of the pockets. "I'll clean it up and put a bandage on it. That rabbit certainly made a spirited attempt to get you."

"It was a snowshoe hare, not a rabbit." Edith winced as Wystan swabbed her wound with an antiseptic wipe. "I'm lucky Rory arrived when he did. I swear it was trying to kill me. It was acting more like a predator than a prey animal."

Rory raised an eyebrow at her. "Do you think it's too late for us to claim it was a very small wolverine?"

Edith had an abrupt, crystal-clear memory of the hare lunging at her, jaws gaping wide… "I think it had fangs."

Rory let out a brief, delighted peal of laughter, making her twitch. "There you go, Wystan. Straight from an impartial witness. Also, I've just recalled that the animal was seven feet tall and breathed fire."

Wystan snorted. "Nice try. You aren't going to live this one down for a long time, Rory."

They thought she was joking.

She opened her mouth to explain that no, she really *did* think she'd seen fangs in the hare's mouth—but stopped. She'd learned long ago to copy people's expressions and tones, mimicking like a parrot, always a second behind.

Rory had seen the hare too, and he clearly hadn't noticed anything odd. Maybe she'd been wrong. And both Rory and Wystan were smiling at her. If she didn't smile back, if she tried to insist that she'd sensed something in the smoke, that there had been something wrong with the hare…

She didn't want Rory's warm regard to turn cold. She didn't want him to stare at her like she was a freak.

"Yes," she said, her voice sounding high and fake in her own ears. "Only kidding. Haha."

"Well, you got off lightly." Wystan finished applying the bandage. "Could have been a lot worse."

"Yes, it could have been," said Rory, his grin fading. He hesitated, rubbing his chin. "Edith, did you notice anything odd about the storm?"

She frowned. "What storm? The lightning came out of a clear sky."

Rory and Wystan exchanged glances.

"Never mind," Rory said. "I, uh, assumed there had to have been storm clouds. Since you saw lightning. Must just have been freak weather conditions."

"Rory!" the female firefighter called from the truck. She and the others had unloaded a pile of gear from the back--helmets, backpacks, digging tools, and a chainsaw. "We're ready. Want me to judge the line?"

"Hang on, I'll be right there," Rory shouted back. He turned to Edith. "I'm afraid we were the only squad in range. The rest of our crew is still back at base. We're short-handed for this fire."

Her heart hiccupped. For a mad, shining, terrifying moment, she was convinced he was about to ask her to work with them. He'd complimented her fireline, after all.

"So this is going to take a while," Rory continued. "Will you be all right here?"

Reality reasserted itself. Of course he didn't need her help. He was a hotshot, an elite wildland firefighter. And she was just…her.

"Yes," she said, trying to smile. "I need to check out the tower equipment, anyway. Lightning hit it pretty hard."

"Take this." Rory unclipped a radio from his belt, handing it to her. "Just in case you need us and don't have comms. Wystan can show you how to operate it. He'll stay here with you."

Wystan stiffened. "I may be green, Rory, but I like to think I'm not entirely useless. You just said yourself we're under-manned for this fire."

"And I don't need a babysitter," Edith said, irritation sharpening her tone. "Or help working a radio."

Rory's eyes narrowed. "You're hurt. I'm not leaving you alone."

"I'm used to being alone," she snapped. "I've been a fire watcher here for years. *You're* the one with a concussion. If anyone here shouldn't be alone, it's you."

"The lady has a point, Rory," Wystan said. "You're acting rather, ah, erratically. Perhaps you should stay here and keep Edith company."

Edith had expected Rory to hotly shoot down the suggestion, but to her surprise he hesitated. His gaze flicking from her to the waiting squad and back again. He ran a hand through his tousled blond hair, mussing it up even further.

"No," he said, shoulders falling in a sigh. He bent to scoop up his fallen helmet. "The squad needs me. But we really can't leave Edith alone here. Fenrir? Would you mind?"

The dog tilted his head. He stood up, shaking himself with a jingle of harness, and trotted over to her side.

"Thanks," Rory said to the dog. He looked back at Edith. "Fenrir will stay with you, Edith. He'll protect you."

He thought a *dog* was more competent than she was.

Apparently taking her outraged silence as assent, Rory fitted his helmet back onto his head. "Call me on the radio if you need anything. Anything at all. And stay in the tower until I get back. Let's go, Wys."

Edith folded her arms, tucking her hands under to hide the way her fingers were twitching with anger. She glared at Rory's back as he headed for the truck.

"Who does he think he is, ordering me around?" she said under her breath. "Condescending ass."

Fenrir made a deep, huffing sneeze that sounded awfully like a stifled laugh. His cold wet nose prodded her side.

Edith felt like pointedly staying outside just as a matter of principle, but the dog poked her again. He was a *lot* stronger than she was. Edith suspected that if she didn't do what he wanted, he was quite capable of carrying her off like a chew toy.

"Fine," she sighed, allowing Fenrir to herd her toward the tower. "What exactly are you supposed to protect me from, anyway? More killer hares?"

The dog's ears perked up. His copper eyes turned hopefully in the direction of the forest.

"It's like you understand every word I say." She reached for his collar, only to discover—to her surprise—that he wasn't wearing one. She settled for taking a firm grip on his harness instead. "Come on, big guy. Let's get you inside, just in case the hare *is* still around."

Even though the animal had attacked her, she didn't want the huge black dog hunting it down. There had definitely been something odd about the hare, but that didn't mean it deserved to be torn limb from limb. The poor creature had probably just been terrified by the fire.

She cast a last backward glance at the forest as she led Fenrir up the stairs. She hoped the hare would be all right.

CHAPTER 4

$\mathcal{T}$he hare's body wanted to run.

It tightened its grip on the animal, squeezing with iron will. The hare had only a small mind, a candle flame of soul. It was easy to dominate.

It crouched in a charred thicket of brambles, wearing the hare's skin, and watched.

Five souls. Dangerous souls, not human nor animal, but a mixture of both.

Shifters.

It knew their kind. Knew enough to be wary of them.

At the moment they walked on two legs, working their way through the forest. It had feared at first that they were hunting for it, but they only scraped at the ground and hacked at trees with cold metal tools. Sometimes they stopped to smother smoldering patches of vegetation with dirt. Fire seemed to be their enemy.

That was interesting. That was what made it creep closer, watching.

That…and one other thing.

The shifter leader's soul was like none it had ever scented before.

Power rolled from him, thick and intoxicating. If it could find a way to wear *that* one's skin…

Nothing would be able to stop it.

The shifter leader was too strong to attack directly. Not yet, not now, when it had only fed on weak, animal hosts. To claim its prize, it would need a subtler approach.

If only it had been able to sink its teeth into the human woman. She was linked somehow to the shifter leader—that was clear from the way both their souls brightened when they were together. Even now, it could smell his sickening desire and longing for her.

She would be able to get close to him. He would never suspect her, until it was too late.

The hare's body would not last long. Already the changes had started—teeth lengthening, nubbins of horns pushing up, fur falling away. In a matter of days the small animal would be twisted into uselessness.

It needed to find a new host. A stronger one, a better one.

And then…

Then, it would hunt.

CHAPTER 5

*E*dith was perfect. That little snub nose, those wide hazel eyes, the freckles dusting her sun-browned cheeks...every inch of her was utterly perfect.

And she thought he was an idiot.

Rory had always secretly hoped that he'd meet his mate while doing something heroic, just like his own father had. When he'd been younger, he'd avidly listened to tales from mated couples about how they'd met. He'd pictured himself taking the starring role, boldly winning his own mate's heart. One day *he* would rescue his one true love from a burning building, or fight a duel for her honor, or save her from a corrupt dragon.

Bunnies had not featured prominently in his fantasies.

Rory was pretty sure that no one, in the entire history of shifter kind, had ever made a less impressive first impression on his mate.

She is our mate, his griffin said consolingly. *We are made for her. She will see that.*

Given that so far Edith had seen him fall down three flights of stairs, get beaten up by a rabbit, and then completely lose coherent speech, Rory did not share his griffin's confidence. Not unless Edith had a secret kink for tongue-tied dorks.

She will *choose us,* his griffin insisted. *Once we prove that she can trust us. That we will always guard her back, always support her and cherish her.*

Yes. Edith needed a mate who was strong, who could protect her. She'd been so wary, so shy. She hadn't even been able to meet his eyes after that first lightning-bolt of recognition.

Just recalling Edith's hesitant, nervous body language filled him with protective fury. Who had hurt her so badly, that she curled in on herself like that? Who had shredded her self-confidence to the point where she stumbled over words as if she didn't believe she had the right to speak at all?

He longed to stroke away the tension in those huddled shoulders. He wanted her to hold her head up high, meeting his gaze boldly, so that he could bask forever in the beauty of her green-brown eyes.

He'd prove that he could be the mate that she needed. That she didn't have to move through the world like a wild creature on the verge of flight. That he could shelter and protect her from any threat.

Rory revved his chainsaw, attacking the next dead tree with renewed determination. From Edith's own fireline, she clearly knew a thing or two about fighting wildfires. She'd understand how much skill and endurance it took to contain even a little forest fire like this one. He had to work faster, harder, to impress his mate-

"Rory. *Rory!*"

Blaise's yell cut through the snarling whine of the chainsaw. Letting the blade power down, he turned. He'd left a messy trail of devastation through the forest, cut-down vegetation scattered haphazardly in his wake. Blaise clambered over a tangle of branches, her heavy work boots stomping through the leaves.

"You're going too fast," she said, jogging up to him. "Joe can't keep up."

Rory glanced impatiently at the fallen material waiting to be cleared. "Joe can learn how to shift his lazy arse."

"I'm *right here.*" Joe's voice came from amidst the trees.

"I know," Rory said. "Move it, prince. We've got a lot of work to do."

Joe reappeared from between the trunks, sweating and scowling.

"Join my squad, Joe," he muttered. "Become a firefighter and heroically save lives with your special skills, Joe." He heaved the next log onto his shoulder, carrying it safely out of reach of the approaching fire. "You'll get to spend hours picking up sticks, Joe. Oh wait, you didn't mention that last one. Must have slipped your mind."

"If you've got breath to complain, you're not working hard enough!" Blaise yelled after him. She turned back to Rory, lowering her voice. "Seriously though, you need to slow down. Even if Joe could swamp fast enough to keep up with you, there's only three of us to cut line. You can't expect the squad to hold this pace all day."

Rory looked back along the line. Wystan and Callum were some way back, digging down to mineral soil along the path that he'd cleared. The paramedic was gamely matching Cal swing for swing, but exhaustion showed in his bowed head and dragging steps. Even Callum was looking a little less crisp and perfect than normal.

Rory clenched his jaw in frustration, but had to concede Blaise was right. "Take a break!" he shouted down to them.

Wystan immediately cast down his tool, flopping to the ground with a heartfelt groan. Callum just settled into something resembling parade rest, feet apart and spine straight, but Rory detected a certain relief to the line of his shoulders.

There wasn't any point in continuing to clear fuel without his squad supporting him. Rory switched his chainsaw off, slinging it over his shoulder. Grabbing hold of the sapling he'd just cut down, he started to drag it away—and discovered that he was trying to drag Blaise as well.

"You need to take a rest too, boss," she said, one foot firmly planted on the slender trunk. "You look like you're about to keel over."

"I'm fine," he growled, barely resisting making it an alpha command. He yanked on the branches, but Blaise kept her balance. "And we need to get this fire under control."

"It *is* under control. Trust me, it's not going anywhere. We're well ahead of the advance, so you don't need to act like there's a wall of flame bearing down on us." She glared at him, her hands on her hips. "I promised your family I would watch out for you. Now come on, before you face plant into the dirt and we have to drag *you* behind the line."

We will be of no use to our mate if we are exhausted, his griffin agreed.

Rory growled again, but let Blaise lead him back to the rest of the squad. Joe had returned as well, and was busy rummaging in his pack for his canteen. Wystan lay flat on the ground, eyes closed. Callum was still standing, staring intently into the bushes.

"Something wrong, Cal?" Rory asked as he set down his chainsaw.

"Hare's back." The pegasus shifter pointed, though Rory couldn't see anything himself. "Shadowing us."

"Watch out, Rory," Joe said, smirking. "It might be looking for another round."

Rory frowned, unslinging his pack. "That's odd. I would have thought it would be miles away by now. You sense anything strange about it, Cal?"

Callum shook his head. "Not a shifter."

"Well, let me know if it does anything. Maybe it's just wistful thinking, but I'm not so sure that was a normal animal." He couldn't help wincing a little as he lowered himself to the ground. Even with shifter-fast healing, his bruises were still tender.

Noticing, Wystan struggled up onto his elbows. "Let me check you over again, Rory. That was quite a knock you took earlier."

Rory waved him back down. "For the last time, stop fussing. I'm fine."

"No, you're not." Blaise sat down cross-legged, taking off her helmet and running a hand through her sweat-damp curls. "I still think he's concussed, Wys."

"I am *not* concussed!"

"Yeah, it'd take more than a twenty foot fall to dent Rory's thick skull," Joe muttered.

"You aren't acting yourself, Rory," Wystan said, looking concerned. "Please, let me take another look. Head injuries need to be treated seriously, even with shifter healing."

They weren't going to let it go. He could use the alpha voice on them, but that would only raise their suspicions even further. He didn't have any choice but to tell them the truth.

"I really am fine." He couldn't stop a silly grin from spreading over his face. "Better than fine. I met my mate."

Joe, who had just taken a drink, sprayed water across Callum.

"*Edith?*" Wystan sat bolt upright. "Edith is your mate?"

"Rory, that's wonderful!" Blaise punched his shoulder, grinning ear-to-ear herself. "Why didn't you say so sooner?"

"Yes," Callum said, dripping. "Why?"

"Because I didn't want you lot gaping at her and elbowing each other." Rory swept them all with a glare. "She's already on edge enough."

"I have to admit, she did seem rather skittish," Wystan said, a faint crease appearing between his brows.

"One wrong move and she'll run for the hills." He settled back on his arms with a sigh. "Let's face it, I haven't exactly covered myself in glory so far."

"Cut yourself some slack," Blaise said. "You've spent, what, an entire ten minutes in her company?"

"And look what I've accomplished in that time," Rory said gloomily. "Just think how badly I can screw things up given a whole hour."

"Hey man." Joe leaned over to rap his knuckles against the side of Rory's helmet, making his ears ring. "You met your mate! Now at least you've got a *chance* to be with her. Do you know how much the rest of us hate you right now?"

"Seething with jealousy," Wystan agreed cheerfully.

Rory couldn't help noticing that—alone amongst the group— Callum didn't look happy. Of course, he *never* looked happy, but at the moment his not-happiness was particularly intense.

"Cal?" Rory said, uncertain what could be bothering the pegasus shifter. "What's up?"

Callum's shoulders were as stiff as a board. "What about the squad?"

They all looked at him in surprise. "What about it?" Blaise asked.

"It's nearly fire season. We'll be working all summer. We could be deployed anywhere in America." For the taciturn pegasus shifter, it was a veritable tsunami of words. Cal *was* worried. "You won't be able to be with her."

This had been gnawing at the back of Rory's mind too. Wildland firefighting was intense and unpredictable. The hotshot crew often spent weeks at a time camped out at remote locations, completely out of reach. And even when they weren't away on active fires, the crew had to be on standby at the base, ready to scramble at a moment's notice.

How was he supposed to find time to win his mate? Particularly when she lived out in the middle of nowhere herself, hours from Thunder Mountain?

For the sake of his squad, he put on a warm, reassuring smile. "It'll be okay, Cal. I know I'm a little distracted at the moment, but I've only just met her, after all. I'll, er, even out."

Callum shook his head. "Not until you're mated."

"Callum's right, actually," Wystan said, tapping a finger against his lips. "A mated couple can endure some physical separation, as long as the bond is stable and secure. But it's different when you aren't fully mated yet. Once a shifter meets their mate, all their instincts are naturally focused toward consummating the mate bond. If they're prevented from doing so—if the mate rejects them, or just if they're physically separated—they frequently start to develop mental problems. I've read some interesting medical research about it."

"Really not helping, Wys," Blaise muttered.

"Unfortunately, it's the truth." Wystan shrugged, glancing apologetically at Rory. "I don't wish to be the bearer of bad news, but you need to know."

Rory rubbed his forehead. This was all he needed. "Are you trying to tell me I'm under some kind of time limit? If I don't mate Edith soon, I'll go round the bend before the end of the summer?"

The paramedic grimaced. "I'm afraid so."

A blissful smile spread across Joe's face. "Oh, *yes*. Thank you, fate."

Blaise shot the sea dragon a look that should have vaporized him on the spot.

"No, I didn't mean it like that!" Joe held up his hands in surrender, as Wystan and Callum glared daggers at him as well. "Look, I'm sorry for the rest of you, but it's no secret I didn't want to be here. This is a win-win for both Rory *and* me."

"Explain," Rory said dryly, "exactly how losing my mind constitutes a 'win'."

"Oh, come on. You found your *mate*, Rory." Joe made a sweeping, magnanimous gesture, like the Pope dispensing a blessing. "Stay. Win her heart. Be deliriously happy. And while you're busy doing *that*, there's no squad. None of us have the qualifications to be boss, and let's face it, we'd be wasted if we tried to work under a non-shifter leader. We might as well all pack up and go home. Or, to pick a purely hypothetical alternative, go spend the summer on a remote tropical paradise populated by lovely, lonely, and very scantily-clad seal shifter ladies."

"A strangely specific hypothetical example," Wystan murmured.

"Some of us don't *want* to go home, you realize." Blaise folded her arms. "Or, for that matter, to Seal Lady Love Island."

Joe opened his mouth, paused, and shrugged. "I can't lie. There really aren't any selkie dudes. That's kind of the whole charm of the place."

"I'm not abandoning the squad," Rory growled. "Don't book your beach hut just yet, Joe."

Joe shook his head, his expression turning more serious. "What's more important, your job or your mate? Get your priorities straight, bro. It won't kill you to take one year off. Think about it. We're supposed to be back at base tomorrow, and then it's balls to the wall training until fire season starts next week. You seriously going to claim Edith *tonight*?"

His griffin saw no problem whatsoever with this plan.

He took off his helmet, running a hand through his hair in frustration. "I could...explain things. Tell her what I am."

"Oh yes," Joe said. "That will definitely go well. Considering she already thinks you have a concussion."

Rory winced. "I could *show* her what I am."

Wystan cleared his throat. "Rory, the poor woman has literally walked through fire this morning. Not to mention been savaged by a rabbit and had lightning hurled at her by an invisible creature she doesn't even know was there. Don't you think she's had enough surprises for one day?"

"And that's another thing." Rory put his head in his hands, pressing his fists against his temples. "You saw that creature today, Joe. How can you even talk about quitting? You want to leave that thing roaming free? Starting more fires?"

The sea dragon hesitated. He muttered a curse in his own language. "No. Damn it, Rory. You're a terrible influence."

"Rory." Blaise rested her hand on his shoulder. "We *could* do this without you, you know."

"Could you?" He looked round at them all. "Really?"

One by one, they dropped their eyes, looking away.

"Exactly." With a sigh, he levered himself to his feet. "Well. Worst comes to the worst, I'll just have to tough it out. Time to get back to work, squad."

He reached for his chainsaw, but Blaise caught his arm. At his raised eyebrow, she shook her head.

"A man in love," she said firmly, "should not be operating power tools."

Joe brightened. "I call dibs!"

Without a word, Callum claimed the chainsaw.

"Awwwww." Joe's massive shoulders slumped. "I never get to do anything fun."

Wystan held out a Pulaski. "I don't mind swamping for Cal, if you want to take a turn cutting line."

"Bronicorn." Joe heaved a sigh, taking the tool. "We need to have a serious talk about your definition of the word 'fun.'"

Blaise still had hold of Rory's sleeve. Her fingers tightened, holding him back as the others moved off, still bickering.

"Rory." Her voice was low and worried. "What *are* you going to do?"

Be with our mate, his griffin said, simply. *As we are meant to be.*

And suddenly, Rory knew *exactly* what he had to do.

"Uh oh," Blaise muttered, staring up at his face. "I know that look. I'm not going to like this, am I?"

"No," he said, his smile widening as he realized how perfect it was. "You really aren't."

CHAPTER 6

"And so this is the transceiver, and this is the control board, and *this*," Edith leaned back in her chair with a frustrated sigh, "is completely and utterly busted."

Fenrir examined the dismantled radio as intently as if it were a dismembered rabbit. "Woof," he agreed.

"Thanks for the second opinion." Edith scratched behind his pointed ears. "You're good company. Most people would have told me to shut up hours ago."

Fenrir leaned into her fingers as she found the good spot. His tail thumped against the bare floor boards.

"I wish people had tails," she muttered. "It would make things a lot easier if I only had to watch their backsides."

Fenrir's tongue lolled out. He pressed against her even harder, nearly knocking her out of her chair.

"Careful, big guy." She dug her fingers into his black ruff, feeling the hard muscles under the thick fur. "You really are huge. What the heck is your boss feeding you?"

He rested his broad muzzle on her thigh, copper eyes rolling mournfully upward. *Not enough*, she could practically hear him saying.

"I'll find you a snack in a minute, once I've dealt with this." Giving

Fenrir a last pat, she started clearing up the radio parts. "Wonder if I'd be allowed to keep a dog in the tower. Want a change of career, big guy?"

Fenrir made one of his deep huffing noises, more snort than bark. He shook himself with a jingle of harness.

"No, suppose not. If I had your job, I wouldn't want to change either." She sighed again. "And there might not be a job here for *anyone.*"

The radio wasn't the only piece of equipment to have been fried by the lightning. She'd managed to get the generator back up and running, so she at least had electric lights, but everything electronic was completely dead.

She'd started repairs filled with fiery indignation, determined to prove to Rory that she *was* competent. Now, however, not managing to impress the hotshot squad boss was the least of her concerns. Dread lay in her stomach like a rock.

No communications, no weather sensors, no data logging system. Of course, she still had her firewatcher—which only needed her own eyes to function—but what good was that without any way to make reports?

The tower could be out of action for the entire summer. And new equipment would be expensive. What if the Forest Service decided not to repair the lookout tower at all?

Fenrir whined. Edith found that she was rocking in short jerks. She took a deep breath, forcing herself into a more soothing rhythm. Gradually, her racing heart slowed.

"The tower will get fixed," she said. "It'll be all right. Soon everything will be back to normal."

Fenrir's whole body stiffened, his head turning. He trotted over to the east window, nails clicking on the floor, and uttered a sharp bark.

"What is it?" She peered out the window herself. "Oh! They're back."

She could just about make out the hotshot crew's yellow jackets through the darkening twilight. They'd regrouped at their transport, discarding helmets and backpacks in a pile by the rear doors. Even at distance, she could see the easy way the squad worked together, moving in practiced unison to load equipment back into the truck.

A stab of longing went through her. She pressed her hand against the glass, imagining for a moment that *she* was down there. Tired and laughing, aching in every muscle but filled with the glow of victory…

She shook herself free from the stupid daydream. "They must be finished. Well, it was nice having your company for one day at least, big guy. Looks like you're heading back to your home base now."

Fenrir yawned extravagantly, lay down, and put his head on his front paws.

"A whole day listening to me babble, and *now* you want to go to sleep? Come on, Fenrir. You don't want them to go without you." She crouched down to tug at his harness. She might as well have tried to drag the entire lookout tower. "I have to take you back to your boss. Much as I'd like to keep you myself."

A deep chuckle floated from behind her. "Trying to steal my crew away from me?"

Edith jumped, whirling round so fast she nearly lost her balance. Rory leaned against the shattered remnants of the door, smiling at her.

At the sight of him, she *did* lose her balance. Her backside connected hard with the floor as her jaw dropped.

He'd been impressive enough in bulky, shapeless turn outs. Now, out of the concealing shroud of the protective jacket, he was revealed as a downright masterpiece.

The doorway framed him like a work of art. A black crew tee with the Thunder Mountain Hotshots logo clung to every line of his broad torso, leaving nothing to the imagination. A light sheen of sweat highlighted the swelling curves of his folded arms. His warm golden tan perfectly complemented the tawny shade of his hair and the deeper amber of his eyes.

He'd left his safety pants on, but pulled the suspenders off his shoulders. The straps hung down around his thighs, pointing like arrows to the parts of him still tantalizingly hidden by the thick fire-

49

resistant fabric. The top button of his pants winked at her, begging to be undone...

Fenrir made one of his deep, huffing laugh-barks. Rory jumped, straightening from his easy pose. He glared at the dog.

"I am *not* flexing," he said.

Edith tore her eyes away guiltily. Had her lust been printed *that* obviously on her face?

"I-I wasn't going to ask you to," she stuttered. She managed to clamp her mouth shut before *though if you wanted to, I wouldn't mind* slipped out.

"No, I wasn't talking to—argh." Rory scrubbed a hand over his face, leaving sooty smudges. "And here I meant to impress you with my dazzling competence and professionalism. Look, can I rewind and try again?"

She let out a breath of pained amusement, recognizing *that* feeling. "Sure, as long as I can."

True to his word, he walked backward, disappearing out the door again. A beat, and then he strode confidently back into view.

"Hello again Edith," he said, dropping his voice into exaggeratedly serious tones. "As a qualified, competent professional, I've come to report that the fire is under control now."

His playfulness surprised a giggle out of her. "I would try to act like a competent, qualified professional too, but I'm still flat on my butt on the floor."

"Ah. Fortunately, as a trained firefighter, I am fully qualified and competent in search and rescue operations." He leaned over to offer her a hand up. "See? Already found you."

He'd taken his gloves off along with his gear. She could touch him, skin to skin...brush her lips against that broad, callused palm, inhaling his scent...

She scuttled back, frightened by the intensity of her own impulses. She forced out a shaky laugh, trying to cover her own awkwardness.

"Well, even more fortunately, I can rescue myself," she said as she scrambled to her feet unassisted. "Fire watchers have to be self-sufficient."

His smile flickered, some other expression clouding his features. Had she insulted him somehow by not accepting his hand? Implied that he wasn't strong enough to pull her to her feet? Surely his masculinity couldn't be *that* fragile. The man looked like a Greek god and had just spent a day in hand-to-hand combat with a wildfire, after all.

"Not that I wouldn't *want* to be rescued by you," she babbled, grasping for a way to recover the situation. "Looking the way you do, people would pay good money to be slung over your shoulder. How do you even walk down the street without causing traffic accidents?"

She knew the instant that the words left her mouth that she shouldn't have said them. The rules around what was and was not appropriate to mention when it came to people's bodies were so dizzyingly complex that she'd long since given up trying to decipher them. It was safest not to comment at all

Fortunately, for once her attempt at a compliment seemed to have been taken as intended. His face broke into a wide, delighted grin that made answering warmth race through her veins.

"I could say the same to you," he said.

While she was still puzzling over *that* one, he glanced down at Fenrir. "So, have you been behaving yourself?"

Fenrir yawned again, looking supremely unbothered by his master's arrival.

"He's been great," Edith said. Even though she'd been irritated at the time to have the dog assigned to her like some kind of four-footed nursemaid, she had to admit that she'd enjoyed the company. "I'm just sorry that he had to be cooped up in here all day. Can't have been much fun for him."

"Woof," Fenrir said firmly.

"He disagrees with you," Rory said, his mouth quirking.

"I swear he can understand every word I say." She shook her head in amazement. "He's the most intelligent animal I've ever met. What kind of dog is he?"

"His own." Rory shrugged. "I can't tell you his background. I found him out in the wilderness last year. Rescued him from a fire."

"Woof."

"Or he rescued me." Rory grinned down at Fenrir, who made a low, grumbling sound deep in his throat. "Depends on your point of view."

Edith stroked Fenrir's soft, thick fur. "Well, I'll be sorry to see him go."

And you.

The thought was ridiculous. Rory was a total stranger. Why was she feeling sad about saying goodbye to someone she'd barely met? She had no business feeling lonely this early in the season. A whole summer of solitude still stretched out before her. *If* she was lucky enough to still have a job.

She smiled wider, covering up the strange sense of desolation hollowing out her middle. "So I guess you've come to fetch him, since you're all finished? Are you heading back to your base now?"

"Actually, no." Rory jerked a thumb in the direction of the door. "We think the fire's knocked over, but it's best to keep an eye on it overnight just to make sure it's completely dead. We're setting up camp. I came to ask you if you'd like to join us for dinner."

"Oh!" Her heart, which moments before had been sunk to the pit of her stomach, leaped so high she physically rose onto her toes. "Yes! Thank you, thank you!"

Rory laughed, holding up his hands, as Fenrir's ears flattened. "Whoa. Don't get *too* excited. It's field rations, not gourmet cuisine."

She realized she'd spoken far too loudly, too enthusiastically, but she couldn't help it. He was staying, if only for one more night. He wanted her company, he'd *asked* her to join them! She bounced on the spot, unable to contain her happiness.

"I don't mind. Can I contribute some food? I have plenty here, enough for everyone." She whirled, masking her excess energy in rooting through her supply cupboard. "Though it's mostly only cans. Beans! Beans are good. I have lots of beans. Does your squad like beans? Are you sure they won't mind me joining you?"

"They'll welcome you with open arms." Rory rescued her from a teetering stack of cans, piling them into the crook of his elbow. He tossed one to Fenrir, who caught it neatly in his jaws. "Especially if you come bearing beans."

Grabbing her biggest pot, she followed them out. The sky was still streaked with the last glow of sunset, but night was gathering in the forest. The rising moon smiled down, veiled and reddish behind the thin haze of smoke left over from the fire.

"Running up and down these stairs multiple times a day must keep you fit." Rory was a broad-shouldered silhouette ahead of her, picking his way cautiously down. "You have to be tough to live up here all alone. You do a lot of hiking?"

"Yep." She didn't even need to hold the handrail; every step was familiar under her boots. "It's part of the job, checking on the area, keeping paths clear. It's my favorite part, actually. I like being in the forest better than being above it."

Moonlight silvered Rory's profile as he glanced back at her. "Why is that?"

She hesitated, struggling to put the feeling into words. "Because… on the ground, I'm part of things. In the dirt. When I'm in the lookout, I'm sealed off. Separated. Locked away behind glass walls."

"A princess in a tower," Rory said, sounding more thoughtful than teasing. "Like in a fairytale."

She snorted. "I'm no princess."

Rory stopped, turning round. Standing a step below her, he was precisely at her eye level.

His voice was as deep and soft as the night. "But you might be in a fairytale."

Close as he was, it was dark enough that she couldn't make out anything of his expression; just the line of his forehead, the curve of his lips. His eyes were hidden in shadow. It was easier to be this close to him when she didn't need to fear drowning in their amber-gold depths.

She breathed in the faintest whisper-trace of his scent; warm and rich, nutmeg and smoke. If she leaned just a little closer—

Fenrir barked from the bottom of the stairs, sharp and impatient. They both jumped, jerking apart.

"Right." Rory let out a rueful laugh, shaking his head as he turned away. "Feed the dog first. Come on, they're this way."

The firefighters had set up camp a little way from their vehicle, halfway between the lookout tower and the fireline. They'd dragged a couple of logs cut from the forest to make seats around a small campfire.

An unpleasant jolt went through Edith's stomach at the sight of the flickering orange glow. After the terror of the blaze earlier, even this tame, homely fire seemed suddenly unsafe. She froze in the shadows.

"It's okay, Edith," Rory murmured, stopping as well. "No rush. Take your time."

She was grateful he seemed to understand the reason for her hesitation. She made herself look at the dancing flames, battling down the irrational sense of fear.

The other firefighters didn't seem to have noticed her hovering on the edge of their circle. They were all fully occupied ripping open self-heating packets of military rations. Judging from the grumbling, Rory hadn't been kidding about it not being gourmet cuisine.

"I'm not sure whether I should eat this or give it a decent funeral." The white-haired paramedic—Wystan, she remembered—held up an unidentifiable brown patty. "What *is* this thing?"

The female firefighter prodded at her own. "I think it's a lightly seasoned hockey puck."

"Apparently it's meant to be brisket," said a huge black man, squinting at a discarded wrapper. "If this ever came out of a cow, it was from the back end. How can you eat this, Cal?"

The final firefighter—a lean, red-headed man with the brooding good looks of a movie star—didn't pause. Alone amongst the group, he was forking up his meal in steady, regular bites. "It's food."

"That's debatable." Wystan sighed, eying his plate without enthusiasm. "Well, I suppose there's nothing else."

It was as good a cue as she could ask for. Edith swallowed, steeling herself.

"I have beans," she volunteered, stepping into the light.

The large black man promptly tossed his prepackaged meal over his shoulder. He slid to his knees in front of her, arms upraised as if in supplication.

"Lo, a goddess has descended from on high to join us," he declared. He had a melodic, lilting accent, as if his native language was something tonal like Mandarin or Cantonese. "Deliver us from this terrible, terrible food, o merciful one. Bestow upon us your blessed beans."

Edith blinked at him.

"Yes." Rory sighed from behind her. "That's the expression people usually get when they meet Joe."

"I'm afraid he's always like this," Wystan added. "We apologize in advance."

"There is nothing wrong," Joe said with dignity, getting to his feet and brushing dirt off his knees, "with injecting life with a little pizzazz."

The female firefighter snorted. "There's nothing little about you, Joe."

Joe's cocky grin widened. "That's what all the ladies say."

"Yes," Edith said, staring up at the towering firefighter. The top of her head barely came to the middle of his chest. "I can see why."

Across the fire, Wystan choked on a bite of food. Too late, Edith realized the innuendo. At least she'd been looking up rather than down.

Joe laughed, loose and easy. "I like you. And not just for your beans. Speaking of which, if you hand them over, I shall concoct for you a creation that will make you feel like angels are dancing on your tongue. May I?"

Edith found herself grinning back at him. Underneath all those flowery words was a simple directness: *I like you.* Her life would be a lot more straightforward if everyone just came out and spoke their feelings like that.

"Here you go," she said, passing the firefighter the pot. "But I'm afraid they really are just plain beans."

"Not for long." Joe reached into his pocket, pulling out a small bundle with a flourish. "Let's see…Tabasco, smoked paprika, a little garlic salt…"

Wystan raised his eyebrows. "You brought culinary spices to a wildfire?"

"Always be prepared," Joe replied cheerfully, busy opening cans.

The female firefighter shook her head. "You are prepared for some weirdly specific situations." She turned to Edith, giving her a casual wave. "I'm Blaise, by the way. And tall, red-headed, and glowering over there is Callum."

The final firefighter made a small nod of acknowledgement, not pausing in his steady, mechanical consumption of his ration.

"Don't take it personally," Blaise said to Edith. "Cal's not really one for small talk."

In that case, they were going to get along just fine. Edith was already feeling uncomfortable, trying to keep track of so many faces and voices. She smiled nervously round at all of them, her tongue thick and awkward in her mouth.

Maybe this wasn't such a good idea after all.

"It's all right, Edith. They won't bite." Rory sat down on a spare log, patting the space next to him. "Come take a seat."

The log was big enough for two, but she'd be hip-to-hip with him. There was no way she could make polite conversation with the warmth of his thigh against hers.

She went to the other side of the fire instead, where Callum was sitting. The firefighter shot her a quick, sharp glance as she hesitantly approached.

"Um. Do you mind if I join you?" she asked, gesturing at the spare space beside him.

Callum considered her coolly. Most people wriggled their faces all the time in a bewildering kaleidoscope of motion, but his was as still as a mountain pond. Edith found his lack of expression rather soothing.

"*I* don't mind," he said, his gaze flickering to the other side of the fire.

A rather awkward silence fell. Edith gingerly perched on the rough bark as far away as she could get from him, trying not to intrude on his personal space, and stared at her hands. As long as she watched them, she could stop them from twitching.

Wystan cleared his throat. "So, um. Have you been a fire watcher long?"

"A few years now," she said, grateful for the conversational lifeline. "Only during the summer, of course. The lookout towers open at the start of fire season."

Blaise cocked an eyebrow at her. "It's not fire season yet. Why are you out here in the middle of nowhere so early?"

"I always come up here as early as I can. Fire watching isn't the best paid career. I can't afford my own place, so off-season I stay with my parents down in San Francisco. They're great, and I love them, but..." She scrunched up her nose, searching for the right words. "They can't help treating me like a child. In their eyes, I'm always going to be the hapless kid who can't be trusted to know what's best for her, you know?"

"Only too well," Joe sighed, not looking up from the beans.

Wystan let out a rueful chuckle. "All of us are somewhat escaping from our families too." He gestured around the circle. "We grew up together. Firefighting rather runs in the blood—our fathers all work together on an engine crew back in England. We had to move five thousand miles just to get out from under their shadows."

"They're that famous?" she asked.

There was a pause. All the hotshot crew exchanged glances with each other, as though having a silent, private debate.

"More like...legendary," Rory said at last. "In certain circles, at least."

She was struck again by how different his accent was from Wystan and Blaise. "You don't sound like you come from England."

"Och aye, lassie, ye must ken my manner o' speakin'," he said, exaggerating his burr to ludicrous extreme. "Half Scottish, half American. My father's side of the family are all true-blood Highlanders. They made it their mission to make sure I didn't end up sounding like a 'soft southerner' despite growing up in England. Left me with an accent that tends to wander around a bit."

"I like your voice," she assured him. "It's big and warm and furry."

Blaise broke into a coughing fit. Wystan covered his mouth with his hand. Too late, her learned social filter kicked in.

"I-I'm sorry," she said, flustered. "That was a weird thing to say."

The firelight flickered over Rory's crooked smile. "No. It wasn't."

In the warm orange light, his eyes almost seemed to glow. She was drawn to them like a moth to a flame. If she stared too long, she would burn up.

She jerked her gaze away, turning to Joe instead. "I don't recognize your accent either. Where are you from?"

"Mid-Atlantic," he replied, not entirely helpfully. Before she could ask what he meant, he handed her a steaming bowl. "Now, taste and tell me if this needs more chili."

Edith obediently took a bite.

"It does not," she gasped, when she could speak again, "need more chili."

Wystan, who had just tasted his own bowl, spluttered. "Good grief. I thought you said this would be like angels dancing on our tongues, Joe?"

Joe pursed his lips, contemplating his creation. "Very large angels. In stilettos."

"Actually," Blaise said around her spoon, "I think it's pretty good."

Edith cautiously tried a smaller, more respectful mouthful. After you got over being slapped in the sinuses by a wave of heat, the beans *did* actually taste good—complex and warming, with a deep, smoky flavor.

"Wow." She smiled at Joe. "You'll have to teach me your secret. Canned food gets kind of monotonous when you're eating it all summer."

"You aren't going to be here this summer though, are you?" Rory hadn't touched his own food. "Not with the tower equipment broken."

She looked at him in surprise. "How did you know that?"

Fenrir, who had his muzzle firmly planted in a large bowl of beans, made a muffled noise.

"Uh, just seemed obvious," Rory said. "I mean, since you had your radio dismantled. I'm guessing there's not going to be work for you here. What are you going to do?"

The beans suddenly seemed tasteless. She mashed them around with her spoon, all appetite lost.

"I'll…I'll find something," she said, trying to paste a smile onto her face.

"Hmmm." Rory leaned his elbows on his knees, watching her through the campfire with odd intensity. "Can I see your Red Card?"

She automatically reached for her wallet—then her brain caught up with her ears. The Red Card was the wildland firefighter equivalent of a driving license. It literally *was* a red card, printed with a record of training and qualifications that showed what roles you were certified to perform. No one was allowed to work on a fire without one.

Every year, she promised herself that she would let her qualifications lapse. Every year, she found herself filling in the forms and taking the required refresher course at a fire academy. All her identity had been bound up in that red slip of card for so long, not to have one would have felt like amputating a limb. Even now it lurked in her wallet, a scarlet reminder of failure.

She swallowed hard. "How did you know I was carded?"

"Like I said, no one cuts line like that without training." He held out his hand. "Please?"

She would have claimed not to have it on her, but he'd already seen her reach for her back pocket. Reluctantly, she dug out the red slip.

Callum plucked it out of her hand before she could get up to take it to Rory. He unfolded it, quickly scanning the contents. His auburn eyebrows shot upward.

"Well?" Rory asked him.

Edith's face burned as Callum gave her a long, considering look. Without a word, he leaned over to pass her card to Wystan. He let out a low whistle as he too read her record.

"My word," the paramedic said, handing the card along to Blaise. "Talk about fate."

"No such thing," Blaise replied as she took it. She paused, her gaze flicking over the card, and her expression changed. "Okay, that's nearly enough to get even me to believe in destiny."

Edith pinned her hands between her knees. "What are you all talking about?"

"You," Blaise said cryptically. She handed the card to Rory. "All right, you win. Don't rub it in."

"Win what?" Edith stared round at them all. "What's going on?"

Rory's face broke into that broad, boyish grin again, wider than ever, as he read down the list. "Type 2 Firefighter certified, Type 1 Firefighter provisional, Basic Feller provisional...this is a hell of a lot more than 'a little training,' Edith. Why on earth are you just a fire watcher?"

She stared at the dirt between her boots, hands gripping each other. For a moment, she was back at another campfire...in the circle but apart, silent and shaking as cruel laughter cut through her...

Something cold and wet nudged her wrist. Edith pulled herself back into the present, to find Fenrir's copper eyes fixed on hers. The enormous dog rested his head on her knee with a quiet, concerned whine.

She stroked his fur, drawing comfort from his simple animal presence. "Fire watching suits my strengths. Wildland firefighting... didn't work out."

Callum stood up abruptly. For a sickening, lurching moment, she thought that he was drawing away in disgust, repelled by her failure—but he stepped aside, revealing Rory. Without exchanging so much as a glance, the two men changed places, as synchronized as ballet dancers.

Rory sank down onto the log next to her. She didn't dare look at him, but she could feel his body heat against her side.

"Why didn't it work out?" Rory asked quietly.

She concentrated on Fenrir, working tangles out of his thick black ruff. "I got the basic Type 2 qualification easily—that was just classroom training. But then... I couldn't get a job. I tried and tried, but the few times I got an interview, they told me I didn't have enough qualifications."

She wished that those crew superintendents had just come straight-out and said it: *We don't want someone like you.* It would have saved her years of humiliation and heartbreak.

She swallowed the pain in her throat. "I took them literally. I thought that if I got the advanced qualifications, the Type 1 certification and the chainsaw handling, then they'd *have* to give me a job. So I searched and searched until I finally found a crew willing to take me on as a trainee. They were dubious about it, but there had been some kind of publicity stink about a lack of diversity in the local fire services, so they agreed to try me out. But they let me go before I even got to work a real fire. I couldn't do the job. I didn't fit on the team."

Blaise muttered a vile swearword. "Let me guess. Was this team all men, by any chance?"

"They were, but that wasn't the problem." She took a deep breath. "*I* was the problem."

Her fingers twisted in Fenrir's fur. The big black dog didn't flinch. He just leaned into her hand, silently supportive.

I'm autistic.

She tried to shape the words, but they hooked into her throat and refused to come out. She couldn't bear to have them look at her like her old crew had done, like some kind of alien inexplicably beamed into their midst. Or, even worse, with the kind, humiliating pity of her own parents. As if she wasn't really a whole person. As if she was broken.

"Bull*shit*," Rory said.

Her whole body jerked, startled by his ferocity. Before she could stop herself, she looked into his eyes. They blazed molten gold, brighter than wildfire, filled with fury.

Not directed *at* her… but *for* her.

"You are not the problem." His Scottish burr had morphed into a feral growl, on the verge of a snarl. "Whoever told you that was a lying asswipe, and he'd better pray I never catch up with him. You're not only competent, you're exceptional. Just look at that line you cut, all on your own."

She shook her head. "You don't understand. I could only do that *because* I was on my own. I—I don't work well with others. In drills, when we practiced, I would just freeze up."

She could still hear the way her squad boss had hurled orders at her like rocks. On and on, a barrage of conflicting demands, until she was disorientated and panicking, not knowing where to go or what to do first.

"Bullshit," Rory said again, even more fiercely. "You responded today without hesitation, didn't you? I bet you didn't even think twice about it. You just *did it*. So congratulations. As far as I'm concerned, you've passed with flying colors."

Once again, she had the sensation of falling through a hole in the conversation. "Passed what?"

"Your job interview," Wystan said, smiling. "Want to be a hotshot?"

She'd never understood why breathtakingly cruel remarks were meant to be funny. But she'd learned the hard way—*only teasing, don't be so uptight, can't you take a joke?*—how to respond in these situations. She forced out a laugh.

No one else did.

"Wait." She stared around at them all. "You can't be serious."

Rory slid off the log, kneeling down in front of her so that their faces were level. He looked more like he was proposing marriage than making a job offer. She fixed her gaze on the top button of his shirt, avoiding the fiery trap of his eyes.

"I have never been more serious in my life." His deep, resonant voice shook her bones. She could feel every word in her chest as if he spoke directly into her heart. "Any crew would be lucky to have you. Come down from the tower, Edith. Don't let your life be defined by stupid words from stupid men, who needed you to be small so that they could feel big. Be bold, be daring, be *you*. The person you were always meant to be. This squad needs you. *I* need you. Join us."

CHAPTER 7

*R*ory's whole chest ached with the effort of getting the words out—not because he didn't mean them, but because he *did*. Edith's whole life history was clear in every line of her posture; shoulders hunched, hands pressed so tightly between her knees that her legs trembled.

He wanted to enfold her in his wings, wrapping her in warmth and reassurance. He wanted to rip apart whoever had convinced her that her dreams were futile. That she wasn't good enough, would never be good enough.

All he could do was draw as hard as he could on his griffin's alpha power. Not to dominate—never that, not to *her*—but simply to convince. He filled every syllable with his trust and certainty and unwavering support. He had to make her believe him, believe in him, as he believed in her—

"No," Edith said. There was nothing but bleak resignation in her own voice.

Rory's lungs felt like they'd turned inside-out. For a moment, all he could do was gape at his mate in utter consternation.

Did she just ignore *your alpha voice?* Blaise said in his head.

He tried again, harder. "Edith. We need you. *Join us.*"

Fenrir flattened against the ground. The rest of the squad all rocked back in their seats as though he'd fired a pistol past their faces.

Edith just looked mildly annoyed.

"I heard you the first time," she said, tone sharpening. "And the answer is still no."

The entire squad stared at her.

She flinched, curling around herself more tightly. "Why are you all looking at me like that?"

"Because we kind of assumed you'd say yes," Blaise said, wide-eyed. "People generally have a hard time saying no to Rory."

"Well, I don't." Edith's mouth set in a determined line, even though her body language was still meek and defensive. "I know that he doesn't really mean what he's saying."

"Trust me." Callum rubbed one ear with a rather pained expression. "He does."

"I do," Rory said, this time being careful not to use his power. "Why don't you believe me?"

Her gaze flicked briefly up from his collar, skating across his face and away again. She *still* wasn't looking him in the eye.

"Because it's unbelievable." Edith pulled her hands out from between her knees to tuck them under her armpits, hugging herself. "Hotshots are the best of the best, the elites of wildland firefighters. People try for years to be good enough to get on a crew. Now you want me to believe that you want *me* in your squad? A random fire watcher you've only just met? I don't know if this is a sick joke, or some kind of misplaced sense of charity, but I'm not falling for it."

She paused, looking down. A crease appeared between her eyebrows. "What's the matter with him?"

Fenrir had crept forward on his belly until his head rested on her boot. He whined, his tail tucked between his legs in a posture of extreme respect. For an enormous hellhound, he looked remarkably like a puppy trying very hard to prove he was a Good Boy.

"I think you've impressed him," Rory said.

Very. No one else has ever been deaf to Birdcat's bark. Fenrir rolled over in full submission, paws waving in the air. *Pack needs her. Run with us, Stone Bitch.*

Fenrir still hadn't grasped the concept of personal names. Or mastered some of the finer subtleties of human language. Rory knew he didn't mean any insult.

His griffin, however, didn't.

Fenrir, Blaise said silently, while Rory was fully occupied with stopping himself from shifting on the spot. *I strongly advise that you pick a different nickname.*

Why? Fenrir asked, sounding puzzled. He was still upside-down, showing Edith his throat. His copper eyes fixed on her face in clear adoration. *Is what she is. Tough. Strong. Break your teeth if you bite her. Stone Bitch.*

"Edith," Rory snarled, his head too scrambled with his griffin's outrage for telepathy. "*Edith.*"

Edith's expression shifted from wariness to baffled annoyance. "I'm sitting right here. You don't need to yell."

Callum stared at the stars. Blaise buried her face in her hands. Joe was biting down on his knuckles, his huge shoulders shaking with suppressed laughter.

May I make a suggestion? Wystan cast an aggrieved glance around the circle. *Shall we try not acting like raving lunatics?*

Rory finally wrestled his inner beast back under control. He briefly contemplated trying to explain that he'd been talking to the dog, and discarded the idea. She already thought he was suffering from some kind of brain injury.

"I'm sorry, Edith." Damn it, he wished she would meet his eyes. "I didn't mean to shout. I swear this isn't a joke. We really do want you to join us."

She shook her head, still looking unconvinced. "Why?"

To keep Birdcat in line, Fenrir said earnestly. *Bite his haunches when he tries to run too far ahead of the pack.*

Blaise managed to turn a laugh into a cough. "Well, for a start, Fenrir likes you. He's generally an excellent judge of character."

"Your Red Card says you're more than qualified." Rory handed it back to her. "And we're one person short."

Fenrir flattened his ears. *Am here. Am pack.*

But technically not on the payroll, Rory sent to him in exasperation. *If you aren't going to shift, you can't complain that humans don't see you as a person.*

"Usually Thunder Mountain Hotshots consists of three squads, with a minimum of six firefighters on each," Wystan was explaining to Edith. "Our Superintendent wasn't pleased with us for being under-manned compared to the other squads—it makes it harder for him to balance tasks across the entire crew when the numbers don't match up. Truly, you'd be doing us a favor by filling the vacancy."

Edith's eyebrows drew down further. "But aren't hotshot crews always flooded with applications? I would have thought that you guys would be able to take your pick."

Wystan winced, glancing at Rory. *Oh boy. How do we explain this one?*

Tell her the truth, his griffin urged.

Rory opened his mouth—and hesitated. If he told Edith about shifters, she'd only demand to know why they wanted *her* on the team, since she obviously wasn't one. Then he'd have to explain about fated mates... and *that* would sound perilously like he only wanted her on the team in order to be close to her.

And he didn't only want her to join because she was his mate. He wanted her because she was, undeniably, a superb firefighter. He'd known that at a gut level, just from looking at her fireline, even before he'd seen the training record printed on her Red Card. It would be criminal to waste such obvious talent in a remote lookout tower.

But she'd locked herself away, because she'd been convinced she wasn't worthy to join a crew. If he told her they were mates, she wouldn't believe she'd won her place on her own merits. Not only would she turn him down, but the little self-confidence she had left would be shattered.

Edith's expression was shuttering down, clearly taking his pause as a bad sign. He had to say *something*. He wished the alpha voice worked on her. It was a little disconcerting to realize just how much he usually relied on his power.

"We did have a lot of applications," he said slowly, picking his words as carefully as threading through a bramble thicket. "But I rejected them all. Our Superintendent gave me full power over hiring decisions for the squad. I'd rather have no one than the wrong person. And I didn't find anyone who came even close to being right for me— for the squad. Until you."

Edith shook her head. "You must have had people better than me. More qualified. More normal."

"I don't want someone *normal*." He made a scornful sound. "None of the rest of us are normal. I need someone *exceptional*."

Edith's face had smoothed out again. Even though she still wasn't looking at him, he could somehow tell that he had her whole attention.

"This isn't just a squad, Edith. This is a family." He gestured around the circle. "A bit weird, a bit argumentative, like any family... but at the end of the day any one of us would run into fire for each other. I can't take on anyone who wouldn't do the same. Today, you didn't hesitate to put your own life in danger. And for what? A rabbit."

"Hare," she said, barely audible.

He grinned at her. "And you don't hesitate to correct me, either. That's the kind of person I want on my squad, Edith. Someone who stands up to me when I'm wrong and has my back when I'm right. Someone whose quirks match ours, who likes Joe's cooking and talks to Fenrir like he's a person. Someone who I can trust, whole-heartedly. That's why I want you. That's why I *need* you."

He held out one hand, palm out. "So. Will you join us?"

Slowly, hesitantly, she put her hand in his. It was only the barest contact, light as a feather. It felt like being kissed by lightning.

"Yes," she said.

CHAPTER 8

*T*he prey was on the move.

The hawk's body was a more difficult host than the hare. It couldn't simply puppet the bird directly; not without falling out of the sky, at least. Instead, it had to keep a light touch on the beast's mind, allowing the animal's own instincts to coordinate wings and tail in the subtle movements required for flight.

It did not like being in the air. The sky was an unnatural domain for it, too far removed from the cold, comforting darkness under the earth. The bright blue emptiness and searing eye of the sun unnerved it.

At least the hawk's mind was a more comfortable fit than the hare's, being closer to its own predatory nature. It only needed to nudge the bird's instincts—*good hunting, prey there, find food*—to get it to follow the shifter pack's boxy yellow vehicle.

To Thunder Mountain.

It knew this place. Or rather, knew *of* it. None of its kind had laid eyes on the mountain for many years. There were forces that even they feared.

Almost, it abandoned the hunt. But it was not a dumb beast, driven only by fear and instinct. It had waited long to re-emerge into the mortal world.

It would not be driven out. If it was to be free to feast and hunt, it needed a strategy. A way to defeat those who sought to destroy it. And this prey—this fascinating, flawed, unique prey—might be the key.

For such a chance, it would risk even Thunder Mountain. It flew on cautiously, alert for any danger.

The jagged peak stood alone in the sunlight. No shadows swept through the clouds shrouding the sacred mountain.

Where were the guardians?

The world had changed greatly since it had last stalked the earth. Human dwellings infested the once-pristine wilderness in astounding numbers now. It could scent their souls, fat and placid and mouth-watering. If the guardians had truly gone…

No. It could not risk feasting yet. The lesser shifters were still here. In the before time, they had always worked for the greater powers, watching over the human herd. This could yet be a trap.

It circled high over the shifter den. Hunger gnawed at it, but it had to move slowly, cautiously. It had to observe these new guardians. Learn their habits, their weaknesses.

Learn how to destroy them.

CHAPTER 9

*E*dith huddled under her noise-cancelling headphones. They muffled the worst of the bone-saw shriek of the hotshot crew vehicle's engine, turning it from agonizing to merely uncomfortable.

More importantly, they gave her an excuse to avoid conversation.

Even a truck this big was a tight squeeze for the whole squad, given the size of the men. She'd ended up wedged into the back row, gear piled around her feet and Fenrir's hot, doggy weight pressed against her side. Joe, Wystan, and Callum shared the middle seats, with varying degrees of muttered grumbling and stoic resignation. She could only catch glimpses of Rory past their broad shoulders.

The squad boss rode shotgun in relative comfort, one arm draped along the open window. He kept turning his head, glancing back as though he could sense her looking at him. Every time, he flashed her a warm, private smile that made her skin tingle. Every time, Edith jerked her eyes away, pretending to be deeply engrossed in her music.

It wasn't just the juddering, jolting ride that twisted her stomach into knots. Edith clenched her hands between her knees, sick with guilt.

I have to tell him.

She knew she should have done so already. It should have been the first words out of her mouth when Rory had made his incredible, breathtaking offer: *I can't. You don't understand, I'm not like other people. You don't want me.*

But his words had been like a spell, transforming her into someone else. For one shining moment, she'd believed herself to be the person that he saw—someone he *could* want. Someone who deserved to have a place on his team.

So she'd said yes. And then sat in mute horror, as everyone beamed and congratulated her and the realization of what she'd done came crashing down on her.

She'd spent her last night in the lookout tower staring up at the familiar ceiling, her head spinning through a million different scripts, trying to find a way to come clean. But her nerve had failed her. Just thinking of how Rory would look at her made her tongue dry up in her mouth.

He would hate her. He would leave. And she'd never see him again.

She'd been a coward. She'd called up her supervisor on Rory's satellite phone to hand in her resignation… and been almost grateful for the blast of anger in her ear. Here was an excuse she could use.

"He says I have to work out my notice period," she'd told Rory, with Warren still ranting down the phone.

The hotshot's mouth had crooked in a way that wasn't quite a smile. He'd taken the phone out of her hand, walking off with it. She hadn't been able to hear what he said, but his shoulders had been loose and relaxed. As far as she'd been able to tell, it had been a perfectly pleasant conversation.

When Rory had handed the phone back to her, a gleam in his eye, Warren sounded very different.

"Yes," he'd said, in a high, peculiar tone that she'd never heard him use before. "Of course. Would two months severance pay be sufficient?"

After that, she'd felt like she was floating free of her body, merely observing as everything happened around her. Surely she couldn't really be packing up her limited possessions. Surely she couldn't really be heading down the tower stairs for the last time. Surely she couldn't really be climbing into the crew truck, as though she belonged there.

She kept waiting to wake up. To be found out. But the dream kept stretching on.

And the weight of the lie grew heavier with every passing moment.

She jumped as a hand waved politely in front of her face. Wystan had twisted round in front of her, as much as the limited space allowed. He gestured at her headphones. Reluctantly, she pulled them down around her neck.

"Apologies for disturbing you," the paramedic said, smiling. "But we're nearly there. You'll need to hang on."

True to his words, the truck lurched as Blaise turned up a narrow dirt track. She had to grab onto the back of Joe and Wystan's seats as the vehicle clawed its way up a steep gradient. Pines rolled past the windows. She noticed that the undergrowth had been cut back, removing dangerous dry fuel. The occasional stump showed where dead trees had been felled.

"Does the crew maintain this forest?" she asked Wystan.

He nodded. "All this land belongs to the Thunder Mountain Hotshots. Our base is halfway up, but we spend a lot of time down here at the foot of the mountain. Hiking, training, and practicing clearing fuel."

She squinted up the twisting road, but couldn't see anything other than forest yet. "Why all the way down here?"

Joe heaved a put-upon sigh. "Because Rory likes making us suffer."

"It's good for you," Rory said from the front. "If I had my way, you'd be hiking to the *top* of the mountain for practice."

"Sadist." Joe put his hand over his heart, lifting his eyes to the ceiling. "Thank you, eagles."

"Eagles?" Edith asked.

"Bald eagle nesting area at the summit," Blaise said from the driver's seat. "We don't go up there, to avoid disturbing the birds."

Callum, who'd been silent and motionless for over three hours, abruptly leaned out the window. Edith tried to see what he was looking at, but all she could make out was a distant dot, keeping pace with the truck.

"Is that an eagle?" she asked him.

"No." His intent focus never wavered. "Hawk."

Something changed inside the truck, in a way Edith couldn't quite put her finger on. As one, the hotshots stared at the sky. Even Fenrir's nose tilted upward. His fur bristled under her palm, a low growl rumbling in his throat.

"Easy, big guy," she murmured, rubbing his neck. "Rory? What's wrong?"

The squad boss didn't answer for a moment, still watching the hawk. Then he shook himself a little, turning to offer her another of those easy smiles.

"Probably nothing," he said. "Don't worry about it. Look, we're here."

The truck rolled through an open gate, past a weathered wooden sign proudly proclaiming THUNDER MOUNTAIN HOTSHOTS. Edith's puzzlement over the squad's odd behavior drowned in a flood of anxiety. She swallowed hard, hands fluttering against her knees.

Fenrir's ear swiveled. His weight pressed against her, warm and reassuring. *All will be well*, the dog seemed to be saying.

The road opened out into a broad area rutted with tire tracks. Three rustic log buildings stood in a wide clearing, one large, two smaller. A number of tiny cabins were scattered haphazardly behind them, closer to the tree line.

"Mess hall and kitchen," Rory said, pointing out the biggest building. "Fortunately the chief hires in a cook, otherwise you'd be periodically subjected to Joe's unique interpretation of breakfast."

Joe folded his arms. "*Everything* is better with chili, bro."

"Not porridge," Blaise informed him.

Rory swung his finger further down the line of buildings. "Superintendent's office and the gym are over there. You'll spend a lot of time in the latter, and hopefully none in the former. The two-story one is tool storage—that's where all the gear is kept. Crew quarters in the little cabins behind. They're basic, I'm afraid, but no worse than your lookout tower. And I guarantee they'll seem positively luxurious after you've experienced the joys of fire camp."

Blaise parked the crew truck at the end of a line of identical vehicles. Half a dozen men were lounging on picnic tables outside the mess hall, drinking sodas. Nearby, another group were playing some approximation of basketball. A large, shirtless man barged into another, knocking him to the ground as he snatched the ball. Noticing their arrival, he held up a hand, pausing the game.

"Oh look," he said as Rory opened the side door. "A-hole squad is back."

"We missed you too, Seth," Rory said, jumping down. "Did it take you all week to think of that nickname?"

Seth's mouth twisted. Without warning, he hurled the ball at Rory's head. Rory caught it easily, spinning it on his finger before whipping it back at twice the speed. Seth staggered as it hit his chest.

"Hope you can catch fires better than that," Rory said, as sniggers rose from the watching crowd. He hauled open the side door of the truck. "Now try to remember some manners. Got someone for you all to meet."

Edith shrank back as the rest of the crew piled out. She jumped as Fenrir's cold wet nose poked the side of her neck.

Courage, Stone Bitch.

Edith blinked. While she was still working out where *that* thought had come from, a shadow fell across her. She looked up at Rory's broad-shouldered form, silhouetted against the brightness outside. Sunlight caught in his amber hair like a halo.

"It's all right, Edith," he said, his voice pitched low and gentle. "Seth is a bag of dicks, but the rest of the guys are solid. Come meet them."

She would much rather have taken up permanent residence in the truck, like a hermit crab in a shell. But Fenrir prodded her again, rumbling encouragement. Reluctantly, she climbed out.

Stares stabbed through her like knives. Her legs locked solid, refusing to carry her any further. The world spun around her in a dizzying swirl of yellow uniform pants and black tees. Her pulse roared in her ears. Her mind seemed to disassociate from her body, looking down dispassionately at the scared, awkward woman cringing at the center of a crowd.

Rory's hand cupped her elbow. It was the barest contact, but it grounded her. Warmth spread through her as if she'd swallowed a shot of whiskey. The threatening roar of impending meltdown receded.

Someone wolf-whistled. Abruptly, she was trying to look through six foot two of firefighter. Rory's black crew T-shirt clung to the tense muscles of his back. The rest of the squad closed ranks around her as well—Blaise and Cal to the left, Joe and Wystan to the right. Behind her, Fenrir snarled.

At her side, Joe drew himself up to his full, impressive height. He glared down at the man who'd whistled, who shrank back. "Not cool, bro."

"You bringing your girlfriends back to base now, Joe?" someone else called. "Chief's going to shit a brick when he finds out."

"She's no one's girlfriend," Rory growled. "She's one of us."

He turned a little, exposing her once again to the barrage of curious eyes. Edith flinched, but let him draw her forward, his solid presence giving her the courage to face the gathered crowd.

"This is Edith Stone," Rory said to the crew. "I've invited her to join A-squad."

Seth spat to one side. "*That* little girl?"

"You're begging me to put you on your ass, Seth," Blaise said. "Again."

"That *woman*," Rory stressed the word, locking eyes with Seth, "happens to be able to cut line like demons are on her tail. She's done all the training, and is just one fire away from completing her work book and being fully Type 1 certified."

"Watch out, Seth," someone commented from the back of the crowd. "Sounds like she could steal C-squad out from under your nose."

"I know who's ass *I'd* rather follow," another man put in. Seth scowled as laughter rose around him.

Most of the rest of the hotshots were exchanging glances. There were too many faces for Edith to even begin to try to work out all the various expressions. She couldn't tell how many of them shared Seth's hostility. She clenched her fists, forcing her hands to stay still.

A wiry man with shaggy brown hair and a beard that could swallow a mouse stepped forward. "Edith, was it?" he asked in a soft backcountry drawl.

She couldn't speak with so many people looking at her, but she managed to jerk her chin down in a nod. The man subjected her to a long, considering look before holding out his hand.

"Tanner Brock, B-squad boss." His palm was rough as granite against her own, but what little she could see of his face was kind. "How'd you impress our boy?"

"Now that," Joe said, grinning, "is a story that needs a lot of time. And beer. You could say it's a *hare-raising* tale."

"Joe," Rory said under his breath. "I will *pay* you to shut up."

"Words spoken by many." Wystan sighed. "And as yet, never with any effect."

"A good story has to run free, Rory." Blaise's wicked grin matched Joe's. "Like a rabbit."

Tanner's shaggy head tilted. "I'm sensing this story has something to do with bunnies, and now I'm doubly curious."

"Hey!" Seth said loudly, drawing attention back to himself. "Tanner, you can't seriously approve of this. Bad enough he's pulled in all his rookie English engine buddies. Now he's hiring some random chick off the street?"

Callum treated Seth to the flattest of stares. "I'm Irish."

"And I was ambulance crew, not fire service," Wystan said mildly. "Anyway, we found Edith in the forest."

Seth brushed the corrections away. "Come on, Tanner. This stinks. You gonna let Rory get away with ignoring all the rules yet again?"

Tanner shrugged. "Rory says a body can fight fire, I believe him. Not me he has to convince, anyway."

"No," said a new voice. "That would be *me*."

There was a sudden mass shuffling, hotshots hastily drawing aside. A man strode through the crowd like Moses parting the Red Sea. He was a good bit older than anyone else, with iron-grey hair and weathered skin, but his shoulders were as broad as any man there. A hawk's beak of a nose gave him a brooding, predatory look.

Rory held his ground as the man's glare fell on him. "Chief. You gave me permission to hire whoever I wanted."

"So I did." The man folded his muscled arms. "Words which I intended you to take as a mission statement. Not a damn blank check."

Rory glanced at the fascinated circle of onlookers. He dropped his voice, to the point where Edith was sure only she and the chief could hear him.

"You told me to find who I needed." Rory's hand tightened on her elbow. "I need Edith."

Edith flinched as the man switched his fierce black stare to her. He looked her up and down without speaking for a long, long moment.

The man muttered a profanity, rubbing his forehead as if he had a headache. "At least tell me she's qualified."

"Chief!" Seth spluttered. "You can't-!"

"Edith's got her Red Card, sir," Blaise said loudly, drowning out Seth's protest. "And we've all seen her work. We can vouch for her."

The man's shoulders fell in a sigh. "Then she's in."

"*Chief!*"

"Take a hike, Seth," the chief snapped without looking around.

From the chorus of groans that went up, he hadn't meant it metaphorically. The crowd broke up, hotshots pulling on discarded shirts and boots. Seth threw Edith a poisonous glance over his shoulder as he led his squad off in the direction of the woods.

"Am I paying the rest of you to catch fires or flies?" Buck swept the remaining hotshots with an impartial glare. "B-squad, those tools aren't going to sharpen themselves. A-squad, why is your truck still loaded up? Are you waiting for valet service, perhaps?"

"Let's go, boys," Tanner told his squad. "Nice to meet you, Edith."

Rory hesitated as Blaise and the others headed back to the vehicle. "Ah, chief? A word?"

"No," the hawk-faced man said flatly. "You do not want me to have words with you right now, Rory. Does this look like a happy, smiling face? Go and get your tools unloaded and out of my reach before I succumb to the urge to beat you over the head with your own Pulaski."

Rory exchanged a glance with Fenrir. The big dog came forward, shoving his head under Edith's hand. She wound her fingers into his fur, grateful for his silent presence as Rory trailed reluctantly after the rest of the squad.

The man waited until Rory had disappeared behind the truck before turning back to her. He didn't offer his hand. "I'm Superintendent Buck Frazer. Crew call me chief to my face, and names I pretend not to know behind my back. You used to hard work?"

Edith nodded mutely.

"No you aren't," Buck said, matter-of-fact. "Not like this. But you will be. I'll be straight with you—this won't be an easy ride. I'll push you to *your* limits, not anyone else's. Don't expect to be able to coast on your abilities."

Her abilities? What abilities? Edith stared at him, wondering if she'd somehow misheard.

Buck glanced around, as though checking for eavesdroppers. His gravelly voice lowered even further. "So…what are you, exactly?"

Her breath froze in her throat. He knew, somehow he knew, he could tell she wasn't like other people…but in that case, why had he agreed to hire her?

Buck's ferocious eyebrows bristled at her. "Spit it out, woman. Whatever it is, it can't be weirder than the rest of them. Though from what I overheard, I have a terrible suspicion that you're about to tell me you're a damn rabbit. If that's the case, I really *am* going to whack Rory with a blunt instrument."

Fenrir barked, sharp and urgent. Rory appeared at her side so fast, she hadn't had time to even begin to formulate a reply. He gripped Buck's arm, which seemed to Edith like a good way to lose a hand.

"Chief." Rory's chest heaved for breath. "We need to talk. In private. Right now."

CHAPTER 10

"*S*he's *not a shifter?!*"

Rory winced. He could only pray that the thick log walls of the office had muffled the chief's explosion. The last thing he needed was for Edith—or any of the other normal humans on the crew—to overhear any of this.

"Chief, I can explain," he started.

"I'm sure you can," Buck cut him off. "But what you are going to do is shut up."

Rory had worked for Buck for three years. He recognized that tone of voice. Usually when Buck spoke like that, he was saying things like "fire on the ridge" or "deploy emergency shelters, *now.*"

Rory shut up.

Buck let out his breath. Deliberately, he placed his large, scarred hands flat on his desk, palm down. Rory had the distinct impression that the chief would much rather be wrapping them around his neck.

"Rory," the superintendent said, still in that frighteningly calm tone. "When I found out you were a shifter, what did I say?"

Rory hesitated, trying to judge if it was a rhetorical question. From the way Buck's eyes narrowed, it wasn't. "That you needed more people like me. Sir."

"And why do you think I want shifters on my crew?"

"Because our powers enable us to fight fire more effectively than normal humans. Chief, I know Edith isn't as strong or tough as a shifter. But she really is a damn good firefighter, and the rest of us can work harder to compensate—"

"I don't *need* a good firefighter," Buck cut in. "I have good fire-fighters lining up to spit-polish my boots at the start of every season. I have so many applications from good firefighters, I could wipe my ass all year with resumes. What I need are shifters."

"She won't slow us down. We'll cut line at the same rate, I promise."

Buck shook his head. "This isn't about fighting fire. Damn it, boy. It never *was* about fighting fire."

Rory furrowed his brow. "Chief?"

Buck let out a heavy sigh. "The fire yesterday, the one at the lookout tower. You said on the phone you needed to talk to me about it in person."

"Uh," Rory said, thrown by the abrupt change of topic. "Yeah. There were things that I couldn't put in the official report."

Buck gave him a level look. "Like the fact that it was started by an invisible lightning-throwing monster?"

Rory stared at him.

"Thought so." Buck pushed his chair back. "Guess it's time we had a little chat about the real reason you're here."

He unlocked a desk drawer, extracting a thick manila folder. He flipped it open, paging through. Rory caught brief glimpses of printed-out news stories—*MYSTERY FIRE CLAIMS THREE LIVES* and *INFERNO STILL RAGES*—before Buck pulled out a map from amongst the clippings.

Buck unfolded the large sheet, spreading it across the desk. Upside-down, it took Rory a moment to recognize it as a detailed topology map of Montana, showing terrain and elevation. Colored blobs had been hand-drawn across the soft, well-worn paper.

Buck put a square, blunt finger on a blue splotch. "Ridge Fire, five years ago. Lightning strike. Jumped four attempts to contain it thanks to repeated thunderstorms." His finger moved across a few inches, to a green blob. "Hook End Fire, following year. Blamed on dumb kids horsing around a campfire, but they swore on the witness stand that lightning came out of nowhere and hit their tents. No one believed them, of course. Blue Mile Fire, lightning. June Bug Fire, a damn nightmare of a blaze, same cause."

"I remember it," Rory said, staring down at the map. "That was my first year. We came in late on that one."

"And I wish we hadn't already been deployed in California when the call went out, because I would give my left nut to have had you on the scene at the start. Might have saved a hell of a lot of acres." Buck leaned back, looking grim. "And lives."

Rory counted blobs. "These are *all* lightning fires?"

"Yep." Buck waved a hand across the map. "Either Montana has personally pissed off Thor... or something paranormal likes to keep its territory nice and toasty. Now, here's the interesting bit. Red, yellow, and purple are the fires from the past three years. What do you notice?"

"There are fewer of them. They're smaller." Something else hit him as he studied the scrawled lines. "And most of them are well away from our base. You think that's because I was here?"

"Exactly. Our firebug is scared of shifters. I've been tracking this creature for a decade, Rory. I was going motherloving bananas trying to work out why it had suddenly started tiptoeing around when it usually rampages across the state every summer. Once I found out what you were, it all clicked into place. And I realized that I finally had a way to put a stop to all this."

Rory had been standing to attention for his dressing-down. Now he sank into a chair opposite Buck. The chief didn't object, simply watching him without expression.

"Why didn't you tell me this before?" Rory asked.

"Because you're pathologically protective with a hero complex," Buck said calmly. "If I'd told you why I actually needed a shifter-only squad, you would never have recruited your friends for me."

Rory clenched his hands on the edge of the desk. "You realize I'm going to tell them the truth."

"Go ahead. Even if you use your power to force them to go home, they're only going to turn around and come straight back the moment it wears off." Buck shrugged. "After all, are *you* going to turn tail and run now that you know the real problem?"

Rory let out his breath, slowly. "No."

"Exactly. You're a firefighter. So are they. Nobody comes into this line of work unless they're willing to lay down their life for the greater good." Buck sighed, suddenly looking every one of his forty-five years. "Look, I'm not going to apologize for manipulating you. I'll do what I have to do to get the job done. But I also won't risk lives unnecessarily. A-squad is my secret weapon. Whenever I get even a sniff of this monster, I'm going to send you out, right into the heat. I need you to kill this thing. That's why I can't put an ordinary human on your squad."

Our mate is not ordinary, Rory's griffin said. *And we need her at our side.*

Rory leaned his elbows on the table, putting his head in his hands. *I know we do. But it's not safe. We have to send her away, for her own protection.*

NO. His griffin's denial was instantaneous, and so fierce that his skin prickled, threatening to erupt into fur and feathers. *We have invited her into our nest, our pride. To throw her out now would break her heart. We cannot hurt her!*

Rory remembered the hitch of old pain in Edith's soft voice when she'd spoken of how her old crew had rejected her. It was clear how much she wanted to be a wildland firefighter. Ever since she'd agreed to join A-squad, she'd been walking around with a dazed, thunderstruck expression, like someone waiting to wake up from a dream. How could he snatch that away from her?

But if she stayed...she would be in danger.

If there is danger, that is all the more reason to keep her close, his griffin insisted. *She will not want to leave us, any more than we would ever leave her in peril. We are mates. Our fates are bound together.*

Cold ran down his spine. His griffin had a point. Out of all the places it could have gone, the lightning-creature had struck at Edith's tower. It had broken its own patterns, attacking even though he himself had been nearby. That couldn't be coincidence.

And there had been the hare. And the hawk that Callum had spotted. The one that had followed them all the way from Edith's tower to Thunder Mountain...

"From the way you're staring into space," Buck said dryly, "I take it you're having one of those weird wrestling matches with yourself again."

Rory pulled himself away from his inner conversation, returning to the outside world. "Chief, these lightning-started fires...has anyone spotted animals acting oddly around them?"

Buck's habitual frown deepened. He shuffled through his folder. "Any critters that hang around a wildfire tend to end up crispy. But I did notice this one, a few years back."

BITTEN OR BURNED? screamed the headline. Rory skimmed the article, his sense of unease growing. *While it was previously thought that the couple had tragically perished in the wildfire, investigators now say that they were actually killed by an unknown wild animal. They believe that a panicked wolf or coyote must have been fleeing from the blaze, and sought refuge in the house...*

Rory pushed the paper away again, feeling sick. "Chief, Edith has to stay."

"Which one of us was sitting on the Superintendent side of this desk, again?" Buck looked around his own office, affecting surprise. "Oh look. It's me."

Rory had only ever pulled the alpha voice on Buck once, and that had been to save the Superintendent's life. Buck had thanked him, sincerely, and then equally sincerely promised to muzzle him if he ever did it again. He was absolutely certain the chief had not been joking.

Which left him with no option but to tell the truth.

"Chief." Rory squared his shoulders. "There's something I need to explain about shifters."

CHAPTER 11

"Edith?" Blaise poked her head around the door, frowning as she took in the pristine state of the small bedroom. "If there's something you don't like about this bunk, we can swap."

"No, no." Edith tried to force a smile onto her face. "The room's fine."

In truth, the mattress was too hard and the pine-tar smell was too strong and the view out the tiny window was all wrong...but none of those was the real problem. She hugged her backpack tighter, running the familiar straps through her fingers.

Blaise sat down next to her on the narrow bed. "Then why aren't you unpacking your stuff?"

She looked down, avoiding the other woman's kind gaze. "I really need to talk to Rory. Do you think he'll be back soon?"

"Hard to say. I think he had a lot he needed to discuss with Buck." Blaise nudged her with an elbow. "But I promise, they aren't talking about kicking you out into the night."

"They should be." Edith stood up abruptly. "I have to go talk to them. I should never have come here in the first place."

Fenrir, who was occupying most of the floor space in the tiny room, made a deep, rumbling growl. He flopped across her feet. The effect was similar to putting a parking boot on a car.

"See, even Fenrir doesn't want you to go," Blaise said, as Edith struggled vainly to extricate her toes from under the dog. She patted the blanket. "Now tell me why you're having second thoughts. It's not that jerk Seth, is it?"

"Not directly." Edith sat down again, since it was clear it would take a backhoe to shift Fenrir. "But he wasn't wrong. I don't really belong here."

"Don't pay any attention to him. It's pitiful, really. Just because we're A-squad while his own is called C, he has to take every opportunity to get into a dick-waving contest with Rory. As though a stupid letter means we're better than him." Blaise grinned. "Though we are, of course. And what's this nonsense about not belonging with us? I thought Rory made it perfectly clear how much he—how much we all want you to be here. You seemed to believe him last night."

Edith bit her lip. "Have you ever been carried away in the heat of a moment, and done something that you would never have done if you'd been thinking clearly, and then realized too late that you've destroyed your life?"

"Ouch." Blaise blew out her breath. "That's a bit close to home. Yes."

Edith traced patterns across the top of her backpack. "Rory's been so kind to me. All of you have. But there's something I haven't told you. And when I do, you're all going to hate me."

"There is literally nothing you could say to Rory that would make him hate you." Blaise shook her head ruefully. "If you told him that you ate roasted kittens for breakfast every morning, he would be scouring the internet for recipes within five minutes."

"But what if, if I was keeping a secret. Not, not anything bad or illegal," she added hastily. "Just something that made me different. Something that I really should have told him straight away, but... didn't."

Blaise leaned back on her hands, staring at the ceiling. She didn't speak for a long, long moment.

"If you found out Rory was keeping a secret like that," she said at last. "Would you hate *him?*"

"No!" The word jumped out of her mouth without conscious thought.

"There you go then." Blaise shrugged. "And as for the rest of us... we all like you, Edith. There's only one thing you could do to change that."

Edith swallowed nervously. "Let the squad down?"

"No." Blaise looked at her levelly. "Hurt Rory."

"I would *never--*" Edith cut herself off as she heard her own voice echo from the walls. She made herself speak more normally. "I mean, I would never want to hurt him. Not deliberately."

"Good." Blaise's mouth curled. "Because you do *not* want to be my enemy."

Fenrir huffed as if agreeing.

Edith jumped as someone rapped on the front door. Neither Blaise nor Fenrir so much as twitched.

"Speak of the devil." Blaise raised her voice. "It's not locked!"

Rory himself came in. He'd swapped his turn out gear for dark jeans and a soft tee that could barely stretch over his biceps. Her bedroom seemed even smaller with his broad, burly form filling her doorway.

"Hey," he said, smiling at her. "You settling in okay?"

He must have come straight from the shower. His blond hair had darkened to bronze, little beads of water glittering like gems amidst the tousled spikes. She was so mesmerized by the slightly damp, gleaming hollow of his throat, she didn't realize he'd even spoken until Blaise slid off the bed.

"I'm gonna go...uh, take a walk," Blaise announced, her gaze flicking from Edith to Rory and back again. "You coming, Fenrir?"

Rory stood aside to let the pair squeeze past. Edith noticed that Blaise caught his eye for a moment, some private message flickering in the air between the two old friends. A pang of envy shot through her at that easy, silent communication.

Rory looked after Blaise as she exited the cabin, his forehead creasing a little. When he turned back to her though, his warm smile was back again.

"We need to get you some gear," he said, holding out a hand. "Buck wants the crew practicing with full kit tomorrow. Let's go see what we can find for you in the storeroom."

She didn't need help getting off the bed, but it would be rude to just leave his proffered hand hanging in mid-air. She tried not to show the shiver that raced through her as his fingers folded over hers.

She hadn't anticipated his strength. A flex of his arm, and she shot up like a rocket, stumbling into him. She caught herself just in time to avoid bumping her nose against his chest, but she *did* get an excellent close-up view of that delicious dip between his collarbones. She wondered if he would taste as good as he smelled...

What was she *thinking*? She stepped back so hastily that she tripped. Only the fact that Rory still had hold of her hand stopped her from toppling straight back onto the bed again.

"I'm not really this clumsy!" she blurted out, blushing furiously. "It's just, just—"

"It's a small room," Rory finished for her, looking a little red himself.

She'd actually been about to say, *just that you make me go weak at the knees.* On retrospect, she was very glad that he'd interrupted.

"Sorry, that was my fault." Rory let go of her hand at last. "I didn't mean to yank you around like that. Come on. Let's go get you kitted up."

"Uh, yeah." Edith swallowed hard, trying to get a grip on her surging libido. "Good idea."

She couldn't have a serious discussion with Rory while she was tongue-tied with helpless lust, after all. Surely it would be easier to maintain a cool, professional attitude once they were away from her bedroom.

There was nothing sexy about putting clothes *on*, after all.

CHAPTER 12

*A*n hour later, and she was seriously wishing they were back in the bedroom.

Rory's bowed head was level with her groin. Her fingers itched to feel the texture of his tousled hair. She stared straight ahead at the wall, and tried very hard not to breathe in his scent.

"It's no good. This pair is too short too." Giving up fiddling with the cuffs of the turn out pants she was trying on, he sat back on his heels. He ran his hand through his hair, making her own hand clench in longing. "You have really long legs."

"Yeah, I know. It's a pain. I can never find pants that fit." She knew she was talking too much, but she couldn't help it. His proximity unhinged her tongue as well as her mind. "All the kids at school used to call me a stork."

He frowned, his eyes darkening. "Teenagers are cruel."

It had actually been back in preschool, when people had only seen her outward differences. Her nicknames later on had been much crueler.

"Well, I *am* a stork." If she didn't move soon, she was going to explode. In a moment of inspiration, she flapped her elbows, making a joke of it. "*Awk, awk.*"

"A sexy stork," he said—and flushed. He cleared his throat, turning away to rummage through the shelves lining the walls.

He thought *she* was sexy?

"Maybe one of the smaller men's sizes would be a better fit." He tossed her another pair of pants. "Try these ones."

As she got changed, she noticed that Rory was carefully keeping his eyes fixed on a shelf of safety helmets. Her stomach sank a little. If he *really* thought she was sexy, shouldn't he be trying to steal a peek?

"These are better, I think." She pinched a roll of extra fabric, wrinkling her nose. "But I'll need a belt."

"Try these." He moved in close, fastening a pair of suspenders to the waistband. She sucked in her breath as his fingertips skimmed over her shoulder blades, adjusting the straps. "There. Move around a bit, let me see if they hold up properly."

She obligingly squatted down, bending and twisting. The pants were definitely roomy around the waist, but they didn't threaten to expose her ass.

"Feels good to me." She straightened, bouncing on her toes. "What do you think?"

He didn't answer.

"Rory?" She turned—and was caught in the full force of his stare.

Heat rushed over her. For all that she was wearing multiple layers of protecting clothing, she felt utterly naked.

But not exposed. She felt...*worshipped*.

Just for a second. He blinked, wrenching his gaze away.

"That looks good." His voice had gone rough and growly. "Take them off now. I mean, uh..." He shook his head sharply, turning on his heel. "Put them with the rest of your stuff. Just got one more thing to find."

She did so, adding them to her growing pile of gear. Protective jacket, pants, backpack, fire shelter, tools...he'd already found her everything on the standard equipment list. She couldn't imagine what else he thought she'd need.

He cleared his throat again, still noisily clattering around at the back of the storeroom. "So. Stork, huh? Any other nicknames?"

There were, of course. Her warm glow faded, quenched by cold reality. She couldn't flirt with him, even if she was *almost* sure now that he might not entirely object.

For all her nervous prattling, she still hadn't told him the truth about herself. Every time she tried, she found herself babbling about something else instead. Like stupid childhood nicknames.

"What was *your* childhood nickname?" she asked.

And there she went, racing away down the slightest diversion. Maybe if she just kept talking long enough, she wouldn't *have* to tell him. Surely he had to have worked it out by now?

If he found her conversational topics odd, he didn't show it. He cast one of those wry, crooked smiles at her over his shoulder.

"Buttbrain," he said, totally without rancor. "At least, that's what my twin called me. Still does, sometimes."

"You have a twin?" Her brain fused and melted at the thought of *two* of him. "Are you identical? Is he a firefighter too?"

"Yes, no, no." He pulled out a crumpled garment, shook his head, and stuffed it back into a box again. "We look pretty similar, but people don't tend to get us confused. Not like Callum and his brothers. They *are* identical. All three of them."

"Wow." She had a sudden terrifying vision of three identical, glowering red-heads. "It must be nice, growing up with someone just like you."

"Don't ever say that to Callum." His mouth quirked. "Though you should definitely suggest that to my twin. I want to see the look on Ross's face."

"Oh, does he live near here?"

He snorted. "Nope. He flatly refuses to even come out to visit. I think he's suspicious I might somehow forcibly recruit him onto the squad. He lives back in England, in Brighton. It's a city on the south coast."

Now she was *really* confused. "Then why would I ever be in a position to be able to say anything to his face?"

He hesitated. "Uh...just a figure of speech. Do you have siblings?"

"No. Thankfully."

He cast her an odd look. "Why thankfully?"

She shrugged. "I'm not great with people. Even my own parents found me difficult. I guess a brother or a sister would have found me equally baffling. It's bad enough being the odd one out when there are only three of you in a family."

"That sounds very lonely," he said, softly.

She turned away from the deep, gentle gold depths of his eyes. "It's all I've ever known. I'm used to it."

He was silent for a moment. She concentrated on folding her new turn outs, aligning the seams precisely.

"Edith."

She jumped, startled by the unexpected closeness of his voice. She whipped round to discover him standing just behind her, a t-shirt in his hands. For such a big man, he was as soft-footed as a cat.

"Last night I told you this squad is like a family." He held out the garment. "I meant it. You aren't alone anymore."

She looked down at the folded t-shirt.

THUNDER MOUNTAIN HOTSHOTS.

She shoved her hands into her pockets, where they couldn't betray her longing. "Rory, I—"

"You still feel like you don't belong. Like you're different." He balanced the crew t-shirt on one hand, taking her arm with the other. Gently but irresistibly, he drew her hands out of her pockets. "Edith, the rest of the squad, we're…we've known each other since childhood. That's all. Just give it time, and you *will* fit in here. I promise."

She was caught in his eyes like a fly in amber. Words fell from her head. The only one that remained was *yes.*

Yes, to anything he suggested. *Yes*, to him.

"Yes," she whispered.

"That's all I ask." He handed her the shirt. "Try this on."

He turned his back, giving her privacy. She shuddered and gasped, the rest of the world coming back like a slap of cold water.

Slowly, she pulled the crew t-shirt over her head. She couldn't think of an excuse to avoid trying it on. And, if she was honest with herself, she *wanted* to try it on. Just once.

Just for one more minute, she wanted to pretend. That she could be a hotshot, someone that Rory could respect. Maybe even someone that he could call *sexy*.

"There." Rory had turned round again. His mouth curved in a smile so purely happy that she wanted to cry. "See? A perfect fit."

It didn't feel like a perfect fit. It felt itchy and uncomfortable, like her own lies. She twitched her shoulders.

"Hang on, the label's sticking out." He put one hand on her shoulder, the other curving around the back of her neck. "Hold still."

She couldn't have moved if the building had been on fire. The discomfort of the new t-shirt against her skin faded into irrelevance. All she was aware of was the warmth of his breath against her skin, the closeness of his body.

Gently, he tucked the label back in. He smoothed the fabric down, making sure it lay completely flat. "There. Perfect."

He still hadn't moved away. Her breath caught. He seemed to have stopped breathing too.

"Perfect," Rory said again, in the barest whisper.

She didn't dare turn her head. She took a deep breath, summoning all her courage. "Rory, I have to tell you—"

A loud cough came from behind them.

Edith sprang away from Rory guiltily. He did the same, although he didn't let go of her shoulder.

"Chief," Rory said, flushing to the roots of his hair. "I was, uh, helping Edith. With her gear."

"So I can see," Buck said, folding his arms. "If you've *quite* finished, I need to talk to her. Alone."

Rory's fingers tightened, as though he'd felt her tense up. "It's okay," he murmured in her ear. "He's cranky, but fair. You can trust him."

With a last parting squeeze, Rory released her. She squelched an urge to clutch at his sleeve and beg him not to go. Something of her dismay must have shown on her face, because he hesitated at the top of the stairs.

"I won't go far," he said. "I'll be right outside."

"No you won't." Buck shooed Rory away as if he was a pigeon. "You will be writing. In my office, where I have thoughtfully left you an incident report form to fill out. With words arranged to form semi-coherent sentences. That I can actually file without having to attach a hand-written note of apology to whoever has to read it!"

He shouted this last bit down the stairs, as Rory beat a hasty retreat. Buck glared after the squad boss for a moment, as though checking to make sure he was really gone, before turning back to her.

"I don't like having you on A-squad," Buck said without preamble.

His words hit her like a gut-punch. He hadn't exactly welcomed her with open arms before, but he *had* said that she was on the crew. What had happened? Had he somehow figured out her secret? Was he firing her?

Buck's mouth thinned. "But I don't have a choice. The other squads are full, so I've got nowhere else to put you."

That didn't sound like an instant dismissal. He *couldn't* know.

Which meant that she had to tell him. Right now.

"S-sir." Apprehension churned in her stomach. She felt sick with dread. "I, I need to tell you—"

"I'm talking," Buck cut her off. "You listen. And you better listen good. Rory needs you here, which means I need you here."

She was reduced to staring at him in confusion again.

"But." The chief raised a finger, glowering more fiercely than ever. "I will not have any more deaths on my head. While you're on my crew, I'm responsible for you. And that means that if I get the slightest *hint* that you are not fit for this job, I will fire you in a hot second. No matter how it messes up my crew or my plans."

"I don't understand," she whispered.

"If you go, so does Rory. Without Rory, all of A-squad collapses." His cold eyes flayed the flesh from her bones. "And I need A-squad. So you better throw everything you've got into persuading me you're an asset and not a liability. Understand me now?"

She didn't. Didn't understand how this could be a man who Rory respected. Didn't understand how he could have called him *fair*.

Didn't understand how anyone could be so cruel, so spiteful, as to chain Rory's fate to hers.

She knew Buck had been angry at Rory for hiring her, but *this* angry? Furious enough to make Rory pay the price if she failed? To fire them both if—when—she made a mistake?

Buck frowned at her. "I expect crew to answer me, Edith. Not a great start."

It took all of her willpower to stop her hands from shaping her distress in the air. Her shoulders and arms were rigid as iron.

"Y-yes, chief," she forced out past numb lips. "I understand."

"Good." His voice softened a fraction. "Look, Rory believes in you. And even if I occasionally wish to skin him and fashion his hide into a fetching hat, I trust him. Give me your best self, show me what he sees in you, and I'll gladly eat humble pie and ask for seconds. Prove his instincts are right. Don't let him down."

Her fingernails bit into her palms. "I won't."

With a small nod, Buck left. She managed to stay standing until he was out of sight.

Then she folded into a huddled ball. She rocked in tight jerks, jamming her fist into her mouth to stifle her involuntary sobs. Buck's implacable voice echoed like thunder in her head.

If you go, so does Rory.

If you go, so does Rory.

"Edith? Are you up here?"

She jerked upright in panic. The light through the windows had darkened into dusk.

She couldn't be seen like this. Other people didn't collapse, shaking from head to toe. Other people didn't zone out and lose chunks of time. Other people didn't have meltdowns.

Above all else, she had to be like other people now. She couldn't afford the slightest hint that she was different.

Otherwise Rory would pay the price.

"Edith?" Blaise called again.

She scrubbed her hands over her face, putting her expression back in order. "Yes! I'm here!"

Blaise's head popped up from the stairs. "There you are! Rory sent me to see where you'd got to. Why are you still up here? Couldn't you find what you needed?"

"I-it took awhile," Edith lied, ducking her head to hide her face. She gathered up her uniform. "But I found it all in the end."

"Great. If any of it turns out not to fit right, don't suffer in silence. Not good for anyone if your gear is giving you blisters out on the line." Blaise hesitated. "Did you talk to Rory about whatever it was that was bothering you?"

"Kind of." She was grateful for the pile of equipment occupying her arms. It stopped her hands from giving her away. "It doesn't matter now."

Blaise eyed her for a moment longer before shrugging. "Well, come on. I'll show you where we stow our squad's stuff, and then you still have to unpack." The other woman bumped her, shoulder to shoulder, in a friendly fashion. "Assuming you've decided to stay after all."

"Yes." Edith set her jaw. Her fingers dug into the rough fabric of her folded turn outs. "I'm staying."

CHAPTER 13

*R*ory was getting dressed when the call he'd been expecting finally came. Shoving his head through the neck of his t-shirt, he lunged for his cellphone. "Dad!"

Framed in the tiny screen, the grainy, juddering image of his father smiled up at him. "So I gather you've found your mate."

The picture-in-picture video showed Rory his own big sappy grin. He didn't care how much of a massive dork he looked. With Edith in his life, he thought he might never stop smiling.

"I'm sorry to give such big news over email," he said to his father. "With the time difference, it was too late to call you last night."

The fine lines around Griff's golden eyes crinkled with amusement. Sometimes looking at his father was scarily like peering into a mirror and seeing his future self.

"Oh, I didn't hear it from your email," Griff said. "Though your mother is still poring over that, ah, extensive essay extolling Edith's many virtues. No, *I* heard the news from Chase."

Rory was taken aback. Chase was Callum's father, one of his own dad's fire engine crewmates. "Cal actually picked up a phone and talked to his family?"

Griff shook his head. "Alas, no. Chase got it from Ash, who of course learned it from Rose. Who in turn was told by your brother, since she overheard part of your phone call with him last night."

That had been inevitable, he supposed. Rose owned the pub where Ross worked as a bartender. She was their godmother, so he didn't really mind Ross sharing the news with her.

"You and Mom aren't upset that I told Ross first, are you?" he asked. "It's just that I knew he'd still be awake, closing up the pub."

"Of course you told your twin first." Griff waved a hand in dismissal. "But *he* immediately called up all your sisters, since he knew his life would be a living hell if they found out he'd kept such juicy gossip from them for even a minute. And *they* called your cousins, who called your aunts…with the result that Chase only managed to be the first to tell me the news because he wasn't shy about waking me up at the crack of dawn. My phone has been going off all morning."

Rory winced. With five siblings, seven aunts, and enough cousins to form a football team, he had a *lot* of relatives. And they were all impossibly nosy. Maybe Edith was right to prefer being an only child.

"Sorry about that," he said. "Why haven't they been calling me?"

"Ross made everyone swear not to hassle you. Said you were going to have enough problems winning your mate without your entire family peering over your shoulder and offering helpful advice."

That was his twin. Combining incredible thoughtfulness with a back-handed insult. *Thanks, Ross.*

Rory folded himself onto his narrow bunk, cupping his phone between his hands. "Well, I could actually use some helpful advice. From one person, at least."

Griff gave him what Rory and his siblings had always referred to as "the dad look." The one that managed to combine total support with a certain wryness; a mix of *you got this* with *gotta let kids make their own mistakes.*

"*Please*, Dad," Rory urged. "I don't have your ability to read people, and my own power doesn't work on Edith. I'm terrified of screwing up and not being able to make it right again."

His dad's image flickered and broke up for a moment, the unreliable internet connection struggling to maintain the call. "I can't tell you your path, son. All I can do is suggest that you listen to your instincts. What does your griffin think?"

Sweep her into the sky, his animal said promptly. *Show her our true self.*

Rory made a face. "My griffin is no help. All it wants to do is mate her immediately. But I *can't,* Dad. I'm her boss, after all. Imagine how it's going to look to her if I hire her one day and start making advances the next. I have to keep my animal leashed, but so far it keeps getting away from me." He winced as he recalled how close he'd already come to disaster. "Yesterday, I almost kissed her in the middle of fitting her out for new gear."

"Well," Griff murmured, smiling. "Firefighter uniforms *are* very sexy."

"Seriously, Dad. You've got more control of your own beast than any shifter I know. How do you do it?"

Griff blew out his breath. "I learned the hard way that if you pit yourself against your own soul, you lose every time. Rory, I understand your concerns, but don't think of this as something that's happening only to you. Even though Edith's not a shifter, she'll be experiencing the mating instinct too. But *she* doesn't know what's really going on. Imagine what that must be like for her."

Was *that* why Edith wouldn't look him in the eyes? "You think she's so timid and uncertain around me because she feels something too?"

Griff cocked an eyebrow at him. "Let's say that I find it difficult to believe that some fragile little mouse could possibly be your perfect match."

Hope bloomed in his chest, but he hesitated. "I don't know. If you saw her, you'd be able to tell how badly she's been hurt. She'd locked herself up in that remote lookout tower like she was scared of the world. Yesterday, when she met the rest of the crew, she looked like she wanted to bolt straight back there. If she's that overwhelmed just by meeting new people, how can I possibly dump shifters and fated mates and lightning-throwing invisible monsters on her head? I can't explain one thing without the whole story coming out."

"Mmm." Griff rubbed his chin for a moment. "Who else knows she's your mate?"

"Evidently, half of England and Scotland," Rory said wryly. "Apart from that…all the squad, of course. And the Superintendent."

The dad look was back again, stronger than ever. "And you see no way this could possibly go wrong."

Rory winced. "Buck won't tell, and I can keep the rest of the squad from spilling the secret too soon. And I *will* tell her. When the moment is right." He glanced at the time. "I've got to go to training. Tell Mom and the girls I'll call when I can."

"We're all thinking of you, son. Stay safe." Griff hesitated. "And Rory?"

He paused with his thumb over the End Call button. "Yeah?"

"*Make* the right moment."

CHAPTER 14

$\mathcal{T}$he right moment, Rory was pretty sure, was *not* in the middle of a crowded gym that smelled of socks.

Nonetheless, when he walked through the door and was confronted by the sight of Edith doing chin-ups across the room, it was all he could do not to drop to his knees and propose marriage on the spot.

Her muscles flexed under a light gleam of sweat. Her shorts and crop top clung to her narrow, straight figure and showed off the powerful curves of her thighs. Tendons stood out in the sides of her neck as she pulled herself up one more time. Strong, controlled, every part of her body working in perfect unison.

Joe came up behind him as he stood there frozen. The sea dragon let out a long, appreciative whistle.

"Bro." Joe draped an arm over his shoulder, nodding in Edith's direction. "Please take this as a totally platonic expression of sincere aesthetic admiration when I say: *Daaaaaaamn.*"

Unaware of her audience, Edith dropped to the ground. She wiped her forearm across her forehead, flushed and panting. She was gloriously female, intoxicatingly sexy, and he was staring at her like a lovesick teenage boy in front of half the crew.

He wrenched himself away, turning to Joe instead. "You want to do some free weights?"

"Not in the slightest," Joe responded. His blue eyes gleamed with wickedness. "But I bet I know someone who does. Hey, Edith! Rory needs a spotter!"

Rory strategically positioned his gym towel in front of his groin as Edith headed their way. "Joe," he growled under his breath, barely moving his lips. "I am going to murder you with my bare hands."

"Just being a good wingman, bro. Whether you like it or not." The sea dragon punched his arm cheerfully before heading off to join Callum and Blaise at the floor mats.

Edith flipped her long honey-gold braid over her shoulder, sweat-damp from her work out. His heart gave a great bound as she lifted her chin, looking him squarely in the eyes. "You wanted me?"

He was so lost in the infinite subtle shades of brown and green patterning her irises, it took him a second to realize she'd spoken at all. A question. She'd asked him a question.

"Yes," he said dazedly. "Always."

Her gaze flickered sideways, breaking the spell. "Um, okay. What did you want to do?"

You, he very nearly said. He clutched his towel more tightly.

"Uh, bench press?" he said at random.

He realized his mistake when he was flat on his back, staring up at the underside of Edith's small breasts leaning over his face. He shut his eyes and desperately imagined the unsexiest things he could. Dung beetles. Foot fungus. Naked mole rats.

Naked mate, his griffin helpfully suggested.

"Too much weight?" she said, clearly mistaking his pained expression.

"No," he grunted, enormously grateful that he'd had the foresight to drape his towel across his lap. "Load me up with more."

Normally he was cautious not to lift anywhere near his actual limit during the morning session, when the other squads were sharing the gym. Apart from Buck, none of them knew about shifters. It was best to avoid attracting attention.

But he needed the burn in his shoulders and chest to drive out the ache in areas further south. And, if he was totally honest with himself, he couldn't resist showing off a little.

He heard Edith's soft intake of breath as he smoothly raised the weights. His griffin preened smugly. He was achingly aware of the warmth of Edith's hands on the bar next to his, not quite touching his own.

He was seriously tempted to power through his reps with his eyes closed, but that would just have made Edith think he was even more of a weirdo than she already did. On the next lift, he opened them, and found himself locking gazes with her. She jerked back a fraction, biting her lower lip, but didn't drop her eyes.

The bar suddenly felt as light as a feather in his hands. She was looking at him, properly looking at him! No more of those fleeting, sideways glances, as though he was some terrifying beast.

See? he said silently to his griffin. *Patience is paying off. She's already more relaxed around us.*

To his surprise, his griffin didn't share his elation. Its feathers flattened in distress, tail flicking from side to side.

No, it whispered. *Look closer.*

Puzzled, Rory studied Edith as best he could while he ran through his bench press routine. His griffin's unease spread through his stomach like ice. Even though he was staring right at her, he had the weirdest feeling that he wasn't *seeing* her.

It was like there was an invisible force-field behind those hazel eyes, walling off her soul. For all that they were physically close, she seemed farther away than ever.

The longer he looked at her, the more he became convinced that she wasn't seeing him either. Before, she'd always been in constant motion, beautifully attuned to the world around her. Now, her shoulders were as rigid as her smile. It was like she was braced against some storm he couldn't see.

"Hey." He pitched his voice low, so that none of the other crew members working out nearby could overhear. "What's wrong?"

"Nothing. Nothing's wrong." Despite her words, her hands spasmed on the bar, pulling him off his rhythm. "Why?"

"You don't seem yourself, somehow."

Her glassy smile cracked. For the barest instant, real panic showed in her face. Her gaze cut away from him at last, fixing instead on the weight rack.

"It's just, just loud in here." She jerked her head to indicate the packed room. "And busy. But I'll get used to it."

"You don't have to, you know," he said, wondering if that really was all that was bothering her. "Did you notice Wystan isn't here? He can't stand the gym—crowds give him a headache. He goes for a long run every morning instead. Don't feel forced to do something just because the rest of us are doing it. Pick something that works for you."

A hint of her usual animation crept back. "Really?"

"Sure. The chief isn't a dictator." Rory paused to catch his breath, his muscles burning. "He doesn't care how we get into top condition, just as long as we do."

She caught her lip in her teeth again, as though debating something with herself. Then she said, all in a rush, "Rory, I'm sorry that the chief is so mad. I promise I'll work hard. I won't let you down."

Was *that* why she was so subdued this morning? He'd assumed Buck had just given her the usual welcome-to-the-crew pep talk.

Of course, Buck's idea of motivational speaking generally involved a lot of colorful language. Not to mention the occasional anatomically unlikely threat.

Anger flooded through him. Edith was so delicate, so sensitive. Couldn't the chief tell that she needed special consideration? How dare Buck treat her like anyone else?

He yanked the dumbbell down so fast, Edith lost her balance. She toppled over, catching herself with her hands against his chest.

"What did Buck say?" he demanded.

They were almost nose-to-nose. She pulled back a little, her eyes widening. Her obvious alarm washed over him like a bucket of cold water. What feral fury was she reading in *his* face, to make her recoil from him like that?

"I-I thought you knew," she stuttered.

"Knew what? I swear, if he's upset you, I'll—"

"No!" She pressed down, adding her own weight to the weight of the barbell, as though frightened he would storm off to punch the chief right there and then. "I mean, you can't. *Please*, Rory. It'll be okay, I swear, I won't let him—please, don't ask me to explain. Just trust me."

"I do," he said, more gently. "But I wish you'd tell me what's wrong."

She was so close that he could feel the warmth of her breath against his lips. Her eyes were the barest ring of hazel around wide, dark pupils. He could see *her* in them again, all her defenses down.

The rest of the world fell away. All he knew was her. If it hadn't been for the cold weight of iron across his chest, he would have cupped his hand round the back of her neck. Drawn her down to him, tasted the trembling softness of her lips...

Heads up, Blaise sent to him telepathically from across the room. *Asshole incoming.*

He had never been less happy to look up into Seth's glowering scowl. Edith went bright red. She sprang away, letting go of the barbell completely. It was just as well he didn't actually need a spotter to help him with the weights.

"You're hogging the bench," Seth snapped. If he'd been a griffin, his feathers would have been puffed out in aggressive display. "I want to use it now."

As always, Rory pushed down his griffin's instinct to put the other male in his place. It wouldn't help to sink to Seth's level. Of course, not reacting to Seth's not-so-subtle dominance challenges *also* didn't seem to help. The man didn't seem able to grasp that they were crew-mates, not competitors.

Rory put the bar back on the stand with barely a *clink*. "Sure, Seth," he said, sliding off the bench. "I was just finishing up anyway. All yours."

Seth took up position under the barbell with a little sneer, clearly feeling that he'd won the round. He tried to lift the bar off the rack. His triumphant expression slipped a little.

Edith was still flushed, but she reached for the bar. "Would you like me to give you a hand with that?"

"*I* don't need a girl to help me lift," Seth snarled. "Back off."

"But it's too heavy for you," Edith said, sounding honestly concerned. "Here, I'll take some of the weights off."

A couple of watching B-squad hotshots sniggered. Seth's expression darkened. With immense effort, he managed to inch the bar off the support.

Rory lunged to catch the bar as Seth's arms buckled. The movement was too fast, too inhuman, but he couldn't let a crewmate get injured. Even if he *was* an asshole.

"There's no shame in knowing your limits," he said, trying to defuse the situation. "It won't help anyone if you hurt yourself and have to sit out the start of the season."

The B-squad firefighters were now openly smirking at the C-squad boss. Still under the bar, Seth flushed dark red.

"Don't you lecture me," he spat. He jerked his chin at Edith. "You pretend you're so perfect, but I saw you drooling over her just now. You only hired her to get into her pants."

His overstretched control snapped at last. Without conscious thought, he let the barbell drop. Seth's eyes bugged out.

"Don't talk about Edith like that." Alpha power rang in Rory's voice like a blade leaving its sheath. "*Ever.*"

Seth made a little mewling sound. His hands scrabbled at the iron bar crushing his chest.

"Rory." Edith tugged at his arm. "Let him go. You're hurting him."

Shame cut through his white-hot anger. The C-squad boss was irritating, but that was no excuse to unleash his shifter powers on the man. Not only was Seth just a regular human, he was fellow crew. Lives depended on them being able to work as a team.

He replaced the bar on the rack. "I'm sorry, Seth. I won't let you disrespect any of my squad, but I shouldn't have lashed out at you."

His apology had the opposite effect to what he'd intended. From the way Seth's fists clenched, Rory might as well have unzipped his fly and peed on his face.

"Damn right you shouldn't have." Seth scrambled up from the bench, pointing a shaking finger at him. "You're going to regret this, you dick."

A growl escaped him before he could bite it back. With his griffin still bristling, now he was one breath away from getting into an undignified scuffle with a fellow crew member. With Edith watching. He was supposed to be acting *normal* in front of her, not letting his animal instincts drive him.

"A-squad!" He turned away, raising his voice. "We're going on a hike. Full gear. Let's go!"

"Hey!" Seth spluttered. "You think you can just ignore me? Hey!"

He walked away, not looking back. The squad fell into step behind him.

"I really wish you would just punch him," Blaise said under her breath.

Rory sighed. "If I thought it would finish anything, I would. But he's so pig-headed, I'd have to seriously hurt him before he got the message. I can't do that."

Callum muttered, "I could."

"No one starts anything with Seth." He used just enough of the alpha voice to make it a command. "Like it or not, he's part of the crew. We all need to do our best to make nice with him."

Joe cast a significant look at Edith. "What if he gives one of us a hard time?"

"Then I'll bounce him like a basketball," Rory growled. "If he takes out his frustrations with me on any of you, let me know. Especially you, Edith."

Her chin jerked down in the barest nod. The stiffness was back in her posture. Where had all her alert, dancing grace gone? It was like she was a puppet of herself. It made him want to rip something apart. Preferably Seth.

"Hey," he said, taking her elbow and drawing her a little apart from the others. He lowered his voice. "It's not true, you know. What Seth said."

She met his eyes. All he could see in them was himself, reflected back. "About you wanting to sleep with me?"

Damn Seth.

"Right," he said, his voice roughening. He wished his power worked on her. "You earned your place on this squad. Don't ever doubt that, okay?"

"Okay," she echoed. She pulled her arm free, stepping back. Her spine straightened. "I believe you. And I meant what I said earlier. I won't let you down."

"I know you won't." His hands felt big and awkward. *He* felt big and awkward. Everything was all wrong, and he didn't know why. "Go get your turn outs and pack. We'll show Buck what A-squad can do."

Rory let out his breath as Edith headed off. That had been a close one. He was doubly grateful now that they'd been interrupted before, in the storeroom. If he'd kissed her then, she'd never have listened to him now. She would have believed Seth's insinuations. Her confidence would have been crushed.

Have to be more careful in future, he vowed grimly.

No more longing looks. No more finding excuses for touching her. From now on, he would be carefully, painfully professional. At least for now.

When she *knew* she belonged in the crew...then, and only then, could he try to win her heart.

CHAPTER 15

*T*he prey was never alone.

The situation was maddening. All it needed was a single unguarded moment, a chance to swoop in and strike...but the pack never gave the opportunity.

They slept together. Ate together. Spent long hours running up and down the mountain and cutting strange, pointless trenches through the undergrowth. There was not a single minute, night or day, when the prey was not guarded.

The shifter pack knew it was watching. One of them seemed to have an uncanny knack of sensing its presence. No matter how high in the sky it flew, the flame-haired shifter's face would turn upward, tracking it through the sky.

Could he detect its true nature? Or had he merely noticed a hawk behaving oddly?

It was tempted to jump hosts again, but caution held it back. Transferring its essence would send out a pulse of energy that could be detected, by those with the senses to do so. The shifters might not be alert to such things...but there was another who *was*.

And it was not yet ready to attract *that* one's attention.

It couldn't decide whether the shifters knew of its plot or not. On the one horn, they hadn't yet tried to attack it. On the other, they stayed close together, like deer scenting a circling wolf.

It had a little more time before it would need to abandon the hawk's body. It could be patient for a while longer.

It circled high above the pack. Waiting. Watching.

For the prey to make a single mistake.

CHAPTER 16

"Spot fire!" Buck called.

From his position at the head of the squad, Rory looked up. The swift, powerful strokes of his Pulaski never paused as he swept the meadow with an assessing glance.

"Bump up," he said calmly. "Edith and Callum, go."

She'd been at the back of the squad, clearing the last debris from the newly-cut line with a MacCleod—a kind of heavy-duty rake with tines on one side and a hoe on the other. Rory's call took her by surprise. She fumbled her tool, nearly dropping it.

"Come on, Edith!" Blaise, who was just ahead of her in line, shoved the Pulaski she'd been wielding at her. "Go, go!"

Up ahead, Callum and Wystan had already exchanged tools like Olympic relay runners passing a baton. Much more awkwardly, Edith swapped with Blaise. The other woman took up the job of raking, while Edith raced after Callum.

He cast her a sideways glance and a nod as she caught up with him. She stretched her legs, chest burning as she fought to match his longer stride.

"Falling behind, A-squad!" Buck roared.

Seth and Tanner's runners were already at work, cutting line around red blankets that Buck had thrown onto the ground. Skidding to a halt in front of their own simulated spot fire, Edith sank her Pulaski into the turf. She dug frantically, keeping an eye on Callum to make sure he was keeping up with her rough cuts. He followed along behind, methodically clearing the ground down to bare soil.

"Wind's shifted!" Buck announced with distinct glee. "Double-strength gusts, straight east. Think fast!"

It was a perfectly calm day. Edith did her best to visualize fire creeping through the peaceful meadow, gobbling up the waist-high grass. She imagined what would happen if a mean, capricious wind suddenly fanned the flames...

"That's it." Callum tossed aside a last clod of cut turf, leaving the blanket isolated in a circle of dirt. "Fire's ringed."

"Wait." She grabbed Callum's sleeve as he started to turn away. "It wouldn't hold. We need to widen it by four more inches on this side."

He hesitated. His gaze flicked back to the rest of their squad, nearly out of sight across the meadow. In the distance, she saw Rory's head turn in their direction.

They didn't exchange any signal that she could see, but Callum nodded. Without a word, he took up his tool again. Working together, they reinforced their line.

"Ha!" Seth's triumphant voice echoed across the meadow. The men he'd sent out had already ringed their pretend spot fire and returned to the body of the squad. "Suck it, losers!"

Edith's heart lurched. She kept cutting line, but her arms felt like lead.

C-squad had won the exercise. She'd let everyone down. She'd fumbled the tool exchange. She'd made a bad call on reinforcing the line. She should have gone back and checked with Rory. Buck would fire Rory and it would all be her fault—

Buck ambled over to the line C-squad had cut around their red blanket. Even from twenty feet away, Edith could hear his sigh.

"Everyone stop," he announced. "Hand your tools to C-squad. They'll be sharpening them for you this afternoon."

"What?" Seth sounded outraged. "But we finished first!"

"And turned the entire crew into toasted marshmallows." Buck spat on the ground. "I said the wind had picked up, idiots. This wouldn't hold."

Edith swallowed hard as Buck wandered over to inspect their own attempt. Her hands twisted on her Pulaski. She made herself stand still.

Buck grunted. "Good."

She was so busy making sure she met his eyes, she didn't realize she should have responded until it was too late. By the time she'd found her tongue, he'd already turned away to check B-squad's work.

"Woohoo!" Joe jogged up to them, beaming ear to ear. "Nice job. And now we get to finish early for the day. Lay on me the highest of fives!"

She grinned back, Buck's grudging praise still ringing in her ears. She jumped up as high as she could, but her own hand barely made it as far as Joe's elbow, let alone his palm. Laughing, he lowered his arm to offer a fist-bump instead.

"Come on." Joe slung an arm over her shoulders. He started to do the same to Callum, but desisted as the other man raised his Pulaski defensively. "We're going to head into town, find some decent food instead of that tasteless mush our so-called cook dishes up. Drinks are on me."

Her satisfied glow flickered and died. "Thanks, but I'm kind of tired. I think I'll just head back to my cabin."

Joe made a face. "All you've done over the past week is work and sleep. You're gonna dig yourself into the ground at this rate. You can let yourself relax occasionally, you know."

That was exactly what she *couldn't* do. Her face hurt from maintaining her mask-like smile. It was all she could do to keep her hands under control.

"Sorry." She moved out from under his arm. "I'm not really a bar person."

Callum frowned at Joe. "I'm not either."

"A picnic then," Joe said promptly. "We'll pack some snacks and drinks, go chill out by the lake. How about that?"

"Sounds good to me," Blaise said, overhearing as they rejoined the rest of the squad. She tightened the straps on her backpack, settling it on her hips. "Might be the last chance for a while. Buck's gone off to call Control and officially put us on the books. As of tomorrow, we could get deployed at any time."

"In that case, we definitely need to celebrate," Joe said. "Come *on*, Edith. We're meant to be a squad, you have to hang out with us. Rory, you tell her."

He was standing quietly a little way off, waiting for the squad to finish packing up. The late afternoon sun lined him with golden light. His eyes caught hers.

"Join us," he said gently. "Please."

He was so beautiful, it hurt her heart. It was hard enough not to stare at him while they were working. Suddenly trying to maintain a polite distance for a minute longer—let alone the rest of the afternoon—was utterly impossible.

"I-I can't." She stumbled back, groping for an excuse. "I...I dropped my canteen somewhere. I'm going to go look for it. Don't wait for me."

She strode away so fast it was almost a run, pretending not to hear Joe's protests. She jogged back along the line they'd cut, dreading at any moment that someone would come after her.

To her relief, no one did. She made it all the way back to where they'd started cutting, on the bank of a small brook. The gentle white noise of the water was soothing, quieting some of the jangly static in her head. She sank down onto a fallen log, hugged her knees, and rocked.

Her senses were scraped raw from constantly monitoring her body language. Every bird call and rustle seemed unbearably loud. Every flicker of motion demanded her attention—a falling leaf, a beetle scurrying over the ground, a hawk circling overhead.

Gradually, her jangling discomfort eased. She let out her breath, tipping her head back. The hawk was still circling above her. The smooth, graceful arcs of its flight against the blue sky relaxed her shoulders even further.

It almost seemed like she'd drawn the hawk's attention too. It dipped lower, balancing on the wind. She glanced around, wondering if it had spotted prey, but the woods had gone silent. The hawk was so low now that she could make out the barred patterns on its wings, the flex of its claws—

"Hey."

In a flurry of wing beats, the hawk swooped away. All the tension crashed back into her body.

Rory sat down on the other end of the log. She turned her face away from the pressure of his eyes, clenching her hands on her knees.

"You did a good job today." His voice was a deep, soft rumble. "Nice call, reinforcing the line around the spot fire."

She picked up some rocks as an excuse to avoid looking at him. "Callum told you about that?"

"Yes. You should be proud of yourself." Out of the corner of her eye, she saw him duck his head to try to see her expression. "So why are you hiding out here in the woods rather than celebrating with us?"

She pitched a rock into the stream. "I just...I'm used to being on my own. It's a lot, always being around other people."

"Edith." His hand covered hers as she drew back to toss another rock. "Look at me."

The warmth of his touch froze the breath in her throat. Longing stabbed through her. She *couldn't* look at him. If she did, she'd shatter. She shook her head mutely.

He took the rock out of her hand. Bereft of the distraction, her palms itched. She rubbed them on the sides of her safety pants as subtly as she could, using the rough texture to anchor herself.

Rory closed his fist over her pebble as though *he* needed something to hold. "Edith, why are you still doubting yourself? You've worked harder than anyone over these past few days. You've proven over and over again that you belong on the squad. But you still look like you expect to be fired at any moment."

Because I could be fired at any moment. And then you would be too.

She clenched her jaw, holding back the words. She couldn't let Rory find out about Buck's threat. If she'd learned one thing about him, it was that he was fiercely protective of his squad. She had no doubt that would outweigh his loyalty to the chief, or even his own self-interest. This was one battle she couldn't let him fight for her.

Rory was still studying her face. "Edith, I can tell something's wrong. You clearly aren't happy with us." His voice dropped a bit. "Is it...me?"

"No!" She jerked her head up, horrified that he could even think such a thing. "You're wonderful. You're kind, and gentle, and—"

Her social filter cut in just in time to save her from blurting out, *and I never get tired of staring at your butt, even when it's mostly hidden under bulky turn outs.*

"I, I mean," she stuttered, heat rising in her face. "Your orders are always clear, and you give us space to do things our own way, and you're always looking out for us. I like working for you. You're a good boss."

"Glad to hear it." He pitched the rock away with considerably more force than she'd thrown hers. It missed the stream entirely, disappearing into the undergrowth on the far bank. "Then why are you holding yourself back from the squad?"

She wished she still had the rock. She tucked her hands between her knees to hide their fluttering.

"I'm just not a very social person," she said. "I don't have to be everyone's best friend to do the job, do I?"

She risked a sideways glance at him, only to be hit by the kilowatt force of his intent stare. She wrenched her eyes away again.

"You just said that I'm doing good work," she mumbled. "That should be all that matters."

He was silent for a long moment.

"What matters to me," he said at last, "is that you're happy."

"Why wouldn't I be happy? All I ever wanted is to be a wildland firefighter. Now I am one. It's a dream come true. And it's all thanks to you. I'm grateful."

"But you aren't *happy*," he said quietly.

She opened her mouth to contradict, but the words stuck in her throat. She couldn't work out why. What was one more lie added to the pile of falsehood?

"I'm as happy as I can be," she said, which *was* true. "To have the chance to do good work, to use my skills to help people...that's more than I thought was possible. It's enough."

And if it came at the cost of hiding her whole self...well, every dream required some sacrifices.

She picked her words carefully, trying to make him understand without saying too much. "Rory, you really are a good boss. Your concern means a lot to me. But please stop worrying. I'm okay. Really. I appreciate the way everyone is trying to include me, but I wish they'd all just *stop*."

He stared down at his folded hands. "I just want—that is, we just want you to feel like one of us. Part of the family."

"I know. But I'm not. You're all so easy and close with each other, and I'm never going to be like that. I don't fit in. I never will. Pushing me to try just stresses me out. Can you explain that to everyone for me?"

He heaved a long sigh. "Okay. If that's what you really want."

It wasn't.

What she really wanted was to press closer to him. To rub her face into the hollow of his shoulder, breathing in his delicious scent. She wanted those big, work-rough hands skimming over every inch of her skin...

But he didn't. He'd been very clear about that. No matter how kind and attentive he was, he'd flat-out *said* that he didn't want to sleep with her.

She squelched her longing down. Just one more part of herself she had to keep locked away.

"It'll be easier if everyone keeps things strictly professional." She tried to smile at him. "Like you do."

He shifted away a little, putting more space between them. "Yeah," he mumbled. "Professional."

CHAPTER 17

*W*rong, wrong!

His griffin clawed at his soul, demanding release. It was a physical effort to keep himself in his own skin. He clenched his fists, trying not to let any sign of his inner turmoil show on his face.

Hold her! his animal howled. *She needs us, she needs us to show her she is cherished and loved. That she deserves to be cherished and loved. HOLD HER!*

He stood up abruptly. It was either that or tackle Edith around the waist. *That* wouldn't have been very professional.

"I have to go do something." Despite his best effort, it came out as a growl. He was about twenty seconds away from shifting on the spot. "I'll see you later, okay?"

"Okay." She gave him a wan, pale smile that didn't reach her eyes. "Thanks, Rory."

He had no idea what she was thanking him for. As far as he was concerned, he'd made everything worse.

With a curt nod, he strode away. It was only sheer luck he didn't pitch himself straight into the stream, he was so blind with churning need. He crashed randomly through the undergrowth until he was certain he was well out of sight of Edith.

Then he tipped back his head, baring his teeth in a soundless scream. He spun and lashed out at a tree. Claws erupted from his finger tips, slicing deep gouges through the bark.

Are you okay? Blaise sent to him telepathically.

She wasn't the only one to notice his turmoil. Joe, Wystan, Callum, Fenrir—tendrils of worry from all of them brushed against his mind.

NO.

His mental roar blasted them all back. He didn't want their support. Didn't *deserve* it. How could he accept comfort from his friends while Edith huddled cold and alone?

His griffin was still raging, demanding that he go back to her and sweep her into his arms. He gritted his teeth, focusing his will. Golden claws slowly shifted back into fingers as he reasserted control over his inner beast.

"Right." Blaise appeared round a tree, the others following close on her heels. She planted herself firmly in front of him, hands on her hips. "What's going on? And don't even think about using the alpha voice on us."

He'd been opening his mouth to do just that, but a flicker of motion overhead caught his eye. He looked up, simultaneously with Callum.

"Oh, for the love of sweet little fishes." Joe shaded his eyes too, looking in entirely the wrong direction. "Don't tell me that bloody bird is spying on us again."

Even with his eyesight, Rory could only make out the bird as a tiny dot in the sky. He glanced at Callum. "Same hawk?"

Callum's mouth twisted. "Same hawk."

The distant speck circled once over their heads, then veered off. With an unpleasant jolt, Rory realized that it was heading for the place where he'd left Edith.

"It did that before." Callum looked even grimmer. "Went for her the instant she moved away from us all."

"Wystan, go," Rory said instantly. "Get her back to base."

Wystan nodded, but hesitated. "What should I tell her?"

"I don't know!" It wasn't like *he* had a great track record of talking to Edith. "Something. Anything. Just get her out of here."

And rest of the pack? Fenrir asked as Wystan sprinted off. *What will we do?*

He might not be able to help his mate. He might not even be able to hold her.

But he could damn well protect her.

Rory bared his teeth in a feral grin. "We're going to hunt."

CHAPTER 18

"*E*dith?" Wystan said from behind her. "Apologies for interrupting. Rory sent me to fetch you."

Keeping her back to him, she scrunched up her face in a silent scream of irritation. She'd thought that she'd reached an understanding with Rory. Yet somehow he seemed to have managed to interpret *please ask the others to leave me alone* as *sure, send them over!*

"I'm sure he meant well, but I'm not in the mood for socializing." She scooped up another rock, pitching it into the stream. "You all go ahead without me."

"Actually, they already have. I'm staying behind too. I, er…need to inventory all the first aid kits. To make sure everything's ready for tomorrow. Rory said you should give me a hand."

"Oh!" She reassembled her face into a more appropriate expression, swinging round. "In that case, of course! I'd be happy to help!"

Wystan's eyebrows lifted a little. "You seem remarkably more enthusiastic about the prospect of counting bandages than you did about an afternoon off."

She fell into step with him. "I'd rather be doing something than nothing. I like to be useful. In fact, if you show me what needs doing, I could take care of it on my own. It doesn't seem fair that you get stuck behind with the chores while the others are off having fun."

"Ah, well." He looked away, his shoulders tightening. "I like to be useful too. And counting bandages is at least something I can do."

"What do you mean, 'at least'?" she asked, surprised by his self-deprecating words. "You do a lot more than that. You're one of the most valued people in the crew. No one else is a trained paramedic."

He winced. "I'm not much of a paramedic. I only lasted three weeks on ambulance crew. I can only hope no one on the crew ever has a serious injury."

"Well, if someone does get hurt, it's better that we have you than no one."

His mouth curved in a way that wasn't quite a smile. "High praise indeed."

With a jolt, she realized that looking in his face was like looking in a mirror. She *knew* that expression. From the inside.

His eyes met hers, and she realized that she was staring. She guiltily jerked her attention to the path ahead. She'd never thought that someone *else* could be doubting that they were good enough for the crew. Let alone Wystan.

Her heart ached for him. She wished she was better at words. She tried to imagine what Rory might say.

"No matter what else, you're a good firefighter," she said firmly. "You're strong and steady, and you're always so polite, even at the end of the day when we're all tired and cranky. The squad is lucky to have you."

"Thank you," he said, his voice softening. "I truly appreciate that."

They walked along in silence for a while. It gradually dawned on her that he kept glancing at her, as though something was preying on his mind.

"Wystan?" she said. "What's wrong?"

"Ah." He hesitated. "I was actually about to ask you the same question."

She tensed, running a quick self-check. Had her expression

drifted? Had her hands slipped free of her pockets? Had she accidentally done something inappropriate? What had he noticed?

"Nothing's wrong," she said nervously. "Nothing at all. Why would you say that? I'm fine."

"Edith." His mouth firmed as though he'd come to a decision. "Forgive me for mentioning it, but you are obviously *not* fine. As the closest thing to a medical professional that the crew has, I'm concerned about you. Long-term stress can have catastrophic consequences."

"I'm not stressed out." She was painfully aware of how her voice had risen, giving the lie to her words. "Really, I'm not."

"It's all right. I'm not trying to declare you unfit for duty or anything of that nature. It's just...I think I know what's worrying you."

Her voice shot up another octave. "You do?"

Too late, it struck her that Wystan *was* a trained medical professional. Of course he'd recognize neurodivergent behavior. He'd probably seen right through her attempts to mask it.

"Yes," he said, confirming her worst fear. "But I need to tell you, it *shouldn't* be worrying you. You don't have to hide it."

That was sweet. And totally wrong. She shook her head. "No. No. I do."

"I mean it," he said earnestly. "Any...urges you might feel are completely natural. No one would think any less of you if you acted on them."

Did he mean stimming? She'd endured enough disapproving stares and loud, pointed comments when she'd accidentally hand-flapped in public to know *that* wasn't true.

"Please don't tell anyone," she said desperately. "Especially not the chief. He'd fire me."

"Mmm." Wystan eyed her sidelong. "You've met Leto, on B-squad, haven't you?"

The sudden topic jump threw her. She dredged her memory, trying to put a face to the name. "Um. He's the guy with the shaved head and tattoos, right?"

"That's the one. Did you know he's Tanner's husband?"

"No." Though, now that she thought of it, they *were* usually together. "I thought they were just cabinmates."

"They're pretty discreet, mainly from habit. They met on the crew, but kept their relationship a secret for a long time because they were worried Buck would split them onto different squads—or even fire them—if he knew. They finally had to come clean when Tanner got promoted to squad boss. Turned out Buck had known all along." Wystan smiled. "The way Leto tells it, Buck chewed them both out for fifteen solid minutes, calling them damn idiots for not having gotten married already. They got engaged more or less by direct order."

"That's a sweet story." Edith still wasn't seeing the connection. She was certain that neither Tanner nor Leto was autistic. "Why are you telling me this?"

"I'm just saying, these things happen." Wystan gave her an indecipherable look. "No one cares what you might choose to do in your own time, as long as you can get the job done on the line."

"Oh!" Relief rushed over her as enlightenment dawned. "You're worried about my *sex life!*"

Wystan inhaled sharply, choked, and broke into a loud coughing fit. Alarmed, she started to pound on his back, but he waved her off.

"My word," he wheezed. "And here I was tying myself into conversational knots, trying to delicately drop hints so as not to offend you."

She shrugged. "It always seemed stupid to me, the way people tiptoe around sex. We're both fully-grown adults. We should be able to talk openly about these things, shouldn't we?"

Wystan did not seem able to talk about *anything* at the moment. He'd gone a very interesting shade of red. His pale eyebrows stood out as if they'd been drawn on with chalk.

Her stomach lurched as she suddenly realized exactly what hints he might have been trying to drop. "Um. Wystan, are you making a pass at me?"

"Absolutely not!" Wystan spluttered, looking even more horrified. "I'm not—that is, I don't—even if that sort of thing was an option for me, you're—no. Just no."

She breathed out a sigh of relief. "Good. Because that *would* be awkward. I like you a lot, but not that way. I'd hate to think that you were pining over me or something."

"*I* am not pining over you," Wystan said, emphasizing the *I* oddly. "But if, hypothetically speaking, someone else was…?"

"Oh no," she said, even more dismayed. "Joe kept trying to persuade me to go bar-crawling, but I thought he meant with everyone. Was he actually trying to ask me out on a date?"

"I am exceedingly bad at this," Wystan muttered. He cleared his throat. "Edith, do you mind if I ask you a personal question?"

"Go ahead." It belatedly occurred to her that there were a lot of things that she *didn't* want him to ask about, so she added, "I mean, as long as it's about sex, that is."

Wystan choked again. "Edith, I'm an Englishman. Don't do that to me."

"Well, why did you bring up the subject if you don't want to talk about it?" she asked, baffled.

Wystan threw his hands in the air. "Because I'm trying to hint that if you're attracted to someone, you should simply go ahead and tell them that directly!"

"I would," she said, even more confused. "You thought I might have a problem being direct?"

"After this conversation, definitely not." Wystan rubbed his eyes. "Your directness is refreshing. But it would be even more delightful if it was aimed at someone else."

"I really don't know what you're talking about."

"Let me try to be as blunt as you, though I confess it does not at all come naturally to me." Wystan drew in a deep breath as though steeling himself. "Edith, *are* you attracted to someone in the crew?"

She hesitated, but she was tired, so tired, of keeping secrets. This one was at least harmless. It couldn't hurt to share it with someone.

"Yes." A tiny amount of weight seemed to lift from her shoulders as she admitted it. "Actually, I am."

He looked even more relieved than she felt. "And the reason you haven't said anything to him is because of a certain power differential?"

She blinked at him.

Wystan sighed. "I am going to need to have a long lie down after this. Edith. Don't you see why I told you about Tanner and Leto? Even though Tanner is Leto's squad boss, they have a relationship. It all works fine. Nobody minds, not even Buck. You shouldn't let your relative positions stop you from approaching...the person we're discussing."

Pieces finally clicked together. He thought she was intimidated by the fact Rory was squad boss. That was so far down her list of problems, she'd never even considered it before.

"It doesn't bother me," she said truthfully. "I mean, it's not like he would be abusing his power over me or anything. I'm a grown woman. I can give consent." She sighed. "I'd be *enthusiastically* consenting."

Wystan was looking at her oddly, as though this conversation wasn't going at all how he'd thought it would. "Then what's stopping you?"

She looked down at her feet. "He doesn't feel the same way about me."

Wystan muttered something that she didn't quite catch. The last few words sounded awfully like, "...*strangle* that idiot."

"Sorry?" she said.

"Never mind." Wystan massaged his forehead as if he had a headache. "Edith, have you *asked* him?"

She bit her lip. "You've just seen how bad I am at talking about these things appropriately. The last thing I want to do is offend him."

"If we are both obliquely referring to the same someone, which I am fairly certain we are, then he definitely won't be offended." One eyebrow quirked. "Edith, I've had nearly this exact same conversation with *him*. Believe me, your attraction is very much mutual. He hasn't said anything to you because he thought you might feel pressured."

Excitement rose through her body, too powerful to contain. Her fingers rippled against her thigh. The best she could do was try to keep the motion small, so Wystan wouldn't notice.

Wystan was Rory's friend. They shared a cabin. If he said that Rory *liked* her, it must be true.

Of course, she realized with a slight lurch, that meant that Rory liked the version of her that he'd seen. The one who was quiet and smiling and still. Not her true self.

Then again, it wasn't like she could show her true self anyway. And if it was the choice between being repressed and stressed all day long, and being repressed and stressed all day long while also spending every night having fabulously hot sex with a sinfully attractive firefighter…well, she knew which one she'd pick.

"You really think he feels the same way about me?" she asked him. "Truly?"

"I don't think it. I know it. Promise me you'll talk to him?"

Butterflies fluttered in her stomach at the thought of confessing her true emotions to Rory. Her racing thoughts spilled over. "I want to, really I do. But I'm not good with words. And maybe it's the wrong moment. We're about to go on active duty. Is it fair to distract him now? Even if he does like me like I like him, we shouldn't rush into anything. It could affect the squad. I think I should wait."

She discovered she was walking by herself. Wystan had stopped in the middle of the path. One hand covered his eyes. His shoulders shook.

"Wystan?" she said, worried. "Are you okay?"

He dropped his hand again. "Excuse me for a moment."

He walked over to the nearest tree. Slowly, gently, and very deliberately, he bashed his own forehead against the trunk several times.

"Uh." She'd never made someone *literally* bang their head against a wall before. "Wystan?"

"My apologies." He turned back to her, offering her a rueful smile. "But you two are unbelievably alike. Edith, I know your head is coming up with a hundred good reasons why you should hide your feelings. It's understandable—baring your soul to someone else *is* terrifying. But if you are honest with each other, truly honest, then all will be well. I promise."

Her throat had gone dry. "How can you be so sure?"

"Because—" He seemed to catch himself, changing his mind about whatever he'd been about to say. "Because he's my friend. I know him as well as I know myself—better, perhaps. And I can't stand to see him suffering needlessly. I beg you, just talk to him. As soon as you can. Promise me?"

She swallowed hard. She couldn't be honest with Rory the way that Wystan meant.

But she could at least be honest with him about *some* things. And maybe…maybe that would be enough.

"I promise. I'll tell him how I really feel." She lifted her chin, setting her shoulders. "Tonight."

CHAPTER 19

"*R*ory, there's been something I've been wanting to tell you." Edith took a deep breath, lifting her chin. "I think that I'm falling in love with you."

She studied her reflection in the mirror critically.

She groaned, hiding her face in her hands. "Now I look like I'm telling him I ran over his dog," she said out loud to the empty bathroom. "He's going to think I don't *want* to be in love with him."

No matter how she practiced, she couldn't get her expression right. Widening her eyes in a winsome fashion had just made her look like a brain-damaged deer. Smiling had given the impression that she was on class-A drugs. *Not* smiling had turned out to be even worse. She'd briefly tried on the Instagram duckface pout, and had immediately vowed never to do so again.

She pushed her hair back, scowling. She rearranged her face one last time, trying to strike that perfect balance between serious and sultry.

"Rory, I think I'm falling in love with you," she declaimed to the mirror. "And now I will club you over the head and drag you back to my sex dungeon. Gaaaaaah. Why is this so hard?"

She wished she could confess her feelings via text. But she knew it was rude to end a relationship over the phone. It was probably even ruder to try to *start* one that way.

It would have been easier if they were in fourth grade. She could have just passed him a note in class: *I LIKE YOU DO YOU LIKE ME Y/N?*

She stuck her tongue out at herself, giving up. She'd just have to wing it. Maybe she could persuade him to come out on a late-night walk, where the darkness would hide her face. Or, even better, dive into a bush and make her confession while completely hidden.

She left the bathroom, emerging into the small corridor that joined her and Blaise's rooms. She hadn't heard Blaise come back into the cabin yet, but she knocked on her closed door just in case.

"Blaise?" she called. "I'm going to dinner. Are you in there?"

Silence answered her. Frowning, Edith checked the time on her watch. Blaise and the others should have been back an hour ago. She couldn't imagine what they could be doing out in the woods for so long. Maybe they'd gone straight to the mess hall.

Her stomach growled at the thought of food. Three hours of daily physical training followed by hikes, briefings, tool practice and equipment checks burned a *lot* of calories. She would have been embarrassed about how much she wolfed down every meal, except that everyone else on A-squad ate at least twice as much. Even Joe usually polished off three helpings, no matter how he grumbled about the hired cook's unadventurous seasoning.

She headed for the mess hall, the setting sun slanting low through the trees. Most evenings, people liked to eat outside—even a room as big as the hall was cramped for the whole crew. Not to mention that at the end of a long day, twenty tired firefighters made for a powerful aroma in an enclosed space.

The majority of the crew were already tucking into their meals, seated comfortably on the picnic tables scattered in front of the large building. She noticed Tanner a little way off, gesturing with his fork while he explained something to his gathered squad. Leto sat next to him, the two men's shoulders and thighs touching. Of *course* those two were partners. It was obvious, now that she knew.

The easy companionship between the two men made a little pang of longing go through her. How nice it would be to sit with Rory like that. Comfortably side-by-side, leaning against his solid, strong warmth...

Tanner noticed her watching. The B-squad boss gave her a little wave, smiling behind his beard. She waved back, shaking herself free of her reverie. The brief daydream filled her with renewed determination. If she opened up to Rory like Wystan had said, then maybe one day it *would* be her and Rory sitting together like that.

Jittery excitement tingled through her limbs. She scanned the gathered firefighters, but couldn't see any of her squadmates. Their customary table was still empty.

Rory, can we take a walk after dinner? She practiced her script in her head as she collected a tray and waited in line for her turn. She barely noticed what the grumpy cook dished onto her plate. *There's something I've been wanting to tell you...*

She took her usual spot, still trying out alternative phrases. *Rory, I've been watching you for some time and...*no, that made her sound like a stalker. *Rory, I admire you so much...*no, too ambiguous. *Rory, you sex god, take me now...*

"Hey. We want to sit here."

She jumped at the unexpected voice. In her preoccupation, she hadn't noticed Seth until he was looming right over her. Two other men from C-squad flanked him. All three wore identical smiles, eyes glinting.

"Uh." She looked around, confused. There were still empty tables available. "Don't you normally sit over there?"

"Yes." Seth put his tray down, shoving hers aside a few inches. "But today we're going to sit here."

Maybe they were just trying to be friendly? They *were* smiling, after all. She smiled back uncertainly.

Rory had said that A-squad should try to be polite to Seth. It would be rude to get up and go somewhere else, or ask them to take a different table. She didn't want to do anything that would give Seth an excuse to snipe at Rory.

"Okay." She scooted over a little, giving Seth room to sit down. "There's plenty of space."

The three C-squad hotshots exchanged glances, as though this hadn't quite been what they'd expected to happen. Then, with a shrug, Seth slid in next to her. She cringed away from the heat of his leg near hers, fixing her eyes on her plate.

"So where's Doofus and the Goon Squad?" Seth asked as he shoveled a forkful of pasta into his mouth. "Got lost in the woods?"

"I-I don't know." His close proximity rubbed against her skin like sandpaper, but she couldn't edge any further away without falling off the bench. "They went off to do something. I don't know what."

"Leaving you behind, huh?" said one of Seth's buddies. With an effort, she recalled his name was Ernie, while the other one was Ed. "Well, we all know Rory didn't hire you for your firefighting skills."

It took her a second to work out what he meant. Heat rose in her cheeks.

"I've never slept with Rory," she blurted out.

"It's all right, princess," Ed said. "You don't have to play the blushing innocent with us. Go on, admit it. I bet you two are going at it like bunnies behind every tree on those 'hikes,' right?"

"No!" How could they think she would be so unprofessional? Okay, so she *might* have had the occasional fantasy... "I swear, he's never touched me!"

Ed made a rude, disbelieving noise. "Yeah, right."

"Hold on." Seth gave her a long, considering look that made her skin crawl. "I think she's actually telling the truth."

"I am." She wished they would go away, or that her own crewmates would come. She let her hair fall forward, hiding her face. "You can believe me or not."

"Huh. That would explain why Boy Scout's been stalking around like a bear with a hangover," Ernie said. "The guy's nuts must be about to explode."

"No kidding." Seth propped one elbow on the table, angling his body toward her. "So why are you teasing your boss, princess? Not that I'm complaining. You frigid or something?"

She *had* to do something to distract herself from how close he was. Her hands wanted to flap, but that would have been a dead giveaway. In desperation, she wound a lock of her hair around her finger, concentrating on the silky texture.

"I'm not teasing him." Her voice had gone high and breathless. She always hated the way she sounded like a little girl when she was mad, but she couldn't help it. "And I'm not frigid. I like sex just fine."

The slight tug against her scalp calmed her a little. It was an old stim, one of the few she'd been able to get away with in front of school teachers who insisted on 'quiet hands' in their classrooms. It gave her space to think again.

"Let's not talk about Rory." She'd gone too long without initiating eye contact. She made herself peep up at him through lowered eyelashes, just to be polite. "I'd rather talk about you."

It was her last-ditch secret weapon, the one that she only pulled out when a conversation was becoming unbearable. Most people *loved* to talk about themselves. Especially men.

"Me?" Seth said. He looked more startled than flattered. "What about me?"

"Well, I'd like to get to know you better." Twirl, twirl, concentrate on soft-silk-slip and scalp-tug-tingle. She managed to lever her lips into a smile. "You're a squad boss, after all, one of the most important men on the crew. How many seasons have you worked?"

She breathed out a silent prayer of thanks as he took the bait at last. She didn't bother to listen to his answer. She nodded and looked impressed and made the occasional encouraging little noise, and Seth did all the rest. She was bored out of her skull, but at least he wasn't needling her any more.

In fact, he seemed to be loosening up. His smile grew broader and bolder the longer he monologued. A couple of times he even brushed against her shoulder or arm, as casually as if they were close friends. Edith tolerated it with gritted teeth, trying not to give any hint of distaste. That would have been terribly rude, and Rory had been very clear that no one should provoke Seth.

Rory, she thought as Seth's knee bumped against hers yet again, *you had better appreciate this.*

CHAPTER 20

"Huh." Rory nudged the dead hawk with the toe of his boot. "Is it just me, or was that weirdly anticlimactic?"

There was no doubt that it was the right animal. The cursed thing had led him and Callum on a dizzying chase through the sky, evading every attack no matter how they'd tried to pin it between them. It had ducked through ravines and made clever fake feints with an intelligence that no normal hawk possessed.

And then, just when it was almost between his claws at last, it had swooped down low, taking cover under the tree canopy...and apparently dropped dead of its own accord.

"Are you *sure* you didn't get it?" he asked Fenrir.

The hellhound's tongue was lolling out nearly to his knees, his black sides heaving. He'd followed them on the ground, ready to catch the creature if it sought cover. *Wish could claim this kill, Birdcat. But found it like this. Dead meat.*

Rory gingerly poked the sad pile of feathers again. His griffin was radiating smugness, pleased by the successful hunt, but he didn't share its satisfaction.

He'd been trying to capture the animal, not kill it. It wasn't just a matter of hoping to learn more about it, and its connection—if any—to the lightning-creature. No matter how suspiciously it had been acting over the past week, it hadn't actually *done* anything to them, after all.

"Maybe it hit a tree during that last dive," he said, feeling guilty.

Callum hunkered down next to the body. He turned the hawk over with his bare hands without the slightest hint of hesitation. His face showed only cool curiosity as he manipulated the limp head.

"Neck's not broken," he reported. "But there's blood on the beak."

"Not mine." The hawk had snapped at him a few times, when he'd come within reach, but hadn't managed to mark him. "It didn't get you, did it?"

Callum shook his head. He bent closer over the hawk, his eyes narrowing even further. "Odd. Look at this."

A rustle in the undergrowth interrupted them. They all tensed, but it was only Blaise and Joe, pushing their way through the bushes. They were both out of breath and grumpy-looking.

"Good. You got it." Blaise pulled her clammy t-shirt away from her stomach, flapping it to cool down. "Did you *have* to chase that thing through every damn bramble-patch on this stupid mountain?"

"We didn't exactly get it." Rory raised an eyebrow at her. "And you *could* have flown, you know."

"*I* couldn't have." Joe scrubbed a hand through his curly blue-black hair, bits of leaf and twig showering down on his broad shoulders. "Next time you decide to chase something, Rory, please make it a fish. Or a beautiful woman. Something that plays to my strengths."

"I hope there won't be a next time," Rory said. "Though I have a nagging instinct this isn't over yet. That was too easy."

Blaise shot him a dark look, still panting. "Speak for yourself."

Fenrir, who'd been sniffing at the dead bird, suddenly jerked his head up. He sprang away, erupting into ear-splitting barks. Callum instantly shifted into his pegasus form, his spread wings accidentally bowling over Blaise and clipping Joe round the ear.

Rory reached for his griffin, ready to shift himself. "What is it?"

Fenrir danced stiff-legged at the base of a tree. *Squirrel!*

Rory sighed, letting his animal sink back. "Not again. Is there anything important about this squirrel, Fenrir?"

Yes. Fenrir sank back to his haunches, quivering with eagerness. His blazing eyes stared intently up into the leaves. *Is squirrel.*

Blaise rolled to her feet, dusting off the seat of her pants. "What *is* it with you and the squirrels, Fen?"

"One day I'm going to have to eat one just to find out what all the fuss is about." Joe rubbed the side of his head where Cal had whacked him. He cast an aggrieved glare at the pegasus. "You're lucky *I* didn't shift on reflex. I'd be scraping you off the grass with a shovel."

Callum shrank back into human form, looking slightly embarrassed. "Sorry."

The squirrel retreated further up the tree, climbing rather slowly. One leg dragged as though injured. Apart from that, it seemed to be a perfectly normal squirrel.

"It *is* just a squirrel, isn't it?" Rory asked Callum.

The pegasus shifter shrugged one shoulder. "As far as I can tell. But I didn't sense anything strange about the hawk either. And look."

Callum pushed feathers apart on the hawk's head, exposing two black, bony nubbins. They looked like baby goat horns, pushing through the bird's skull.

"Well *that's* not creepy at all," Blaise commented, shuddering.

Rory studied the bird more closely. There was an odd reddish tinge to the glassy, staring eyes. The beak was wrong too, serrated and jagged, like fangs. Even though the body was fresh, a fetid, rotting smell hung around it.

"Definitely not a normal animal," he said, standing up again. "Let's take it back to Wystan. Maybe he can do an autopsy or something."

"What a treat for him," Blaise said dryly. "And who's going to carry it?"

They all looked at Fenrir. The hellhound wrinkled his lips back from his fangs.

No, he said, his mental tone final. *Bad meat.*

"This from the shifter who considers week-old raccoon a delicacy." Joe sighed, pulling off his shirt. He rolled the bird into it to make an anonymous bundle. "I'll carry it. We should be getting back, we're already late for dinner."

"I'll take Blaise," Rory and Callum said simultaneously.

"I'm not *that* heavy," Joe said in a wounded tone.

"You're nearly seven feet tall and built like a cathedral door," Blaise informed him. "Also, you're carrying a dead monster that stinks to high heaven. I'll go with Rory. Cal's a stronger flier, after all."

Rory wanted to object to this assessment, but that would have gotten him stuck with Joe and his evil-smelling bundle. Pride took a back seat to pragmatism.

"We'll meet you back at base," he said to Fenrir. The hellhound had his own ways of travelling quickly. "Let's go, squad. Edith and Wystan will be wondering what's happened to us."

He shifted, holding still as Blaise swung herself up. When she was safely settled on his neck, gripping his feathers, he took off. Callum followed, carrying Joe with a resigned air.

You really should *fly yourself, you know,* he sent privately to Blaise.

"No. I can't." Her flat tone of voice told him there was no point trying to talk her round. "Got any theories about the hawk?"

None whatsoever. I've never even heard of anything like it. His wings ached, still tired from the hours chasing the hawk across the mountains. *Maybe your dad will have some suggestions. He's seen a lot in his time.*

"Maybe." Blaise sounded dubious. "Though he hasn't been able to track down any leads on your lightning-throwing arsonist yet, last time we talked. I'll call him again tonight, anyway."

All these weird things skulking around. Rory's talons clenched in frustration. *If only they'd just come out and attack already. That I would know how to handle.*

"Be careful what you wish for." Blaise poked the side of his neck, where the feathers blurred into fur. "Speaking of things you don't know how to handle, how are things going with Edith?"

Don't ask.

"Ouch. That bad, huh?"

I'm going out of my mind. It's taking everything I've got to control my beast. But no matter how slowly and gently I try to take things, she isn't relaxing around me at all. Around any of us. She can tell there's something off. She knows there's something different about us.

"Edith's no fool, Rory." She stretched out along his back, tucking her feet up. "You really should just tell her, you know."

Rory thought back to his earlier conversation with Edith. She's looked so small and lonely, huddled on the log next to him. *I don't fit in. I never will.*

She felt alone. She felt so alone that she'd given up on ever *not* feeling alone. She thought that the best she could hope for was to do a good job and maintain a professional relationship with the squad. No matter what she claimed, that couldn't really be the fulfillment of her dream. Yet somehow she'd persuaded herself that it was good enough. That it was all she deserved.

He'd been avoiding telling Edith the truth because he'd been worrying it would change how she saw him. But *not* telling her was worse. It was changing how she saw herself.

He set his beak. *You're right, Blaise.*

Blaise pretended to swoon in exaggerated shock. "Of course I am. But you're actually *admitting* that? Who are you, and what have you done with our boss?"

Ha ha. He rolled in the air, making her swear and grab onto his feathers to avoid sliding off. *I do have to tell Edith the truth. Not just about me, but about all of us. That's what's stopping her from feeling like she's part of the team. It's not fair on her. No matter how it affects things between her and me, I have to tell her. Tonight.*

Blaise surprised him by leaning down and hugging him round the neck, hard.

What was that for? he asked.

"Being brave," she said, ruffling the short bronze feathers on the top of his head. "I'm proud of you, big almost-brother."

It was just the wind that made him have to blink moisture out of his eyes. That's what he would have told her if she'd asked, anyway.

Just be ready to provide a shoulder to cry on when it all goes horribly wrong, he said gruffly.

Callum had overtaken them, his flame-red wings catching the last of the sunset as he began to spiral down to the base. Rory followed him, banking in wide, sweeping arcs. The rest of the crew were already at dinner, sitting on the picnic tables outside the mess hall. None of the humans looked up, oblivious to the invisible shifters passing over their heads.

They touched down outside his own cabin. Wystan opened the door as they landed, hurrying out.

"How did it go?" he asked.

"Weirdly." Joe slid off Callum's back, handing the shirt-wrapped bird to the paramedic. "We brought you back a present."

Wystan unwrapped a corner of the fabric. A pained expression crossed his handsome face as the smell hit him. "Why thank you. It's just what I always wanted."

Rory shifted as Blaise jumped to the ground. "We're hoping you can tell us what it is."

"It's certainly very dead." Wystan rolled the bird back up again. "What happened to capturing it alive?"

"Change of plan," Blaise told him. "Speaking of changes of plan, Rory needs to talk to Edith. Right away, before he loses his nerve."

Sometimes, Blaise was a little bit *too* much like one of his actual sisters.

"Actually, I think that's an excellent idea," Wystan said, his mouth crooking in a small, mysterious smile. "I saw her heading to dinner a little while ago. Let me just stash this away somewhere, and we can go find her."

As Wystan disappeared into the cabin with the bird, Blaise laced her arm through Rory's. It wasn't really a casual, friendly embrace. More of an armlock.

"I am *not* going to lose my nerve," he said in exasperation.

"That's what you say." Her fingers tightened. "Get his other arm, Joe."

Grinning, Joe complied. Rory found himself being frog-marched toward the mess hall, like a prisoner under police escort. Blaise and Joe still had tight hold of his arms as they rounded the final corner.

And that was the only reason he didn't murder Seth on sight.

CHAPTER 21

"Oh, there's my squad!" Edith interrupted Seth's monologue, relief flooding through her. She jerked her hand out from under his. "I'm really sorry, but I have to go."

"Aw, forget those losers." Seth caught her sleeve as she tried to stand up. "Stay here with me. We're having a good time, aren't we? And everyone's watching. Prove to the crew you aren't really Rory's little bi-"

"I think Blaise wants to talk to me." Edith managed to jerk herself free. She backed out of reach, plastering what was probably a too-wide smile of apology onto her face. "So sorry. Another time."

Blaise *was* heading straight for her. Edith had never been so glad to see someone in her entire life. She hurried to meet her.

And walked straight into Blaise's stiff-armed shove.

Edith staggered back, a picnic table catching her painfully across her hip. The breath whooshed out of her lungs. Not from the impact —but from the punch of Blaise's contemptuous glare.

"*Seth?*" the other woman hissed, clenching her fists. "Seriously?"

"Wh-what?"

Blaise's lip curled. "Don't play dumb. We all saw what you were doing."

What she'd been doing? Eating dinner? Suffering through an incredibly tedious conversation? Edith had absolutely no idea what she was supposed to have done wrong.

She looked around for help. Callum stood a little way off, arms folded over his chest. She'd never seen him look so cold.

Wystan and Joe had turned their backs on her entirely, as though so repulsed they couldn't stand to spend a moment more in her presence. There was something weird about the way they were lurching away. It looked almost like they were wrestling something invisible between them.

Rory. She needed Rory. He was the only thing that always made sense. She'd been sure she'd seen his stocky form between Joe and Blaise when she'd first caught sight of the squad, but he wasn't anywhere to be seen now.

"Where's Rory?" she asked.

"Getting changed," Callum said.

"Come on, Cal." Blaise turned on her heel. "Let's go help."

"Wait!" Edith hurried after them. "Why does Rory need help? What's wrong?"

"He saw you!" Blaise wheeled round again, eyes blazing. "He *saw* you, Edith! Do you have any idea what that did to him?"

Someone whistled from the C-squad table. "Oooh, catfight!"

"Y'all are attracting attention, friends." Tanner drifted over, frowning. "Something going on?"

Words were slipping from her mind like water through a sieve. She could only stare at Blaise wide-eyed, in mute confusion.

Blaise flung her one last scorching look. "I told you there was only one thing you could do to make us dislike you. Congratulations. You did it. Just stay away from us for a while. Especially me."

She felt cold from her fingertips to her toes. She turned to Tanner as Blaise and Callum stalked away. "I-I don't understand."

"Don't think she takes kindly to people helping themselves to more than one pie." Tanner gave her a long, level look. "Can't say I do either. Think you should pick a stool and sit on it, if you take my meaning."

She didn't. She'd been sitting in the same place as always. And she hadn't been eating pie. Why was everyone staring at her like that?

"Hey." Seth's broad chest blocked out the accusing eyes. He took her arm, drawing her aside. "Ignore these assholes, Edith. You're no one's property. You want to get out of here?"

He was smiling.

Out of the entire crew, he was the only person who was smiling at her.

She nodded.

~

Close. Too close.

It made the squirrel crawl along the ground, ignoring the way red pain shot through the animal's injured leg. There had been no time to take care with the transfer, or to find a better host. With the shifters a heartbeat away from catching the hawk, it had been forced to dive and snatch the first creature it saw.

Even so, it had thought that it had been caught. When the black-furred shifter's burning eyes had fixed on it, it had braced itself for a fight. Almost, it had relinquished its host and taken its true form, regardless of the risk.

But the shifters had turned aside from it. They'd taken the hawk's empty body away like a trophy. From that, it now knew they didn't understand its ability to move from host to host.

It still had the advantage of surprise.

It dragged the squirrel's body out into a clearing. All the little creature's instincts fought, filled with terror at being exposed in the twilight. It tightened its will, forcing the squirrel to stay motionless.

It did not have to wait long. A passing fox surged out of the bushes, all lean purpose and hunger. A pounce, a bite, teeth sinking into flesh...and it had a new host.

It shook the fox's body like settling a coat, then set off purposefully through the trees. The fox's sharp nose easily picked out the scents of men twisting through the forest. A simple matter to track them back to the shifters' den.

As it drew closer to the angular man-dwellings, it picked up a different, subtler aroma. Not one that could be detected by any earthly creature, but intoxicating to its own unique senses.

Rage. Disgust. Anger. Shame.

The emotions hung thick over the shifters' den. Something had happened. Something which had turned the bright, repulsive scents of *friendship* and *trust* and *loyalty* into a delicious stew of chaos.

The fox's mouth watered in echo of its own hunger. It made the host creep cautiously through the base, slinking from shadow to shadow. Dangerous, to come so close to the shifters. But it could not resist that alluring scent.

Perhaps...perhaps it would finally be able to claim its prey.

It watched from under a log pile as the human woman stumbled away from the shifter pack. Shame and confusion clung to her like smoke. The shifters turned their backs on her, crowding around one of their own, pulling him into the privacy of the forest.

They didn't see her climb into a vehicle with a smirking, shadow-souled human man. They didn't see the headlights cut through the night, or hear the coughing roar as the truck pulled away from the camp.

For the first time, the shifters had left her alone. Unguarded.

Unprotected.

Its excitement made the fox's heart pound in its narrow chest. It steered the animal back into the trees. It took care to loop round wide, avoiding the shifter pack.

It had been waiting for this chance. It had prepared. Located a special host, saved just for this eventuality.

A thousand scents filled the fox's nose. It picked out the one it needed—pungent, earthy, dangerous. The spoor made the fur on the fox's back stand on end. The animal did not want to go anywhere near *that* scent.

But the fox had no choice. It drove the animal onward, already planning its next move.

Risky, to jump hosts so many times in short succession. It would attract attention.

But if its plan worked...that would not matter.

It lolled the fox's tongue out in a predatory grin, and ran on.

CHAPTER 22

*R*ory awoke to a scaled, blue-black weight crushing him to the ground.

His chest burned. With the last of his strength, he pounded as hard as he could on the side of the tail wrapped around his body. The gleaming coils shifted a little, allowing him to suck in a desperate lungful of air.

"Get *off*, Joe," he managed to wheeze.

He was too groggy to make it an alpha command, but the sea dragon released him anyway. The scales filling his vision were replaced by a ring of anxious faces.

"Oh good." Wystan blew out a sigh of relief. "You're human again. How are you feeling?"

"Like a dragon sat on me." Wincing, Rory levered himself to his elbows. He was going to have some spectacular bruises. "What was that for?"

The rest of the squad exchanged glances.

"You don't remember?" Blaise said cautiously.

His head throbbed like he'd just woken up from a week-long drinking bender. Deep in his soul, his griffin was screaming, clawing at his bones, trying to wrest them back into its own shape.

"Last thing I knew, we were going to dinner," he said, having difficulty hearing his own words over the din his inner animal was making. "Then I went round the corner, and saw—"

Memory returned.

He surged upward, his griffin's anger transmuting into his own. *"I'm going to kill him."*

"Sit on him again, Joe!" Blaise yelled.

Joe's tail slammed across him, knocking him flat once more. Wystan and Callum pinned his arms. Fenrir hurled his full weight across his head.

"Rory, of course you're upset," Blaise said, speaking so fast her words blurred together. "You've got every right to be. But you have to *calm down.* You can't just slaughter Seth in front of a dozen witnesses."

He couldn't breathe. Blackness swirled at the edges of his vision, replacing the red mist of rage.

She was right. He needed to get a grip. He had to be perfectly rational and civilized and draw Seth aside for a private, man-to-man discussion.

Then he could slaughter him.

Let me go, he said telepathically, since his mouth was full of dog fur.

This time, he had the control to make it an alpha command. They all fell off him. Rory got to his feet, brushing himself down.

He frowned as he looked around the group. "Wait. If you're all here, who's with Edith?"

A guilty flicker crossed Blaise's face. "If I'd stayed with her, I would have done something we'd all regret. You weren't the only one who needed to cool off."

"You left her alone?" His heart lurched. "With *Seth?*"

"Now, Rory." Wystan's tone dropped into his most soothing, trust-me-I'm-a-doctor bedside manner. "I'm sure she was just flirting a little. I don't think anything will have actually happened. Certainly not in the last half hour."

"Edith? Flirting?" It was such a nonsensical statement, he thought for a moment Wystan was joking. "Seriously, that's what you thought was going on?"

"Uh, yes?" said Blaise. "I mean, you did go utterly berserk the instant you saw the two of them."

Rory pressed the heels of his hands to his eyes, fighting down an urge to throttle them all. "Are you people *blind*? Edith wasn't flirting."

"Bro." Joe had shifted back to human form. He spread his hands, looking uncomfortable. "Don't want to set you off again, but take it from an expert. When a woman does that thing with her hair, she's definitely flirting."

"Not Edith. Couldn't you see how stiff she was? She was trying to *hide* from Seth. He was the one leering and pawing at her. She just wanted to get away." Rory dropped his hands, raking them all with his glare. "And you *left her with him.*"

"Oh," Blaise said, in a very small voice.

"'Oh' is right. You are all going to owe her a huge apology."

As was he. If he'd had more control over his own animal, he could have helped her like a man rather than succumbing to feral instincts. By his own nature, he'd failed his mate.

He wouldn't do so again.

He turned to Callum. "Where is she now?"

Callum's eyes unfocussed for a moment. He hesitated.

"*Callum*," Rory growled. "Spill it."

"Heading into town," the pegasus shifter said reluctantly. "And she's not alone."

CHAPTER 23

*I*n her numb shock, she'd only cared about getting *away*. She didn't actually register where Seth had guided her until the tooth-itching snarl of the truck engine cut through her misery.

"W-wait," she protested, as the door locks clicked down, trapping her. "I didn't mean—I can't-"

"Sure you can, princess." Seth floored the accelerator, making her lurch back in her seat. "Come on, it's our last chance for a little fun. Fire season opens tomorrow, and the chief never lets us leave base while we're on the books. Forget your troubles for an evening."

"Th-that's very kind of you." The lights of the base had already disappeared behind them. She swallowed an irrational surge of panic. "But I have to get back to my squad."

"Those dorks?" Seth caught her eye in the rear view mirror. "The ones that told you to piss off? Didn't sound like they wanted to be with *you*."

She could still feel Blaise's shove, as though it was branded on her skin. Confusion closed her throat.

"Don't worry, princess. I'll take care of you. I'll be a perfect gentleman, I promise." Seth was taking the hairpin bends at a horrifying speed. "Look, after that little scene, you definitely need a drink. Just one drink, then I'll bring you straight back. Okay?"

She didn't have any choice. She could hardly fling herself out of the vehicle.

She twisted her hair again, trying to stay calm. "Okay. But just one drink. Promise?"

Seth held up a hand as though swearing an oath. "Scout's honor."

In short order, they pulled into Antler, the tiny cluster of houses that was the nearest thing to a town within twenty miles. She'd never been here before, though Joe had often tried to persuade her to join him on one of his regular visits to the place. Thanks to the local logging industry and the nearby hotshot base, the town boasted no fewer than five bars.

Seth pulled up in front of what Edith was pretty sure had to be the dirtiest and seediest of them.

"Aw, don't look like that, princess." Seth grinned as he helped her down from the car. He didn't let go of her hand once her boots were on the ground. "This place is great. Best tequila in town."

The parking lot was littered with battered pick-up trucks. Music spilled out into the night, harsh and pulsing with a deep bass beat. Even before Seth pushed open the door, her head was pounding.

She balked on the doorstep. "Just one drink, right?"

"Just one drink," he agreed. His hand ran down her back....and lower. "And maybe a little dance once you're relaxed, hey?"

Her head spun like a kaleidoscope, a horrifying new pattern emerging. His hand on her butt was a signal even she couldn't miss.

Somehow, she'd given him the impression that she was *interested* in him.

She jerked away from him. If he hadn't still been holding her wrist like a manacle, she would have backed away. "Wait. There's been some misunderstanding-"

Too late. He tugged her across the threshold, into a wall of blinding light and noise. The hot, musky fug from dozens of sweating bodies choked her nostrils. Completely disoriented, she staggered. Only Seth's arm kept her upright.

"See?" he yelled in her ear over the din. "Just what you need. To lose yourself for a bit."

Her head spun. The shrieking music stabbed through her head, scattering her thoughts. She clung to Seth as he steered her to a bar stool.

"P-please," she managed to get out. "I can't. I want to go."

He wagged a finger in her face. "You promised me a drink, princess. Hang on, I'll be right back."

He abandoned her in the midst of the chaos. She dug her finger-nails into the wooden bar, desperately trying to cling onto her own sense of self.

The growling beat seized every bone in her body, shaking her like a snarling dog. An answering shriek built in her throat, unstoppably.

Her mind detached. With icy clarity, she knew she was about to have a meltdown. In front of Seth and all these strangers, she was going to lose control like a toddler throwing a tantrum.

They'd all see. Buck would find out. He'd fire her and fire Rory and she *couldn't stop it*—

Strong arms wrapped around her, holding her together. "I have you. I have you, Edith. It's all right."

Rory.

Impossibly, wonderfully, Rory.

"Come on." He lifted her clean off her feet, half-carrying her through the crush of bodies. She caught a brief, confused glimpse of Seth staring at them, a bottle in each hand, before they were out, into the clean night air.

She buried her face in his chest, drawing in great gasping breaths. His smoke-spice scent was pure oxygen in her lungs. She shook from head to toe in sheer relief.

"I'm sorry, I'm sorry," he was saying, over and over again. His fingers tangled in her hair. "I'm so sorry."

Wasn't that what *she* was supposed to be saying?

Rory pulled back a little, his fingers stroking down over her cheek. He tried to tip her chin up as if to search her face, but she jerked away, hiding against his shoulder. Eyes were too much at the moment. Even his eyes. *Especially* his eyes.

A low growl echoed through her ribcage. "Whatever Seth said or did to scare you so badly, I swear he'll regret it."

She shook her head jerkily, still pressed against him. "No. Not Seth. Me. My fault."

His hands swept down her spine in long arcs, as if she was a cat. The touch was a little too light, too tickly, to be soothing, but she could tolerate it as long as he kept holding her.

"You've done nothing wrong, Edith," he said. "Blaise and the others misunderstood, that's all. And I…wasn't there for you. We're the ones who need to apologize, not you."

"I do." Her secret spilled out of her at last. "It's my fault I didn't understand Seth. My fault I couldn't cope with the noise, the crowd. I'm autistic."

He paused. "Is what I'm doing too much right now? Do you need me to stop?"

She'd told him.

And the first thing he'd said was not *why didn't you tell me* or *oh* or *that explains a lot.*

But to ask what she needed.

Tears leaked out of her eyes. "No. It's helping. Harder, please."

His muscles tightened, holding her closer. His solid heat grounded her. His hands defined her edges, shaping her back into herself.

"I know what it's like to have different senses, different instincts and reactions, to most people," he murmured into her hair. "Whatever you need, I'm here. It'll be okay."

"No it won't!" She gripped his arm in sudden panic. "You can't tell anyone, Rory. Especially not Buck. He'll fire me. And then he'll fire you too. He said so."

"Buck said what?" Rory sounded puzzled. Then, to her astonishment, he chuckled. "Wait. Did he tell you that if you left, I'd go too?"

She nodded, her cheek rubbing against his soft T-shirt.

He laughed again, low and easy. "Oh, Edith. That's not because he'd fire me. That's because I'd resign."

She tilted her head up at last, focusing on his mouth. He was smiling. "What? Why?"

His thumb brushed across her own lips. His voice dropped to a soft, deep rumble. "Because I'm crazy about you. I'll follow you anywhere, always. No matter what."

Baffled joy rose in her like sunlight, starting at her toes and sweeping up to the top of her head. She felt light as a balloon. If he hadn't been holding her, she would have floated away.

"I'm crazy about you too," she mumbled. "As well as just being crazy."

"You're not crazy. You're *you*. And what you are is perfect." His fingertips traced a path from her lips to the corner of her eye. "I've just realized. You don't like looking at people directly, do you?"

"Only in small doses. Otherwise it's too much." She tried to think how to explain. "It's like getting too close to a wildfire. It can be done, but it takes preparation. Effort."

"And here I was trying to stare deeply into your eyes at every opportunity like a lovesick idiot. I'm sorry." He dipped his head a little, carefully keeping his eyes in shadow. "Would it be too much if I kissed you?"

"I don't know." She could barely breathe. "Only one way to find out."

His hands cupped her face. She rose up on her toes, meeting him halfway.

Slowly, gently, their lips touched.

A tingling sensation spread across her skin—not the painful needles of sensory overload, but something sweet and true, soft as spring rain.

She wasn't swept away. She didn't lose herself.

She was Edith. Simply, entirely, Edith.

In his arms, under his touch, she was more present, more *herself*, than she had ever been in her entire life. Every nerve ending of her body sparked. Every slight movement of his mouth against hers echoed right down to the tips of her toes. The background pounding of music faded into irrelevance. The only thing that mattered was him, and her.

Someone cleared his throat behind them. "Rory."

She jumped, but he didn't. His fingers tightened a little on the sides of her face. He finished the kiss leisurely, drawing out the moment, before finally lifting his head.

"Cal." Rory's voice was deeper than she'd ever heard. It vibrated through her body, making her legs buckle and heat flash through her. "Something had better be on fire."

"Not yet. But look."

Callum's grim tone cut through her post-kiss daze. She twisted around in Rory's arms. Callum stood a little way off, every line of his lean body tense. He wasn't looking at them.

He was staring upward, at the night sky. His eyes moved a little, as though tracking something flying overhead.

Edith looked up herself, as Rory did the same. She didn't see anything...but Rory's muscles abruptly went hard as iron under her hands. He breathed out a soft curse.

"Exactly," Callum said. "We have a problem."

CHAPTER 24

"What is it?" Edith twisted in his arms, scanning the sky. "What are you both looking at?"

She couldn't see it. Couldn't see the dense knot of clouds swirling on the horizon.

The storm was coming in fast. Gathering strength. Gathering speed.

And moving against the wind.

He didn't need to ask Callum what his pegasus shifter senses had detected in the heart of that unnatural storm. He already knew full well what was homing in on them like a missile.

"Edith," he said, still staring upward. "Go with Cal."

"What? Why?" She tightened her grip on him. "Rory, what's going on?"

He bent down and kissed her again—hard, this time, claiming her lips as swiftly and fiercely as his animal craved. He closed his eyes, memorizing the heat of her mouth, the press of her body against his. Promising without words that he was hers, all of him, always.

She was his mate. He had to protect her.

It was an effort to wrench himself away, but he had no choice. As gently as he could, he unwrapped her arms from around his waist.

"There's something I have to take care of." He brushed her hair back from her dazed, uncomprehending expression. "I promise, I won't be long."

Her brows slanted down. "You aren't going to go beat up Seth, are you?"

"Nothing to do with Seth." *That* would have to wait until later. "But I really do have to go. The rest of the squad is waiting back at the base. Cal will take you there."

Callum shot him a rather ironic look. "How?"

Rory clenched his jaw, realizing the flaw in his plan. In their haste to reach Edith in time, they'd flown straight here. They didn't have a vehicle.

Here, ride this pegasus! was not the way he wanted to introduce her to the existence of shifters. He fully intended to reveal all his secrets tonight—especially now that she'd revealed hers—but he couldn't cram it all into the next ten seconds.

Antler was far too tiny and remote a town to support a taxi service. He searched the parking lot for inspiration…and found it.

"Stay here for a sec," he said, letting go of Edith's hands. "I'll be right back."

Without waiting for a response, he turned and strode back into the bar. He winced as the so-called music assaulted his ears. If Edith's hearing was anything like shifter senses, no wonder she'd been on the verge of overload.

Seth was hunched over a row of empty tequila glasses at the bar, looking morose. His expression darkened even further as he noticed Rory. The C-squad boss shot to his feet, overturning his bar stool.

Rory caught Seth's fist as the other man tried to throw a punch. "I need your car."

Seth gaped at him like a fish, struggling to jerk his hand free. "You —what?"

He didn't have time for this. *"Give me your keys."*

He could make full-grown *dragons* curl up and whimper. Seth never stood a chance.

The C-squad boss disintegrated like wet tissue paper, his face crumpling with terror. With shaking hands, he fished out his key ring.

Rory plucked it out of Seth's weak grip. Leaving the man to collapse into a trembling heap, he strode out again.

"Here." He tossed the keys to Callum. "Courtesy of Seth."

Edith drew in on herself, tensing. "Is he coming with us?"

"No. And he'll never come near you again." He took hold of her shoulders, rubbing his thumbs in firm circles until her taut muscles eased. "Edith, I promise I'll explain everything as soon as I get back. But right now, I need you to trust me."

Her eyes were still wide and confused, but her jaw set. "I do."

If he stole one last kiss, he didn't think he'd be able to let go again. He made himself step back.

"Go with Callum." He looked past her to Cal. "Take care of her for me."

Callum nodded. "I'll come back as soon as she's safe."

"*No.*" His griffin's growl put force behind the word. "Stay with the others. Tell Buck what's going on. If anything happens to…if anything happens, you and the others will be the last line of defense. I need to know that you're there, ready to keep everyone safe."

Callum's mouth twisted unhappily, but he nodded again. Without another word, he drew Edith away. Rory's last sight of her was her pale, anxious face, pressed against the window as they drove away.

As the truck pulled out of sight, he let out his breath. He tipped his head back, narrowing his eyes. The storm was nearly overhead now. Lightning flashed through the clouds like claws unsheathing. A low, rumbling growl of thunder shook the air.

"Fine by me," he said to his unseen opponent. "If you're done with skulking and spying, then let's finish this."

His griffin's power surged over him. Fierce focus washed away human doubts. He was made for this, to protect and defend. Lion-strong, eagle-swift, he leaped into the sky.

But as he extended his claws to meet his foe, a nagging worry still whispered at the back of his mind.

Why now?

~

"Will *you* tell me what's going on?" Edith asked Callum.

He shook his head. He drove fast but steadily, slowing for bends and intersections. His gaze kept flicking from the road to the sky and back again. It was as if he was monitoring an approaching snowstorm...except that it was summer.

Edith ducked to peer upward through the windscreen herself, but still couldn't see anything unusual. "What do you keep looking at?"

"Nothing."

Nothing seemed to be awfully interesting. But it was difficult to prize words out of Callum at the best of times. It was clear he wasn't going to say anything more.

Edith sank back in her seat, abandoning the mystery for now. Her lips were still tingling. She touched her fingertips to them, feeling the shape of her own dazed, incredulous smile.

Rory had *kissed* her. She'd told him everything, admitted her secrets, and he'd still kissed her. He'd said he was crazy about her.

Not even his weird behavior afterward could cloud the glow within her chest. No matter what, he absolutely, definitely wanted her. After that, nothing could spoil her happiness—

Without warning, Callum spun the steering wheel hard, stomping on the brake. Edith's seatbelt snapped tight across her torso, driving all the air out of her lungs. Tree trunks whirled past the windows as the truck skidded. For the briefest instant, she saw something huge and dark looming out of the night.

Then they were past, the truck still turning, travelling backward. A jolt rattled her teeth so hard she tasted her own blood. The vehicle slammed to a halt, tilted crazily with two wheels lodged in a ditch.

Her ears rang. She clawed at her seatbelt. It seemed to take an age before the strap finally released its stranglehold on her neck. She sucked in a grateful, shaking breath.

"Cal?" she croaked.

The engine had cut out, but the headlights still stared blindly into the dark. The harsh glow illuminated Callum's slack face. He hung from his own seatbelt, slumped over the steering wheel. Blood masked his features.

"Cal!" She scrambled across to him. He didn't rouse at her touch. His pulse beat weakly against her searching fingertips.

Something moved in the beams of the headlights. Something big and shambling, with shaggy brown fur. Eyes glittered red, meeting her own through the windscreen.

It was a bear.

A grizzly bear. An adult male, the biggest she'd ever seen.

She froze, not daring even to breathe. The bear rose onto its hind legs, towering as high as the truck, still holding her gaze. Lips wrinkled back from finger-long fangs. It wasn't a snarl.

The bear looked like it was *smiling.*

The massive paws slammed down. She shrieked, covering her head, as the windscreen cracked and crazed. The bear's claws screeched across the glass.

She yanked frantically at Callum's seatbelt as the bear drew back for another blow. With the strength of desperation, she wrestled him free, hauling him out of reach just as the bear's paw smashed through the glass.

She scrabbled into the back of the vehicle, dragging Callum's limp body over the rows of seats. It wasn't much more cover, but at least the bear couldn't just scoop them out like shucking an oyster.

A big black nose poked through the hole in the windscreen. Nostrils flared, huffing. The snout withdrew, replaced by a beady, gleaming eye. It studied them for a long moment.

The eye blinked, and disappeared. The truck bounced as the bear took its paws off the hood. In the narrow gap between the seats, she caught a glimpse of the massive silhouette dropping to all fours again. She could hear its claws clicking on asphalt as it circled the vehicle.

It was coming round the back. No point ripping apart the front of the truck when it could just tear off the rear door.

That's not right, it's not possible, bears don't do *that!* some distant part of her brain was yammering. But there wasn't time for disbelief.

Instinctively, she groped in the darkness. The bear's heavy, panting breath sounded from outside the truck, barely a foot away. A weapon, she needed a weapon. Something, *anything*—

Her hands closed on a familiar shape.

Bless Seth and his arrogant disregard for regulations.

She'd never thought she'd be thankful for B-squad's sloppiness, but she was now. Encouraged by Seth's lax attitude, they always took every chance to cut corners and shave a few minutes off their chores.

By, for example, leaving their gear in their truck rather than properly returning it to the tool store.

Claws scrabbled at the rear door. With a shriek of metal, the hinges gave way.

In one smooth, practiced motion, Edith yanked the chainsaw to life.

The blade roared like an animal in the confines of the truck. The bear recoiled, only just managing to jerk its foreleg back in time. It stumbled backward, tripping over its own paws in its haste to evade her swing.

She screamed wordlessly at it, brandishing the snarling chainsaw. Any ordinary animal would have fled in panic, but the bear just retreated a few more steps, ears flattening.

The heavy muzzle swung, looking from her to the sky. The bear shifted its weight on its paws as if in indecision.

Its eyes met hers again. It wasn't the still, enigmatic regard of an animal. A cold, assessing intelligence cut through her as though spreading her out for dissection. There was a *person* behind that stare.

A low growl built in the bear's throat. The huge muscles of its shoulders bunched.

With a roar, it charged.

Time seemed to slow. The bear was a tsunami of teeth and claws, blocking out the world. The chainsaw felt as useless as a toy sword in her hands. She braced herself anyway.

A tawny blur streaked out of the sky, smashing the bear aside. The huge animal roared in pain and outrage, tumbling head-over-paws and crashing into a pine tree.

Edith stared.

A *creature* crouched between her and the bear. Golden wings spread wide, shielding her behind vast pinions. A tufted tail like a lion's lashed from side to side. Powerful muscles gathered to spring.

She recognized those feline haunches, that eagle head. She knew what it was.

It was...utterly impossible.

The bear rose to its full height, rather more stiffly than before. Blood streaked its fur. It roared at the creature in challenge.

The griffin's huge beak opened. Its answering shriek split the air. It rose up on its hind legs too, dwarfing even the grizzly. Every golden talon unsheathed, razor-sharp and ready.

The bear flinched. It looked past the griffin, straight at her. Hatred burned in those red, alien depths.

Then it turned tail, and fled into the woods.

The griffin took one great bound after it, then stopped. Its enormous wings shivered for a moment, as though it was on the verge of taking to the air in pursuit of the bear.

The griffin shook itself a little, turning with swift, predatory grace. It folded its wings, the glimmering feathers tucking neatly against its sides. Deep golden eyes fixed on her.

For all the griffin's size and strength, its gaze was as gentle and warm as sunlight. A strange jolt of recognition gripped her heart. Somehow, she *knew* those eyes.

The griffin cocked its head, its attention sliding past her to focus on Callum's unconscious form. It hissed, surging forward.

She'd almost forgotten she was still holding the idling chainsaw. She raised it again, though it felt even more ludicrous to threaten this glorious creature with such a mundane tool.

"P-Please don't try to eat him," she said, blocking the griffin's path. "I don't want to hurt you."

The griffin blinked at her.

It settled back on its haunches. And then it settled back *more*, its outline blurring, shifting into—

"Edith." Rory straightened, holding up his hands. "It's me."

CHAPTER 25

Seth tripped, one boot jarring into the weeds. Cursing, he cast around with the feeble beam of his cellphone flash, finding the edge of the road again.

The growl of an approaching engine brightened his black mood. He turned hopefully, sticking out his thumb.

"Well, screw you too!" he yelled, as the headlights swept past without pausing.

Seth set off again, punctuating every step with curses. Antler was just a distant cluster of lights behind him. He had no idea how far he'd walked so far, or how much further it was back to base.

"I'm a dam' hotshot," he muttered to himself, squinting through the warm fog of tequila. "Don' care about a lil' hike. Do it ev'ry day. Easy peasy."

He didn't care if it took all night. He'd be damned if he called for someone from his squad to come pick him up, like a little girl crying for momma. No way was anyone *ever* finding out about tonight.

Except if Rory told them.

Which he no doubt was, right at this very minute.

Likely he was back at base already, that hot-ass Edith chick snuggled up against his side. The two of them spreading the story across the whole crew. Everyone laughing their heads off.

Seth's fists clenched at his sides. When he finally got back to base, he was going to...to...

Piss his pants again, probably.

Just the thought of confronting Rory again made his bladder squeeze ominously. He had to stop and take a long pull from his bottle of liquid courage to steady his nerves.

He wasn't a coward. He *wasn't*. The only explanation was that Rory had used some kind of trick on him. Seth had always known in his gut that there was something weird about that guy. Something weird about *all* those foreign freaks on A-hole squad.

It wasn't fair. There was no way he could go toe-to-toe with psycho Rory and his hypno-stare. It wasn't a fair fight.

So he wouldn't fight fair either.

Oh, he would have his revenge. On freaky Rory *and* that little tease Edith.

Yes.

All this was her fault. She'd led him on, and then dumped him without a backward glance. Likely the two of them had planned the whole thing, just to humiliate him.

Maybe he'd punish her first. Rory was crazy about her, plain as day. Hurting her would be the best way to hurt *him*. Yes.

Yesssssss.

The thought echoed oddly in his skull, hissing. He frowned at his tequila bottle. Maybe he was a teeny bit drunker than he'd thought.

He shook his head to clear it, and set off again. The road swerved and swayed under his boots. His feet were starting to hurt. Another thing to add on to the end of his long, long list of grudges. Oh, Rory and his bitch were going to *pay*.

Lots of ways someone could get hurt out on the line. A faulty chainsaw. A misheard command. A rip in a fire shelter.

I have a better way.

He stopped, tripping over his own feet as he tried to see who had spoken. "Who's there?"

Silence. The road stretched out in both directions, empty. The only thing he could hear was his own harsh breathing. The forest was pitch-black and impenetrable.

A twig snapped, somewhere in the darkness under the trees. A deep, ancient instinct prickled down his spine. He hefted his tequila bottle by the neck, holding it like a club.

"Don't come any closer!" He brandished the bottle at the lurking shadows. "You don't want to mess with me!"

I want to help you.

The voice didn't come from the bushes. It sounded in his head without involving his ears at all. That couldn't be real. He was definitely drunk.

I can help you get revenge. The voice coiled through his mind like a snake. *We have the same enemy.*

Even his hallucinations were pissed off with Rory now? Heh. Maybe he could get a dancing pink elephant to squish the bastard.

"Yeah?" he said, entertained by the experience of talking to his own subconscious. He should get this drunk more often. "Awesome. Got any suggestions for me?"

Let me in.

"You're already in my head, dumbass." Wait. Was he insulting himself?

Let me in fully. If you let me in of your own free will, I will be more powerful than you can imagine. More powerful than our enemy. I promise you, everything you desire will come to pass, if you just let me in.

He shrugged, taking another swig of tequila. "Sure. Whatever."

Laughter filled his mind, drowning out his own muzzy thoughts. Something huge lunged out of the bushes. He was abruptly, icily sober...but it was too late.

Fangs bit down.

And there was nothing left of Seth at all.

CHAPTER 26

"Hang on." Edith stared around Rory's crowded cabin. "You're *all* were-griffins?"

"We're called shifters." Rory leaned back against the log wall, giving Wystan as much space to work as he could in the small common-room. "And we're not all griffins. My type of shifter is very rare."

"Not as rare as mine," Wystan murmured, his sensitive fingers probing at Callum's skull. "Or, for that matter, Blaise's."

"Yeah, Rory, don't go giving Edith the impression griffins are special or anything," Joe said, grinning. "I mean, there are a whole *five* of you guys in the whole world."

Five griffins seemed like a lot to her. It was certainly five more than she'd expected. If she hadn't already been sitting down, her knees would have buckled.

All the squad looked so *ordinary*. Well, not ordinary, exactly—Rory could make anyone walk into a post, and all the others were just as good-looking in their own different ways. But she'd seen them drinking coffee and scratching bug bites and washing their socks. What sort of magical shapeshifter washed *socks*?

"So if you aren't griffins," she said faintly, "what are you?"

"Pegasus," Callum said, as if simply stating that his hair was red.

Joe waved a casual hand. "Sea dragon here."

Fenrir barked. The dog stood up, shook himself…and blurred.

Edith jammed her knuckles into her mouth, biting back a shriek. She shrank back in her chair as the enormous, bristling *thing* padded toward her on feet the size of dinner plates, claws clicking ominously.

The creature stopped, tail drooping. Red eyes like burning coals gave her a distinctly wounded look.

"You can't act all injured," Rory told the monster that had been Fenrir. "What did you expect would happen, springing your full shift form on her without warning like that?"

The monster grumbled low in its throat, sinking back onto its haunches.

Rory's mouth quirked, as though someone had said something funny. "Yes, but *I'm* not a hellhound."

Edith unstuck her fist from her mouth. "H-he's a shifter too?"

"Yeah," Blaise said. She was perched cross-legged on the back of the battered sofa, behind Callum. "There's a reason I told you not to let him sleep on your bed."

Rory shot a dark glare at the hellhound. "That better have been her idea, not yours."

Fenrir looked as innocent as a pony-sized wolf with hellfire eyes *could* look.

"Um." As much as Edith tried to tell herself that he was still Fenrir—sweet, clever, loyal Fenrir—her monkey hindbrain was screaming *wolf wolf run aieeeee!* "Can he turn back into his real self now, please?"

"Actually, he can't." Wystan didn't look round, still busy checking Callum for concussion. Cal winced as the paramedic shone a penlight into his eyes. "Or at least, he claims he can't. He's always in his shift form. He can tone it down enough to pass as a regular dog, but he isn't a dog who can turn into a hellhound. Somewhere under that fur is a man. Animals can't be shifters."

Fenrir rumbled again, showing a hint of fang.

"You *are* a shifter," Rory said firmly. "No matter what you think."

Edith looked from one to the other. "Wait, you can understand him?"

"Yes, but not the way you think. Hellhounds talk to their pack members telepathically. We're his pack, so we can hear him in our heads." Rory rubbed the back of his neck, looking a little awkward. "In fact, the rest of us can talk to each other mind-to-mind too, since we're all mythic shifters. Sorry."

Edith was confused. "Why are you apologizing?"

Rory blew out his breath. "Because we've occasionally done it in your presence, to talk about things we couldn't share with you. I know you felt excluded. I'm sorry for that."

"It was unconscionably rude of us," agreed Wystan. "Please accept my sincere apologies, Edith."

"Mine too," said Joe, his usual grin sliding away for once. "You're our bro, Edith. We should have been straight with you from the start."

The others nodded as well. Even Fenrir hung his head, tail curling against his belly.

Edith looked round at all their solemn, disconsolate faces. A giggle bubbled up, turning into a full-blown belly laugh. She toppled sideways, shaking with uncontrollable mirth.

Now they were all staring at her as if she'd lost her mind. Understandably.

"We broke her," Callum said.

"N-no," she hiccupped out. "Can't you see how funny it is? All this time, I thought it was *me*. I always miss things that everyone else finds obvious. But for once it's not because I'm autistic!"

She hadn't meant to say it. The word had just slipped out, carried on her wave of giddy relief. Her laughter caught in her throat. She froze.

Blaise started giggling. Joe joined in as well, with his loud, unrestrained whoop of exuberant joy. She found that she was smiling again too, though she wasn't sure why.

"Oh man." Blaise wiped her eyes, shaking her head. "Is that what you've been hiding from us all this time? That must have been awful for you. And all along we were keeping our real selves secret too."

Callum's mouth actually crooked up. She'd never seen him smile before. "Ironic."

A warm hand fell on her shoulder. She looked up at Rory's profile. His eyes were on the rest of the squad, but his voice was pitched for her alone.

"I told you that I needed someone whose quirks matched ours." Heat seemed to flood out from his touch, filling her with fire. "You fit with us. We all know that. I hope that you do too."

Fenrir crept forward. Tentatively, he laid his head in her lap, as he'd done so many times. Out of sheer habit, she scratched behind his ears. His tail wagged.

And just like that, it didn't matter that his eyes were red flames, or that her leg instantly went numb from his weight. He was himself, and she was herself.

And they were exactly as they should be.

Rory's hand tightened a little on her shoulder. When he spoke, though, it was to Wystan. "You haven't told her your animal, Wys."

Edith shook her head, grateful for the distraction from the confusion of emotion welling within her. "By this point, I'm not going to be surprised if he turns out to be a unicorn."

"Ah." Wystan grimaced. "Good."

Blaise and Joe exchanged a glance, and started laughing again, harder than ever.

Edith stared at the paramedic. "You're an *actual unicorn?*"

Wystan rumpled his white-blond hair, looking embarrassed. "Somewhat. In a manner of speaking."

"You can't be *somewhat* a unicorn," Edith said blankly. "It's a binary state. You're either a unicorn or you aren't."

"He's a unicorn," Callum said, casting a faintly disgusted look at Blaise and Joe, who'd now chortled themselves into incoherent heaps.

Wystan sighed. "Yes, technically speaking I can turn into a unicorn. But if I was a *real* unicorn, Callum wouldn't have a bandage on his head right now. My father and grandfather can heal people just with a touch of their horns, but I don't have any powers myself. I'm just a very pretty horse with a pointy bit."

"That's literally the dictionary definition of a unicorn," Edith said. "I should know. When I was eleven, I collected every book about them that I could find, including academic theses. My bedroom was wallpapered with unicorn posters. My parents started getting concerned when I ran out of space and began pinning them to my ceiling. I was *obsessed* with unicorns."

"Not griffins?" Rory sounded a little crestfallen.

"Bro." Joe gave him a look. "No-eleven-year-old girl collects pin-ups of griffins."

"Actually, I did," Blaise said. "But only because I had a thing for Ross."

Rory spluttered. "My *twin?* You had a crush on *my twin?*"

Blaise shrugged. "He was always the bad boy in your family."

"What kind of creature are you, Blaise?" Edith asked her.

The amusement slid off Blaise's face. "It doesn't matter. I'm like Fenrir, but the other way round. I never shift into my animal form."

"Why not?"

"I don't like to talk about it." Blaise held up a hand, forestalling her as she opened her mouth. "I'm not mad or upset that you asked, but it's a painful topic. The rest of the guys have learned not to bug me about it. I just ask that you do the same, okay?"

On impulse, Edith pushed Fenrir's head off her lap, getting up. Blaise shot her a startled look as she approached.

"Okay." Edith held out her hands. "But I'd really like to give you a hug right now, if that's all right."

Blaise's eyes widened. Not looking at all her usual badass self, she ducked her chin in a shy nod. Edith folded her arms around her, feeling her stiff uncertainty.

"Thanks for being direct with me," Edith whispered in her ear. "And if you ever do want to talk, I'm here."

Blaise's hands came up. All the breath whooshed out of Edith's lungs as the other woman hugged her back, fiercely.

"Woohoo!" Joe lifted both fists into the air, nearly punching the ceiling. "Squad pile!"

Edith squeaked as Joe swept both of them up in his enormous

arms. Wystan squawked in protest as Joe seized him too, dragging him into the crush. Then Fenrir was there, thrusting his cold wet nose into their midst, his tail wagging madly. She even felt Callum's hand briefly squeeze her own.

Fenrir's tail hit her thighs like a baseball bat. Their mingled scents swamped her, a heady perfume of animal fur and clean sweat and wildness. Bodies were packed so tightly against her she could barely tell where she stopped and they began. She couldn't breathe.

She'd never been so happy.

Just as she thought her heart couldn't get any more full, Rory's arms enfolded her as well. Even in the chaos of the laughing, wrangling puppy-pile, she felt his touch as though no one else existed. She turned her head, meeting his deep, gentle eyes.

He leaned his forehead against hers. "Welcome to the family," he murmured, his breath whispering against her skin.

Then he raised his voice. "All right, that's enough! Let's not crush her to death with sheer enthusiasm. And there are some things I need to discuss with Edith. *Privately.*"

"Right." Wystan extricated himself, straightening his rumpled shirt. "Joe, put Callum down. The man has a head injury."

"Good point." Joe released them all at last. He winked at Edith. "In fact, don't you think you'd better stay in our cabin tonight, Wys? To keep an eye on Cal, of course."

"I was just thinking that myself." Wystan headed for his bedroom. "I'll get my things."

Callum glowered. "I'm fine."

"Bro." Joe's arm fell heavily across Callum's shoulders. He turned Cal to face Rory and herself. "You feel terrible. You're seeing double. You probably have a concussion. You definitely need a trained paramedic to watch over you tonight. *Don't you?*"

Callum paused. "Yes."

Blaise was already holding the door open for Fenrir. The squad streamed out. The room suddenly seemed a lot bigger...but not even remotely empty. Rory's presence was enough to fill it from wall to wall.

Even though he'd moved back to let the others pass, her body still held the memory of his warmth. She was abruptly, acutely aware that they were a) alone, and b) less than five steps away from his bed.

Rory's gaze flicked from her to the bedroom door, as though he'd just been struck by the same thought. He shifted his weight, clearing his throat. He looked almost…nervous.

That was patently ridiculous, of course. He'd faced down the monstrous grizzly without even blinking. He could turn into a griffin. Why on earth would he look at her as though *she* had the power to rip him apart?

"Let's take a walk," he said. "There's still something I need to tell you."

CHAPTER 27

$\mathcal{I}$t was the same, and yet totally different.

Just like before—could it really have only been this afternoon?—they sat on the log overlooking the stream, not quite touching, the gentle murmur of the water whispering in the background. Just like before, Edith scooped up a handful of pebbles, pitching them one by one into the shallows. Just like before, she watched the water rather than his face as he spoke.

But this time, he didn't worry that he didn't have her attention. He knew better now. The way she focused on the water, the way she rubbed each rough rock in little circles with her fingers, the way she tilted her head; they were all signs that she *was* listening, with her whole being.

He found himself mimicking her, without really meaning to. He sat side-by-side with her, looking more at the water than her face as he talked. Though she barely said a word as he explained the attacks and the storm-creature and Buck's plans for A-squad, he slowly began to understand her better.

It *was* easier to talk when she was just in the corner of his eye. His words flowed more easily when he wasn't scrutinizing her expression for every hint of reaction. Not to mention that it was easier to keep himself on topic when he wasn't constantly getting lost in her beauty.

"So that's why I took off like that this evening." He leaned his elbows on his knees, watching the crystal-clear water hurry past. He was exquisitely aware of the heat of her hip near his. "I had to stop that monster from starting a lightning fire here."

Plunk went one of Edith's rocks into the stream. "Do you think Buck's right? That it's afraid of you?"

"Well, it didn't hang around when I went after it." Rory shrugged one shoulder. "I didn't even get close enough to get a good look at it through all that cloud. I think its main weapon is its lightning, and that's too slow and inaccurate to hit me in mid-air. It flew around for a bit, as if it was trying to get past me, but when I turned back to come after you, it didn't follow. Last I saw, it was headed for the horizon again."

Edith frowned, her forehead creasing. "It doesn't sound like a real attack."

"That's exactly what I've been thinking. I suspect it was just trying to keep me busy. Lure me away long enough for that bear to go after you."

The line between Edith's eyebrows deepened. "It definitely wasn't a normal bear. You're sure it wasn't a shifter?"

"Pretty sure. It's not totally accurate, but we can generally scent each other. And that hawk I caught earlier definitely wasn't one of us. I think they're animals that the storm-creature has corrupted, somehow. Turned into its minions."

Edith rolled a pebble between her palms, apparently giving it her full attention. He could almost hear her mind working furiously.

"Maybe." She sounded dubious. "But something doesn't seem quite right to me."

He let out a snort of laughter. "You mean, apart from all the demonic wildlife trying to attack you?"

She wrinkled her nose at him, her own lips twitching up. "I'm not saying that isn't weird. And it certainly seems like the bear and the, the storm-thing were acting in concert today. But then there was the hare. It doesn't fit. You didn't see how terrified it was, how desperately it was searching for a way through the flames. Why would the storm-thing incinerate one of its own servants?"

Rory shrugged again. "Collateral damage? Maybe it had been using the hare to spy on you, and wasn't too bothered about it getting caught up in the attack. I mean, we're talking about a monster that regularly sets fire to tens of thousands of acres of forest. I don't think it has much of a conscience."

Edith made a noncommittal noise, looking unconvinced. She tossed her last pebble into the stream. Her hands fluttered for a moment as though in search of something to hold.

Catching sight of him watching her, she flushed. Her hands stilled, flattening between her knees with what was clearly a deliberate effort. He'd noticed her do that before.

"Why do you do that?" he asked, nodding at her hands.

Her blush deepened. "Hand flapping? It's a form of stimming, getting sensory feedback. It's…natural, for a lot of people like me. Like facial expressions are for other people. I can't really explain it any better than that."

"No." He touched the back of her wrist, very lightly. "I mean, why do you make yourself stop?"

Her fingers wound together. "It's a dead giveaway. It's inappropriate, and makes people uncomfortable. My teachers taught me how to control it. *Quiet hands.*"

Her shoulders jerked a little on the last two words, as though they were an old, unhealed wound. He clenched his jaw against his instinctive protective fury.

"I love your hands." He took them in his own, resting her palms atop his. Her fingers trembled a little. "Beautiful hands. Dancing hands. Loud hands."

He opened his grasp, as though releasing a pair of birds. Shyly, hesitantly, her hands took flight. She let out a soft sigh, some of the tension draining out of her body. In the graceful flutters of her fingers, he could see her smile.

She tilted her head, giving him one of those subtle sideways glances that never failed to make his heart stutter. "Rory. What are *you* stopping yourself from doing?"

He realized his own hands had clenched into fists, knuckles whitening. Edith might not stare, but she missed nothing.

"Touching you," he said, honestly.

His breath hitched as she shifted a little closer. Her thigh nudged his. "Why don't you?"

"Because...because I still haven't told you everything." He closed his eyes, fighting for control. "You're braver than I am, you know. You dared to bare your true self to me...and yet here I am, still hesitating because I'm scared of how you'll react."

"Rory." The warmth of her hand covered his, fingertips tracing delicious circles over his skin. "I've worked it out, you know. The bear and the other creatures...they were targeting me. But I'm no one special. Unless...unless maybe I *am* special. To one person. The one person that the lightning-thing can't attack directly."

His heart was pounding so hard, he was sure she could hear it. "You're right. This is going to sound horribly egotistical, but I think that creature is going after you as a way to get to me. Because if it captured you...there's nothing, *nothing* I wouldn't do or give to get you back. I'd let it burn down the state, if that kept you safe."

"Why?" she whispered.

"Because you *are* special to me. More special than you can know." He took a deep breath. "It's a shifter thing. All shifters have a true mate, a perfect match. Just one person in all the world. And we know when we meet that person."

Her fingers stilled. "How?"

He shook his head. He still had his eyes shut, not daring to look at her. "I can't explain it. The animal in us just *knows*. It's like a little voice in our heads whispering, *yes, that one*. And after that...there will never be anyone else for us. We're completely fixed on our mate, forever. No matter what."

"Oh." Her voice was softer than the sound of the water over stones. "And I'm...?"

"Yes. You're my mate. I knew the moment I looked into your eyes."

Silence.

Then she took her hand away.

His heart seemed to disappear from his chest entirely. He felt as though he'd fallen through ice into a frozen lake. He couldn't feel her warmth against his side anymore.

"I know it sounds impossible," he said hastily, grasping for words that might bring her back. "To fall in love in an instant like that. And maybe you think it's unhealthy, to be so bound up in someone that you literally can't live without them."

Her hands closed on the sides of his face, stopping his desperate babble. He opened his eyes at last, and discovered that she was standing over him, looking down. The full moon backlit her, hiding her own expression in shadow.

"Rory." Her thumb brushed his lips, silencing him. "That doesn't seem strange to me. I know what it's like, to be so wrapped up in one thing that it's all you want, even when it seems stupid to everyone else."

She slid onto his lap, still holding his head. The warmth of her strong thighs shook him to the core of his soul. She pressed her forehead against his, lips almost touching his own.

"I've always been told that sort of obsession is wrong," she whispered. "But I never understood why. It's stupid, how other people put limits on how much they let themselves love. I don't."

Her hazel eyes filled his world. He looked into them, and saw her love shining back.

Without restraint. Without limit.

He closed that last gap between them, kissing her fiercely, not holding back anything. Everything he gave, she gave back, magnified and doubled. His need was hers; her joy was his.

Her hands were everywhere—tangling in his hair, caressing his face, trailing fire down the side of his neck. He explored her with equal fervor, learning the sweep of her spine and the exquisite curve of her hips. All the time, he devoured her mouth, glorying in her heat, her softness, the boldness of her tongue against his own.

He scooped her up, never breaking the kiss. Her legs wrapped against his waist, her strength holding her in position as much as his own arms. He'd had a vague plan of carrying her back to the cabin... but the night breeze whispering through the trees gave him a better idea.

"Edith." With an effort, he pulled back far enough to speak, though his mouth never quite left hers. "I need you."

"Good." She nipped at his lower lip, making him groan in response. "Because I need you too."

"I want to make you my mate." It was hard to keep hold of human words, with his animal need pounding through his blood. "Tonight. Right now."

She broke off tormenting him with her kisses, looking puzzled. "I thought I already was."

"We're mates, but we're not *mated*. It's different. A joining of souls. A bond between us. Kind of like marriage, but deeper and more primal."

The faintest frown crossed her face. "Would I...become a shifter?"

"No. But we'd feel each other, in our hearts and minds, always."

Her expression cleared, shining like the dawn. "Yes. Oh, yes. I want that."

His griffin surged forward, but he held himself back. Just for one second more.

"It's forever," he warned.

She kissed him in answer, claiming his mouth with a passion that left him breathless. "I want you forever."

His griffin roared in triumph. Gently, he unwound Edith's limbs from around him, letting her slide to the ground. The feel of her lean, taut body against his nearly undid him, but he made himself break off the kiss. Her eyes widened in sudden worry as he stepped back.

He squeezed her hands. "Don't be afraid."

He let go.

CHAPTER 28

*E*dith had one heartstopping moment where she was convinced that she'd done something wrong, or misinterpreted his intentions...but Rory smiled at her, washing away her fears. His face was alight with joy and anticipation.

And then he was *literally* alight, moonbeams warping around him. In a flare of gold, the man was gone.

In his place stood the griffin.

The sight of him stole her breath away. Before, she'd been half out of her mind with terror, unable to fully appreciate his splendor. Now he stood posed in front of her, wings spread and one foot upraised, as though he'd stepped off a medieval knight's shield.

He was magnificent.

She trembled, not from fear, but from awe. Even motionless, he had the swift grace of an eagle in flight, the liquid strength of a stalking lion. He gleamed in a thousand subtle shades of bronze and gold, rich and vibrant even in the pale, washed-out light of the moon.

And he was *huge*. The top of his feathered head towered four inches above her own. His hawk-like front talons could have easily circled her waist. No wonder the storm-creature—whatever it was— had fled rather than face him.

He was holding very still, just the slightest movement of his furred flanks and the tiniest twitch of his tail betraying that he was a living creature rather than some elaborate work of art. Her fingers longed to explore that powerful shape.

"Can I touch you?" she breathed.

He dipped his beak in a nod. A little tentatively, she stroked the fine, dense feathers on his throat. Soft, so soft. The exquisite delicacy of the sensation thrilled through every inch of her skin.

His huge head lowered, his hooked beak caressing her hair. She flung her arms around his neck as far as she could reach, burying her face in those cloud-soft feathers, breathing in his rich, warm scent. Nutmeg and clove; burnt wood and smoke. She'd always thought that faint, ever-present trace of wildfire came from his well-worn uniform, but now she realized it was just *him*.

Pressed against him, she could feel his great heart beating powerfully in his broad chest. The rhythm echoed through her own bones, her blood singing in answer. He was immense, magical, and *hers*.

She wanted to be his, too. Forever.

"I want us to be mates. Fully, like you said." She pulled back so she could look up into those luminous golden eyes. "What do we have to do?"

He knelt, folding his front legs with easy grace, until his back was level with her waist. One wing unfurled in clear invitation.

Giddy delight filled her. Without hesitation, she scrambled up onto his back, perching just in front of his wings. The feel of his hot, powerful form between her thighs made her tingle in delicious anticipation.

She leaned forward, wrapping her arms around his neck again. "I'm ready."

His muscles bunched under her. In one incredible bound, he leaped into the air.

The wind snatched her gasp from her lips. Heart hammering with excitement, she huddled against his warm strength as the world fell away. In a matter of seconds, the base looked like a child's model; toy houses and matchstick trees. Antler glittered on the horizon, just a handful of lights in the vast darkness of the National Park.

She gazed down in wonder as Rory swept steadily higher in a wide spiral. Despite the chasm of air underneath her, she didn't feel the least bit afraid. Rory wouldn't let her fall.

Cold, clammy fog wrapped around them, making her shiver and bury herself even deeper into his feathers. Then they were through the cloudbank, out into breathtakingly clear night air.

She found herself staring *down* at the forbidden peak of Thunder Mountain, usually hidden behind its ever-present veil of cloud. Bare, stark rocks gleamed in the moonlight. The very top seemed oddly flat, as though it had been sheared off with a knife—and then Rory banked again, his broad wing hiding her view. By the time he'd curved round again, the mountain was too far below to make out any more details.

She looked up instead, into the sea of stars. They glittered in impossible profusion, far denser and brighter than she'd ever seen. It was getting hard to breathe now, the air thin and sharp in her throat. Even Rory's mighty wingbeats seemed to be becoming more labored. She couldn't guess where he was taking her, except possibly the moon.

Just as she was starting to seriously wonder if he *was* taking her to the moon, he leveled out. She could feel how his own breath rasped in his chest as he went into a smooth, circling glide.

His head turned, one eye fixing on her. He made a little inquiring, encouraging noise, somewhere between a chirp and a meow. It was such an incongruous sound from that axe-blade of a beak that she couldn't help giggling.

"I'm fine," she said, and meant it. "This is wonderful. What happens now?"

He turned to catch the wind, his wings beating hard so that they came practically to a standstill. His beak turned to point straight downward. His feathered ears flattened against his head.

Even without words, his intention was obvious. She gulped, taking a firmer grip on his feathers. Her knees pressed into his sides. He stayed steady, balanced on the wind, waiting for her signal.

"I trust you," she whispered. "Go."

He folded his wings, and dove.

She couldn't have screamed even if she'd wanted to. The wind was a howling hammer-blow against her face, trying to rip her from his back. She clung to him with all her strength, eyes scrunched shut. Her world narrowed to the rhythm of his heartbeat thundering through her blood, his soft-strong heat, the burn of her muscles as she locked her limbs around him.

He was hers. She was his. And she would never let *anything* separate them.

She was so focused on holding tight that she didn't realize they were back on the ground until the warmth of his wings closed over her legs. She blinked, head spinning from the dizzying dive. He'd landed just outside his cabin, not far from where they'd started.

Before she could try to unclench her numb fingers, his form *blurred* underneath her. For a stomach-lurching instant, she was falling again—and then his arms caught her.

"Edith." His fingers tightened, pulling her against his chest. "Oh, my Edith. You were magnificent."

"I did it right?" she managed to gasp out, still breathless from the wild flight.

In answer, he kissed her again, even more fervently than before. There was a new feral urgency about him that made her already trembling legs go completely boneless. If he hadn't been holding her up, she would have been a puddle on the floor.

His hot, demanding mouth left her lips, roving across her jaw and down her neck. He tasted her as though he was starving, her skin a feast.

"Higher the flight, stronger the bond," he gasped into her neck, between savage, toe-curling kisses. "Griffin tradition. Edith, oh, *Edith*."

She pressed against him, nipping at his own smoke-spice skin with equal passion. "What—what next?"

An animal growl rumbled through his chest, making liquid heat pool within her. He swept her up in his arms as easily as if she weighed nothing at all, kicking the door of his cabin open.

Good thing Wystan had to go watch over Callum, Edith thought distantly as he carried her inside. Though with the need burning within her, she wouldn't have cared if the entire squad was still present. Every part of her was on fire, craving more.

Fortunately, Rory seemed to have shed the last remnants of his careful control. He practically threw her onto the bed, ripping at her clothes in a fevered frenzy.

All thought disappeared as he laid her bare. All she knew was the heat of his mouth, the roughness of his work-hardened hands skimming exquisitely over her curves.

He explored every inch of her as though gloating over a priceless treasure. He seemed to know what she needed even better than she did—lingering here, teasing there, until she was arching her back and crying out, hands fisting in his hair.

Even as his clever mouth made ecstasy crash through her, she needed more. Her muscles quivered with aftershocks of pleasure, yet she yearned for him worse than ever. She yanked at his shirt, near blind with desire.

He made a deep purr of masculine satisfaction. With a last teasing lick, he straightened up, pulling his shirt over his head in one fluid movement.

All the breath sighed out of her. She'd thought she'd known the shape of his body, but she'd never seen him bare like this before. His fully glory was revealed at last, every plane and ridge honed to sheer perfection.

She ran her hands greedily over his chest as he worked at his belt, reveling in the feel of his sleek, hot skin. She dug her nails into his sides and was rewarded by a hitch of breath, the muscles of his abdomen tightening. His hands worked even more feverishly at his clothes.

At last, at last, he was stripped naked for her, his desire clear. Part of her wanted to linger over him, exploring his velvet length with fingers and tongue as he'd explored her—but he caught her wrists, pinning her back against the bed. She was more than happy to accede to his urgency. She wrapped her legs around his lean hips, thrusting her own up in invitation.

As his body covered her, he turned his head aside a little, in a way that didn't seem quite natural. Her heart melted as she realized that even now, in this intimate position, he was avoiding locking eyes with her.

"Rory." She twisted her hands free, taking hold of his face and turning it back to her. "Look at me."

His eyes were dark and fierce with hunger. They blazed like eclipsed suns, a thin rim of gold around wide, black pupils.

She fell into those burning depths boldly, without fear. She *wanted* to be flooded by his presence, to embrace his mind as much as his body.

"Yes," she gasped, opening willingly to him. "*Yes.*"

He slid into her with a single hard thrust, filling her utterly with white-hot pleasure. It was more than the overwhelming sensation of his body buried deep in hers. *He* slid into her too—his love, his awe, his deep, true joy.

My mate! His mind joined with hers even as their hands linked in shared ecstasy. *My mate!*

CHAPTER 29

$\mathcal{E}$dith awoke to a satisfied ache between her legs, a heavy arm draped across her chest, and a cold wet nose poking her cheek.

"Yuck!" She groggily batted away the morning dog-breath panting in her face. "Fenrir!"

Up, Stone Bitch. Sun rises. Pack calls.

The deep, unfamiliar voice made her come wide-awake in an instant. Rory made an indistinct sound of protest as she sat bolt upright, taking the sheet with her. Clutching it to her chest, she stared around—but all she could see was Fenrir.

The dog's tail swished like a windscreen wiper. *Morning, Stone Bitch.*

She wasn't hearing the voice with her ears. It was in her head. Just like she'd heard Rory last night…

"Edith?" Rory mumbled. Somehow she could feel his surge of concern, like a light brightening in her heart. "Wha' wrong?"

"Nothing." She fumbled for his bare shoulder, patting it in reassurance. "Go back to sleep."

He sighed and relaxed again, his muscles unknotting. That strange sense of him in her chest faded again, though it didn't disappear entirely. She could sense it pulsing gently, in time with his slow breathing.

Fenrir peered with interest at Rory's slack, slumbering face. *Good. Worn out. Serviced Stone Bitch well?*

Edith stared at the dog. His mouth wasn't moving. "That *is* you talking, isn't it?"

Fenrir flicked an ear. *Have always talked. Stone Bitch just started listening. Is pack now.*

"Um. You know my name is Edith, right?"

Yes, Fenrir said serenely. *Stone Bitch.*

As nicknames went, it was…pretty badass. She'd take it.

"What do you call Rory?" she asked, curious.

Fenrir's jaw dropped in a sly doggy grin. *Birdcat.*

Edith choked back a laugh, not wanting to wake Rory up. "Does he mind?"

Immensely. Fenrir sounded distinctly satisfied.

Now she knew how to tease Rory, if she ever needed to. Not that she could imagine ever *wanting* to. She gazed down at him, the warmth in her heart expanding to fill her whole chest. He was perfect.

And he was *hers*.

She wanted nothing more than to spend all morning—all *week*—in bed with her mate, but she made herself roll away. From the angle of the light filtering through the curtains, it was just past dawn. Soon the whole crew would be up, beginning the now-familiar morning routine of breakfast and exercise.

Or possibly not. A shivery tingle went through her as she realized that it was the first day that the crew was officially on call. From now on, they could be deployed at any moment, anywhere in the country.

Today might be the day she fought her first real wildfire as a hotshot.

Yesterday, that would have made her stomach twist with nerves. Now, with the mate bond beating steadily in her chest, she just felt excited. This was what she'd been training for, what she'd dreamed about for so long. She was ready.

Yes. Too long in den. Fenrir's eyes gleamed like molten copper, as though he too felt the same restless energy. *Pack needs to hunt.*

She started to throw back the sheet, and then stopped abruptly. A blush heated her face.

"Uh, Fenrir?" Wystan *had* said that the dog was really a man, after all. "Would you mind turning around? I'm not wearing anything."

Fenrir wrinkled his nose. *Two-legs. Never understand you.*

Nonetheless, he obligingly fixed his gaze on the wall. Edith scrambled out of bed, hunting for her clothes. Her shirt was a tragic casualty of the night before. She had to steal Rory's crew tee, although it hung from her much narrower shoulders like a tent. His spice-smoke scent wrapped around her like an embrace.

Got to get some clothes from my cabin, she decided as she pulled on her boots. *Otherwise I'm going to be drifting round all day smelling myself and walking into things.*

Rory didn't stir as she got dressed and bound her hair into a messy braid. He was even more beautiful in sleep, all control relaxed at last, the lines made by worry and responsibility smoothed away. The rising sun turned his hair the innocent gold of an angel's. He looked strangely vulnerable, in a way that he never did when he was awake.

She couldn't bring herself to disturb his well-earned rest. There was still time to let him sleep a little longer. She tiptoed out, Fenrir at her heels.

The front door of the cabin was still closed and bolted. She glanced at Fenrir as she opened it. "How did you get in here, anyway? I thought you never shifted."

He snorted. *Two-legs as foolishly proud of hands as they are ashamed of their hides. Overrated. Watch.*

His body expanded into the bristling, flame-eyed monster wolf. In *that* shape, she half-expected him to huff and puff and blow the whole cabin down. But to her surprise, his hulking coal-black form *faded*, going thin and shadowy. In seconds, he'd vanished entirely.

Before she could call out, his distinctive bark sounded from outside the cabin. Opening the door, she found him sitting right in front of it, looking rather smug.

"Wow." She had to reach out to touch him, just to make sure he was really there. "How did you do that?"

Don't know. He rumbled in pleasure, nudging into her hand until she hit just the right spot. *Just do. Is like Birdcat's voice, or Shadowhorse's nose. Natural.*

She frowned as she started toward the mess hall. "Shadowhorse? Do you mean Callum or Wystan?"

Mean Shadowhorse. Fenrir shrank back into his dog form, padding along at her side. *Flies. Quiet.*

"Oh, Callum." Her frown deepened. "But he doesn't have black hair or skin. Why do you call him Shadowhorse?"

Fenrir shook his head as though not understanding the question. *Is shadow.*

And apparently that was all she was getting on that topic. "Fair enough, I guess. So what do you call Wystan? And Joe?"

Icehorse. Seasnake.

Seasnake was obvious enough, since Joe had said he was a sea dragon, but Wystan's nickname puzzled her. "Because...a unicorn horn is like an icicle?"

Fenrir gave her a deeply puzzled look. *No. Because is behind ice. Can't smell him.*

Now she was going to have to work out a way to politely sniff Wystan. "And what's Blaise's name?"

Not for speaking. Makes her sad.

"Edith."

The familiar, unwelcome voice made her whole spine tense up. She hadn't noticed Seth lurking in the shadowed gap between two cabins.

The C-squad boss looked awful. He was still wearing the same clothes as last night, muddied and wrinkled. A pair of mirrored sunglasses hid his eyes. As he stepped out of his hiding-place, he winced as though the pale dawn light hurt even through the smoked lenses.

A deep growl shook the air. Seth halted abruptly.

"Call off your dog." Seth tugged his baseball cap a little lower, shadowing his face. "I only want to talk."

Ugh. She was done with maintaining polite fictions for the sake of others' comfort. "I'm sorry, Seth, but I think you got the wrong idea yesterday. I'm not interested in you. I'm actually in a relationship with Rory."

There. He couldn't possibly misinterpret *that.*

"I know." He took a step closer. "I wanted to...apologize. In private. Can we go somewhere?"

She cast a puzzled glance around. They were the only people in sight. "This is private."

His gaze flicked to the still-growling Fenrir. But that was silly. Seth didn't know Fenrir was anything other than a dog. Did he?

"Just come with me." He edged closer. His tongue darted out, licking his lips. "It'll only take a second."

"No, thank you," Edith said firmly. "Apology accepted, but I think it would be best if you stayed away from me. Rory doesn't like you very much. And to be blunt, neither do I."

Fenrir stayed between her and Seth as she marched past. Even with the hellhound guarding her back, her skin crawled. She could feel Seth's fixed stare burning the back of her head.

"Gah." She shivered with relief as they went round the corner of the office building, finally escaping Seth's unnerving attention. "Trust Seth to find a way to make an apology creepy. I wonder if he meant it?"

If he did, he should have brought you a squirrel. Fenrir's ears perked up. *Why is Man-Alpha howling?*

It didn't take a great feat of deduction to work out that *Man-Alpha* was Buck, considering that she could hear the chief's steady, methodical, and heartfelt cursing from clear across the parking lot. The Superintendent was standing with folded arms in front of the battered C-squad truck. The few crew members already up were giving him a wide berth. He fixed her with a scowl as she approached.

"What," he demanded, stabbing a finger at the truck, "is *this?*"

Edith looked. "It's a hole in the windscreen."

"I can see it's a damn hole! What I want to know is how it got there!"

Well, he could have *said*. "A bear punched it."

"A bear punched it," he repeated. He closed his eyes, bringing one hand up to pinch the bridge of his impressive nose. "A *bear* punched it. Of course it did. *RORY MOTHERLOVING MACCORMICK, GET YOUR FURRY ASS OUT HERE!*"

His roar rocked her back on her heels, but her sense of the mate bond stayed quiet. "He can't hear you. He's still sleeping."

Will go fetch him. Fenrir backed away, ears and tail flat. *Stone Bitch can handle Man-Alpha.*

"Gee, thanks," she muttered, as Fenrir beat a strategic retreat.

Buck glared at her. Then his eyes narrowed. "That's a very interesting interpretation of uniform you're wearing this morning, Edith. Do I take it that Rory's night has been filled with even more excitement than mere bears?"

Heat colored her cheeks. She tugged self-consciously at her borrowed t-shirt. "Yes, chief. We're fully mated now."

Buck grunted. "Congratulations. I'll send you a card and a damn waffle-maker. I hope that means Rory will stop dragging about like a sad puppy. All that pining was setting my teeth on edge."

"I'm sorry about that." She hesitated. "And...I'm sorry that you're stuck with me, chief. I know you only hired me because I'm Rory's mate."

"True," Buck said—not meanly, just as a simple statement of fact. "But I also told you that I'd fire you if you weren't up to the job. And yet, here you still are."

Now, she decided, was definitely not the time to mention her autism. "I—I promise I'll keep working hard. I won't hold the squad back."

"Just don't let Rory hold you back," Buck said, mysteriously. Before she could ask him what he meant by *that*, he went on, "He *did* tell you everything about himself and the rest of A-squad, didn't he? Otherwise I will kick his ass up and down this mountain."

"Yes, he told me. Everything. He kind of had to, what with the thunder-monster and the demon-bear and everything."

Buck stared at her. Then he turned his attention to the sky.

"One day," he announced, apparently to the clouds, "I am going to permanently staple a radio to that boy's forehead. Maybe then he'll remember to actually *report things*."

Edith! She jumped as Rory's voice crashed through her mind. His concern washed over her like a bucket of ice water dumped on her head. *Are you okay? I'm coming, don't worry!*

"*You're* the one who's worrying, not me," she said out loud. She twitched, struggling to separate his emotions from hers. "And there's no need for you to be concerned. I'm perfectly fine."

Buck muttered a curse. "And now she's talking to thin air too. Since when is telepathy a damn STD?"

Edith made an apologetic gesture at him, mouthing *sorry* as if she was on an invisible phone. She turned away a little, concentrating on her inner sense of Rory. She could feel him tearing around, throwing on clothes in a mad panic.

I'll be right there, he said in her head. *I can't believe you left her alone again!*

She was pretty sure that last bit had been addressed to Fenrir, not herself. She could feel him in her mind too, a kind of hazy mental picture of drooping ears and shamed tail.

"Don't yell at Fenrir," she said, a little annoyed. It wasn't like she'd left the base again, after all. What could happen to her in the midst of the crew? "And I'm not alone. Buck's here."

This seemed to be the opposite of reassuring, as far as Rory was concerned.

"It's all right," she added quickly. "He's not mad."

"Buck is very mad," Buck corrected her. "Buck is just very good at suppressing his emotions, for which everyone should be heartily grateful. Is Buck going to continue to have this conversation in the third person and through a third party, or might a certain squad boss deign to put in an appearance sometime before noon?"

"Um." Edith eyed the chief. "On second thought, Rory, maybe you'd better hurry up."

Rory turned up in person less than thirty seconds later. He had his shirt on back-to-front, and had forgone his boots entirely. But despite his obvious haste, he looked at *her* first, not the fuming chief. A small, wondering smile curved his lips.

"Hi," he said softly.

The mate bond filled her with light.

"Hi," she said, smiling back.

"Don't mind me," Buck said loudly. "I mean, I'm just your boss. No one important."

Rory ripped himself away from her, straightening into something that wasn't far off a military salute. "I'm sorry I didn't report to you earlier, chief."

Buck gave him a level look. "Didn't have time?"

Rory colored under his tan. "It was, uh, a very busy night."

"Well, I hope you found time in your packed schedule for some actual sleep, because it's going to be a busier day." Buck shook his grizzled head. "Much as I'm dying to hear this semi-mythical report, it'll have to wait a few more hours. Come on, lovebirds. All-crew meeting, right now."

Edith's heart missed a beat. "You mean...?"

"Yep." He turned away. "We've got a wildfire."

CHAPTER 30

*F*ire crowned the mountain. Liquid rivers of orange light trickled down the sides, dividing and multiplying as the blaze found more fuel. With no rain in the area for weeks, the forest was tinder-dry. The fire perched on the peak like a hungry dragon, eying the houses in the valley below.

And he'd brought his mate here.

His mate. Just thinking the words made his heart fill with awe and pride, even through his worry. He felt the mate bond glowing in his soul, twice as bright as the raging wildfire.

Rory snuck another glance at Edith, unable to stop herself. She was helping the rest of the squad set up the rough camp that would be their home while they fought the blaze. Even at this distance, her excitement was obvious. When she wasn't carrying equipment, her hands swooped and darted in constant motion, wordlessly speaking her joy.

This was her dream. It was the same as his own—to protect people from the wildest forces in nature. To be the thin line between destruction and civilization.

She was going to march up there, into the very fires of hell, armed with nothing more than hand tools and dogged determination.

And he would lead her.

She'll be fine, he tried to tell himself. She was far safer on his squad than any other wildfire crew. If the worst came to the worst, he could always snatch her up and fly her to safety. He could protect her.

But still, unease crawled down his spine.

He was so caught up in his inner turmoil, he almost didn't react in time. Only shifter reflexes saved him. A flicker of motion, a sudden surge from his griffin—and he found himself holding a pinecone.

"That's the closest I've ever gotten to hitting you." Buck had his arm half-cocked, another missile ready to launch. "You want to pay attention while I explain how we're all going to avoid becoming deep fried chicken bits today, or have you got better things to do?"

"Sorry chief." With superhuman effort, Rory managed to turn his back on Edith. "I'm listening."

Buck grunted, looking like he might be considering hurling another pinecone at his head anyway. "As I was saying, Control's tried to drop smokejumpers in, but the fly-boys couldn't cope with the winds up there. They're scrambling more ground teams as fast as they can, but for the moment, we're the cavalry."

"Lucky this one is practically in our backyard." Tanner cast a worried glance at the distant town. "Know some nice folks down there in Blackbeck. Has an evac order gone out?"

"Yeah, local sheriffs are getting people to pack up and skedaddle. Let's try and make sure they've all got homes to come back to." Buck hunkered down, spreading a map out on the ground. "We've got two choices. Play it safe and let the fire have its way with the trees while we cut line lower down, or race the blaze and try to save as much of the forest as possible."

"We should cut it off high up," Rory said without hesitation. He traced a line across the map. "Here."

Tanner sucked his teeth. "That's awfully close to the head, Rory. No room for mistakes."

"We can do it." He caught Buck's eye meaningfully. "Send my squad in, on our own. We'll strike hard and fast. B and C can cut line lower down, just in case it gets away from us."

"No," Seth said, predictably. No matter how sensible and obvious a plan was, if it came from Rory, the C-squad boss *always* disagreed.

What Seth said next, though, surprised Rory. "My squad should go with Rory's."

"I don't need any help," Rory said, annoyed. "We work better on our own."

Buck glanced up at them both, eyes narrowing. "I do not have time for pissing contests today, boys. Rory, you'll go faster with C-squad following along to make good. Seth, if you go in, it'll be to support Rory's squad. He'll be in charge. You going to be able to follow his orders without any lip?"

Seth pushed his mirrored aviators a bit higher. What little of his face Rory could see looked pale and gaunt. He didn't know how the C-squad boss had gotten back from Antler the previous night, and didn't much care. An all-night hike wasn't nearly enough punishment for what he'd done to Edith.

"Yes," Seth said, to Rory's astonishment. He gestured at the burning mountain. "That's what's important. We have to save the forest."

Tanner's eyebrows ascended. "Since when do you care about trees?"

"It's old," Seth sounded oddly intense. His whole body was wound tight. It was difficult to tell, but Rory thought his hidden gaze was fixed on the distant fire. "Untouched. Mustn't burn."

"We'd have a hell of an easier time if someone *had* let it burn," Buck said grumpily. "Buttload of dead crap in that undergrowth. We should have been doing controlled burns on this place years ago, but it's a nature reserve or something. Never could get approval. Now it's just a giant all-you-can-eat buffet for that damn fire."

"So do we abandon it?" Tanner asked.

"No." Rory found himself saying the word simultaneously with Seth. It was pretty much the first time the two of them had ever agreed on *anything*.

He'd thought that humiliating Seth by using his alpha voice would have made the C-squad boss even more pissed off with him, but the opposite seemed to be true. Seth was staying as far away from him as possible, shoulders hunched and cap drawn down as though trying to hide under the brim.

Huh. Maybe Blaise was right, Rory thought, bemused. *Should have kicked his ass a long time ago.*

Buck heaved a sigh. "Okay, we'll try it Rory and Seth's way. A-squad goes first with rough cuts, with C-squad following behind to shore up. Tanner, you start a backup line at the foot. I'm going to stay here where I can see everything, and coordinate on the radio. If I yell, you boys pull out *fast*, got it? Brief your squads. Make sure everyone's bringing their best game, because there's no margin for error on this one."

Rory hung back as Tanner and Seth headed to their respective teams. "Chief. Do we know how the fire started yet?"

"No. It was only just spotted at ass o'clock this morning, so the sheriffs haven't had time to sniff around for any guilty kids or careless campers." Buck shot him a keen look. "Why? You got a hunch?"

"Yeah. My animal's restless." The back of his neck prickled. He resisted the urge to glance over his shoulder at Edith again.

He studied the map instead, following the route from Thunder Mountain to their current location. It *was* practically in their backyard, only a few hours' drive from base. Much closer than the lightning-creature had dared to come before, but still...

"It was heading this way." He traced a straight line from Antler to Blackbeck. "The lightning-creature, I mean. When I chased it away from our home turf, this is the direction it fled. I think it's responsible for this fire."

Buck folded his map decisively. "Then we've definitely got to cut this sucker off early."

"Why?"

Buck's smile gleamed like a knife. "Because in every case where its fires were caught and contained straight away...it came back to restart them."

CHAPTER 31

*T*hey weren't going fast enough.

Edith dug and scraped at the back of the squad, her worry growing as the sun arced through the sky. She knew from her years as a fire watcher exactly how fast a blaze would spread in these conditions. As they cut line, she kept a running mental map in her head, comparing their progress to the rate that the fire was advancing.

They weren't going to make it.

Ironically, the squad was working *too* hard. They were cutting too wide. And they weren't pacing themselves properly, either. They were clearing too much. At her position right at the back, behind Wystan, she barely had anything to do, the line already scraped to bare earth by the superhuman efforts of the shifters ahead of her.

Seth and C-squad, following along a few hundred feet behind them, were completely redundant. She was amazed he hadn't caught up with them yet, or at least sent a runner ahead to demand to know why they weren't leaving any work for his squad. Then again, it *was* Seth. He was probably dawdling deliberately, enjoying getting paid for doing nothing.

She'd always had an intuitive grasp of numbers and equations. She modeled variations in her mind like a computer simulation—a line four inches narrower would still hold back the fire, and would let them advance that critical bit faster.

She bit her lip, fighting the urge to say something. People hated being told that they were doing things wrong. It was one of the first social rules she'd learned, painfully.

Rory had to know what he was doing. He was a veteran hotshot. It wasn't her place to criticize his leadership, even if she was his mate. She was the newest on the squad, a rookie, and only human to boot.

He'd taken lead, as he always did. Normally he handled his chainsaw with ease, but today his cuts were rushed, sloppy. He was trying to do too much at once—watch the sky, judge the line, monitor the fire, check in with Buck on the radio, supervise the squad.

And still, every few minutes, he looked round at her. As though *she* was his most pressing concern.

It was sweet. And also stupid.

He wasn't the only one who was distracted. Callum was nowhere near his usual precise self. His head snapped round at every noise. At one point, he'd been so busy staring into the forest, he'd embedded his Pulaski deep into a stump. It had taken three of them to get it free again.

She edged closer to Wystan, who was just ahead of her in the line. He'd fallen a little bit behind the others, battling a stubborn tree root.

"I think you should check on Cal," she said, keeping her voice low. "I'm worried he might still have a concussion. He's not acting himself."

"He's fine. Just preoccupied." Wystan didn't pause chopping at the root. "Rory has him constantly monitoring the position of every animal bigger than a beetle for a two mile radius."

"He's doing *what?*"

"It's his special power. Most mythic shifters have one. He's watching out for our mysterious lightning-throwing friend, and also making sure no surprise bears or hares or anything else decide to make our day even more interesting."

"Oh. Um." The way he was bashing at the root was setting her teeth on edge. She *had* to say something. "Wystan, you want to leave this one to me?"

His Pulaski whistled through the air with inhuman strength, finally cleaving through the gnarled wood. "I can handle it."

"I didn't mean to imply that you can't. But it'll go faster if we share out the work."

"I may not have any useful powers, but I'm still a shifter," Wystan snapped. "I am considerably stronger than you. And don't stand so close to me."

His unexpected attack made her blink. It was so out of character for him that she was more startled than hurt.

Before she could come up with a response, he sighed, letting his tool drop. "My sincere apologies, Edith. I'm appallingly cranky. It's something of a strain for me to be around people who have recently been..." He cleared his throat. "Er, intimate. It's a unicorn thing."

"Oh! Like in the legends, where unicorns can only be approached by virgins?"

A blush crept up his pale features. "I'm not *that* badly affected. My father used to be crippled by migraines in this sort of situation. I just get a bit irritable. Normally I'd manage it better, but I'm not my best self today. I didn't get much sleep. Joe is not the most restful person with whom to share a cabin."

Edith glanced over at Joe, who was working with Fenrir to drag cut branches safely away from the fireline. The sea dragon also wasn't his usual self, going about his tasks without a word of complaint or a single terrible joke. She'd thought he was just focusing on the job, but now she realized his dark skin was ashen with more than just fallout from the wildfire.

"He doesn't look like he slept well either," she said.

"Nightmares, I believe. Though about what, I don't know. Whatever he was yelling was in sea dragon language." Wystan rubbed his forehead. "I suppose the attack last night has put us all on edge."

He was right. The whole squad was acting strange. Fenrir was trotting around with his usual alert energy, but his tail was low and wary rather than waving like a flag. The fur on his neck bristled under his harness. And as for Blaise…

She barely seemed to be aware of any of them. She'd been laughing and relaxed at the start of the job, but her confident air had evaporated as the line lengthened. Now she hacked at the ground with single-minded focus, as though the forest floor had done her a personal injury.

Maybe Blaise was just tense because she too had figured out that they weren't cutting line fast enough. But in that case, why hadn't she said anything? In training, she'd never hesitated to comment if she felt someone wasn't performing their best. Everyone respected her.

Yes, Edith decided with a twinge of relief. Blaise should be the one to quietly point out to Rory that they needed to change their strategy. *She* was a confident veteran firefighter, and a shifter. He would listen to his old friend.

She sidled over to Blaise and cleared her throat. The other woman didn't look up.

"Blaise." When Blaise didn't react, she tentatively put a hand on her arm, stopping her swing. "Blaise? Can we…"

She trailed off. Blaise's bicep was as rigid as iron. She was gripping her Pulaski so tightly, Edith could see her hands shaking. Her breath rasped between her teeth.

Edith knew only too well what an imminent meltdown looked like. She grabbed Blaise's tool, wrenching it away. "Blaise!"

Blaise's eyes were wide and unfocused. Flames reflected in their dark depths…even though she was facing away from the approaching fire.

"Burning," she said dreamily. "Burning."

"*Rory!*" Edith shrieked.

He was at her side so fast, his chainsaw blade hadn't come to a complete stop. He took one look at Blaise and threw the tool aside. He snapped his fingers in front of her slack face.

"Look at me," he commanded. There was something odd about his voice, an awful jarring note like claws scraping over a blackboard. "*Look at me.*"

Blaise's head turned like a puppet on a string. When she spoke, she sounded both more and less like herself. More, because at least it wasn't that alien sleepwalking drone...and less, because her voice had gone high and tight with fear.

"Rory," Blaise gasped. "It's too close. Help."

"You are in control. You will not shift unless you want to." Rory gripped Blaise's face between his palms, his golden eyes locked on hers. "You will not shift. *You are in control.*"

A shudder went through Blaise's whole body. She relaxed at last, slumping forward. Rory caught her in a hug.

"It's okay," he said, his voice softening back into his usual deep, warm register. "We're here. We've got you. Do you need to get off the fireline?"

"No." Blaise stepped away, back straightening. "I've got it locked down again now. Thanks for the assist." She turned to Edith. "And thanks for realizing something was wrong. Even though you didn't know what."

"No problem," Edith said, relieved that Blaise seemed to be back to normal. "What was it, a panic attack?"

"Something like that." Blaise reclaimed her Pulaski. "Let's get back to work. We're running out of time to get this line finished."

"It's too late already," Edith blurted out. "We aren't going to make it."

Rory blew out his breath, his mouth setting in a grim line. "We'll just have to step up the pace."

His physical closeness made the mate bond glow brighter in her heart. The steady warmth bolstered her courage.

"It's not going to work, Rory." She took his hand, a little thrill shooting through her just from that small contact. "Can we talk?"

"Five minute break!" Rory called to the rest of the squad. He let her draw him aside. "Are you holding up okay?"

"I'm fine. I'm barely working up a sweat, to be honest." She lowered her voice. "But I'm the only one who's holding it together. I don't know why, but no one is working effectively. Look at them."

His jaw clenched. She could sense that he accepted the truth of her words. Her stomach churned with his worry and…guilt?

"Why do you think that this is your fault?" she asked, confused.

"Because it is." He took off his helmet, raking a hand through his damp hair. "I'm the squad boss. And more than that, I'm the alpha. It's a shifter thing. Like in a wolf pack."

Edith frowned. "I thought that whole alpha-beta-omega status theory had been discredited."

"For regular wolves, maybe. But it's true for shifters. We tend to be strongly hierarchical. And you've seen how we share thoughts. Emotions bleed through too. I think I'm throwing everyone off their game. Because…because I'm distracted."

She felt as though someone had whipped the ground out from under her feet. "You're distracted because of me."

He looked miserable. He also didn't deny it.

It was her old crew all over again. Once again, her very nature made her the weak point. She'd been so caught up in her joy over mating Rory, and her relief at finally having all their mutual secrets out in the open, that she hadn't stopped to consider what it actually *meant* to be the only human on the all-shifter crew.

No wonder he was half out of his mind with worry. He loved her—she'd never doubt *that*—but the fact remained that he'd seen her in full meltdown. He knew how much she struggled with things other people found trivial.

She was a liability.

"Do you want me to go?" she forced out, through her tightening throat.

"No!" He grabbed hold of her shoulders, fingers digging in as though he thought she might try to slip away. "That would just make it worse."

"But I'm holding you back."

"I need you here." He shook his head savagely, face contorting. "My instincts are all confused. You're in danger here, but if you're somewhere else I won't be able to protect you—"

"Rory," Callum said.

Rory whipped round without letting her go, so fast that her head spun. "What is it?"

Callum pointed at the sky in answer.

There was a smudge of cloud on the horizon. It shimmered oddly, like a mirage.

Rory's hands spasmed on her shoulders. "It's coming."

CHAPTER 32

"That's the thunder creature?" Edith asked. Rory could sense her surge of apprehension down the mate bond. "But I can see it. Kind of."

"Really?" Wystan shot Edith a sharp sideways glance. "That's interesting. People who are mated to shifters can generally see through our invisibility tricks. Our friend over there might be one of us after all."

"I don't care what it is," Rory growled. "Callum, any unusual activity in the forest?"

Callum shook his head. "No animals at all. Only living things around are us and C-squad."

The news should have been a relief. Instead, his tension only increased. His griffin paced like a caged lion, every hair and feather on end. Somehow he knew, *knew*, that his mate was in terrible danger.

He came to a decision. "Everyone pack up. You're pulling out."

"What do you mean, 'you'?" Blaise said, eyes narrowing.

"I'm staying to face down that thing." He unclipped his radio, passing it to her. "Call Buck and let him know what's happening. Then go back and meet up with C-squad. Tell them we're abandoning the fireline up here."

Edith cleared her throat, looking a little tentative. "We could still save the forest. That's what I was trying to tell you a minute ago. If we focused on rough cuts and combined forces with Seth's squad, we could-"

"Edith, it's too risky." He turned her to face him again, locking eyes with her. He knew she didn't like it, but it would stop her from arguing. "This could be another distraction. You can't fight fire and look out for ambushes at the same time. It's best if you get to safety."

"But I'm worried about *you*." He could tell the effort it took her to shape words without looking away. "I know I can't help, but the others can. They should stay."

"They can't." If only the alpha voice worked on her. She could already be on her way to safety. "I need them all to protect you."

Then pack should stay together. Fenrir showed his teeth. *All together.*

"I have a really bad feeling about this, bro." Joe had a haunted, strained look. "I can't explain why, but I know you're going to need backup."

"I've fought this thing before," Rory snapped, irritation rising. "I can handle it alone."

"We don't *know* that." Blaise matched him glare for glare. "It could have just been sounding you out before, learning your patterns and probing for weaknesses. It certainly doesn't look at all hesitant now."

Blaise was right. The cloud was coming in fast, growing thicker and darker by the second. He was running out of time.

"Go with Edith." He put all his force into the alpha command. *"Protect my mate."*

All five of them closed around Edith like a fist. She stared around in confusion at the sudden wall of muscle circling her.

"Rory," she started.

He *had* to make her leave. The alpha voice didn't work on her, but he hardened his tone anyway, cutting off her half-formed protest. "You have to go, Edith. Now. I can't fight if I'm worrying about you."

She flinched as though he'd snapped a whip in her face. His heart broke at the way she crumpled, shoulders and head bowing in a huddled, defensive posture as she turned away. He knew from the mate bond just how much his words had hurt her.

Almost, he called her back. It took all of his willpower to clench his jaw, shielding his emotions so that she wouldn't feel his regret. He would apologize to her later.

Right now, he had to protect her.

He focused on his approaching enemy. Despite the speed of its approach, it was still miles off. He had a little time to prepare.

He slipped off his backpack, relieved to be free of the heavy weight. He tried to loosen his muscles. He'd been cutting flat-out for hours, working hard enough to tax even a shifter's stamina. He was uneasily aware that he wasn't at his freshest.

He took a deep breath, rolling his shoulders. He could do this. He *had* to do this.

He couldn't let anything hurt his mate.

A twig crunched behind him. He bit back a curse.

"I *told* you—" He cut himself off as he turned. It wasn't Edith, or any of his squad.

"Seth." Wonderful. This was all he needed. "Didn't Blaise tell you to clear out?"

"Yes." Seth's mirrored sunglasses reflected the dull red light of the approaching fire. "But she said you were staying up here."

"I don't have time for a debate." He barely held back the alpha voice. It wouldn't help to reduce the man to a sniveling wreck again. "Buck put me in charge. I'm ordering you to leave."

Instead, Seth came closer. He licked his lips. "I already sent my squad away. Now yours is gone too. It's just you and me."

The back of his neck crawled. If he'd been in his griffin form, his hackles would have raised. "Seth, whatever idiocy you're thinking of committing, don't. Last chance. Get out of here."

Seth took another step forward, as if he hadn't spoken. His voice dropped to an oily hiss. "I've been waiting for this."

His griffin snarled, straining against his control. *Kill! Tear out its throat!*

It wasn't like his animal to be so bloodthirsty. He shook his head, trying to push back the odd, growing rage. Seth was emptyhanded, not even armed with a shovel. The man couldn't possibly hurt him.

"You've made this easier than I expected, sending them all away like that." Seth's mouth stretched in a thin, close-lipped smile. He was almost within arms'-reach now. "I thought I'd have to catch *her* alone. Take her in order to slip past your guard."

"Okay, we're done," Rory announced. He switched to the alpha voice. *"Back off."*

Seth lunged. It was so utterly unexpected, Rory was taken completely off-guard. The man moved fast as a snake, far faster than any human *should* be able to move.

Seth's weight crashed into him. They both went over, Seth on top. His cap and sunglasses flew off.

Rory stared up into glittering red eyes. Small horns bulged out from Seth's distorted forehead. Seth's lips peeled back to expose needle-like fangs.

"Now your strength will be mine," the creature hissed, and sank its teeth into his neck.

CHAPTER 33

*E*dith knew it was the right thing to do. She knew she was just a distraction. She knew she couldn't help him.

And yet, she also knew that this was *wrong*.

It was wrong, all wrong, to be walking away from Rory. She had the oddest sense of being *stretched*, as though there was an invisible elastic band between them. With every step, her discomfort grew.

"We should go back," she blurted out.

Callum stared straight ahead, striding so fast she could barely keep up with him. "Can't."

"But Rory needs us." She tried to stop, but she was stuck in the midst of the squad. She had to keep going, or get run over. "I don't know how I know, but I *do*. We have to go back."

Callum shook his head sharply. His steps never paused. "*Can't.*"

"Joe." Edith twisted round, seeking an ally. "You said yourself that he needed help. I'm begging you, go to him."

Joe twitched, grimacing in a parody of his usual easy smile. "I wish I could. But Callum's right. We can't. None of us can."

"It's the alpha voice," Wystan said, his face as white as his hair. "Rory's special power. When he uses it, we can't disobey."

"Not for a while, at least," Blaise spat out. Her fists clenched, shoul-

219

ders rigid. "That short-sighted, arrogant, overgrown...when this finally wears off, I swear I will *roast* him."

Edith stared around. There *was* something unnatural about their gaits. It was like they were being forced along at gun-point. Fenrir kept snarling and shaking his head, paws stumbling as though fighting against an invisible choke chain.

"Well, I'm not a shifter." She planted her boots in the ground. "*I* don't have to—ooof!"

Joe swept her up like a snowplow. She found herself being practically carried along, her feet barely making contact with the ground.

"Stop it!" She struggled against Joe's chest. "Put me down!"

With a slight twinge of guilt, she kicked Joe hard in the shins. He let out a pained grunt, his grip slackening for a second. She twisted free, dancing frantically away from them all.

"I'm terribly sorry." Wystan advanced on her like a quarterback, ready to tackle her. "We don't have any choice. Rory ordered us to get you to safety."

"No he didn't," she gasped, back-pedaling further. "He told you to *go with me*. And I am going back to my mate!"

All the shifters froze.

"Is she right?" Joe asked, glancing around at them all. "Does that work?"

Callum's eyes lit up. "Yes. It does. Try it."

Wystan straightened, rocking a little as though testing uncertain ground. "The alpha voice *is* very literal. I'm only feeling compelled to stay near her. Edith's right. He ordered us to protect her, not to forcibly carry her off the mountain."

Clever, clever Stone Bitch! Fenrir frisked around her like a puppy, his tail windmilling madly. *Yes, lead us, lead the pack!*

Blaise grinned, showing all her teeth. "Edith, I could kiss you. Let's go."

They pelted back the way they'd come. Edith led the way, following their own trampled trail through the dense undergrowth. Her heart lightened with each step.

Even if she couldn't help Rory herself, she could *bring* him help.

A bolt of pain stabbed through her chest, so sudden that she thought she was having a heart attack. She dropped like a shot deer, gasping with shock.

"Edith!" Wystan was on her in a second, stripping off his gloves. His cool fingers pressed against her pulse. "What is it? What's wrong?"

"Rory," she managed to force out. The mate bond twisted around her heart. "It's Rory. Something's wrong. Don't wait for me, go, hurry!"

Can't leave you. Fenrir swelled into his hellhound form, the elastic straps on his harness barely managing to stretch far enough to accommodate his greater size. He crouched down on his belly. *Up, Stone Bitch.*

Wystan and Blaise grabbed her arms, bodily lifting her onto Fenrir's back. She grabbed hold of his harness straps, clinging on for dear life as he bounded forward. The others kept pace, running far faster than any human athlete.

The mate bond stuttered like a fading heartbeat. She gripped tight to it, as hard as she gripped Fenrir's harness.

We're coming, she tried to send to him down their bond. I'm coming, Rory!

...no...

It wasn't her thought. She knew it was his. It sounded like he was shouting from a very long way away, his voice echoing up weakly from some deep, dark chasm.

...No...stay away...NO!

She clenched her jaw, refusing to listen to that faint, agonized plea. She was coming for her mate.

Whether he liked it or not.

Fenrir broke into ringing, full-throated barks, like a hunting hound scenting its quarry. *There!*

They broke out of the undergrowth onto the line they'd cleared earlier. Her breath caught at the sight of a limp form sprawled on the ground.

Wystan was already there, rolling the collapsed man over. His hands moved swiftly—then stilled.

"It's Seth," he said, looking up at them all wide-eyed. "He's dead. And he's...mutated. Just like the hawk was."

Callum's head swiveled. "This way!"

He swerved off the fireline, vaulting over a felled tree. His body stretched in mid-air. When he landed, it was on four hooves.

Edith grabbed onto Fenrir as the dog surged after the copper-red pegasus. A silver glimmer caught her eye. Despite everything, a jolt of sheer wonder went through her.

Oh, she thought, awe-struck. *He is* definitely *a real unicorn.*

The shining, pure-white creature moved with such grace, he seemed to float through the forest. The moonlight glow of his horn cut through the swirling smoke. Blaise and Joe clung to the unicorn's back, half-hidden in his streaming mane.

Ahead, she saw a flash of yellow through the trees. Rory was lurching through the forest like a drunk, all of his usual fluid grace lost. He moved with an odd stop-start rhythm, freezing in place for a second and then hurling himself forward. It was like *he* was fighting the same sort of compulsion he'd laid on the rest of the squad.

"Rory!" she yelled.

He spun round, eyes widening. His mouth stretched in a strange, thin-lipped smile.

"Good," he said—and then he stiffened, his head twitching in a quick, sharp jerk. *"No! Go away!"*

Fenrir yelped, his paws freezing. Unprepared for the sudden stop, she tumbled from his back. By the time she'd rolled to her feet, the rest of the squad had retreated, leaving her alone.

She could tell it wasn't by choice. Fenrir was snarling, his jaws flecked with foam. Callum and Wystan stamped and snorted, equine ears pinned flat back against their heads. Rory's words must have been an alpha command.

But he couldn't command *her.*

CHAPTER 34

"*N*o," he forced out, blood filling his mouth as he fought for control of his own body. "Edith, no, *run!*"

She did, but the wrong way. She ran *toward* him, her braid flying behind her, a look of fierce determination on her freckled face.

Oh, yessss.

The voice hissed through his mind, vast and alien and amused. Cold, scaled coils curled round his soul, crushing and silencing his griffin.

Your mate. He couldn't stop the whispering foreign presence from slithering through his memories. It chuckled as it picked over them like a vulture tearing choice bits from a carcass. *See her come, so brave, so blind. Shall I welcome her?*

Another's will curved his lips. Not of his own volition, his arms lifted, spreading wide.

He barely managed to wrench himself aside before Edith flung herself into the trap. He took two jerky steps away before the *thing* grabbed control back from him, forcing him to stop.

"Rory, what is it?" To his relief, Edith hesitated. Her gaze searched his face, skipping past his eyes.

Hissing laughter filled his ears. *She can't* look into your eyes, *can she?* *She can't see me here. How delicious.*

"What's wrong?" She took a step closer, reaching out to him. "Please, talk to me. I don't know what's happened, but I can feel how much you're hurting. Don't shut me out."

How much she loves you, the voice taunted him, as he fought with every ounce of his will to keep his distance from her. *How much you're hurting her, refusing her touch. How exquisite her pain will be, when I close your hands around her soft, fragile neck.*

"No," he gritted out. He jerked his hand away from Edith again. "No!"

You wish me keep her alive? the voice asked, dripping malice. *Then stop resisting me. Submit to my will, and she will walk free.*

"Why are you acting like this?" Edith glanced past him, scanning the sky. He couldn't waste effort trying to look up himself, but he could tell from the way that her eyes widened that the storm-creature must be getting close. "Rory, you have to release the others. You aren't in any condition to fight that thing alone. You have to let them help."

The creature within him surged forward, swelling with eagerness and rage. *Yes, yesssss. Tell your shifter pack to attack the guardian. Tell them to kill it. Now!*

He bit his tongue to stop it from using his voice. Blood ran down his chin. He had no idea why the alien thing wanted to attack its ally, but—

You thought it was my ally? It laughed harder than ever, shaking the foundations of his mind. *Oh, foolish, foolish prey. No. Always, the guardians have hunted my kind. But at last, at last, we shall be free. You and your shifter pack will kill the last guardian. No longer will we have to hide under the ground, weak and starving. We shall emerge. And we shall* feed.

Its cold glee turned his bones to ice. With the monster coiling through his soul, he could see glimpses of *its* memories. His mind shuddered away.

He couldn't let it have its way. He fought harder than ever, reaching for his griffin.

You animal cannot help you, the creature hissed in his mind. *You may be able to keep your power from me, but you cannot stop me from using your body as I please. If you do not do as I wish, I will kill your mate. Slowly. If you want to save her, do as I say. Kill the guardian. Now!*

He couldn't let the creature hurt his mate. She was his *mate*. But he wasn't strong enough to resist. He couldn't find his griffin in the utter blackness coiling through his soul.

But in the crushing darkness, one flicker of light remained.

"Rory, I'm your mate." Though Edith's expression was confused and hurt, her love shone in his heart. "You don't have to do this alone."

Her strength beat through his soul. Stronger than the darkness. Stronger than anything.

He couldn't save her.

But she could save him.

With the last of his own strength, he gripped her hand.

Edith, he sent down the mate bond, praying that she could hear him. *Help me.*

CHAPTER 35

*T*he instant his fingers brushed her, she *knew*.

Edith snapped her head up, meeting Rory's eyes. The impact pierced through her—not warm like sunlight, but *cold*.

"You're not Rory," she breathed, staring into that foreign gaze.

White-hot fury filled her. She tightened her grip on his hand, fingers digging in. His eyes widened, the parasitic presence behind them recoiling.

"Get out!" she yelled at the top of her lungs, right into his face. "Get out of my mate!"

The crimson tinge in his eyes flickered. The mate bond roared between them, fierce as a wildfire. Warmth flooded through her, *his* warmth.

Rory doubled over, gagging, though he didn't let go of her. She clung to him as he hacked and fought, his whole body jerking in great wrenching spasms.

She could *feel* the surge of his soul as he tried to force out the thing inside him. She added her will to his. The alien presence cowered, backing away from their pure, bright love.

Thick, oily smoke poured out of Rory's mouth. It continued to stream out of him for far longer than his lungs could possibly have contained. The dark coils twisted and lashed on the ground, wriggling away.

"*Rory!*" Blaise screamed from the distance.

The other shifters were trapped by Rory's previous command. They must have been fighting against it, trying to move as slowly as possible, but he'd told them to *go away*. They were almost out of sight already.

The smoke thinned at last, trailing off. Rory collapsed to his knees. She held his shoulders, supporting him as he gasped for breath.

The darkness that had spewed out of him thrashed like a wounded snake. It drew itself up, coiling and congealing. Smoke hardened into thick, plated scales. Long, demonic horns branched outward, sharpening to wicked points. Two red, slitted eyes opened.

She froze, caught in the malice of that inhuman gaze as it fixed on her. At her side, Rory managed to suck in air at last. He lifted his head.

"*Help!*" he roared.

The monstrous serpent lunged—and recoiled, shrieking, as brilliant light burst in front of them like an exploding star. Edith flung up a hand to shield her own eyes, momentarily blinded.

She blinked, tears streaking her face. The white unicorn stood in front of them, hooves braced and head lowered. His horn blazed like bottled lightning, holding the towering serpent at bay.

Rory's arms closed around her protectively. "Don't let it bite you!" he shouted. "It can take over your body!"

Wystan danced aside as the horned serpent struck at him. It hissed, sweeping its tail round. Busy trying to avoid its head, the unicorn couldn't react in time.

"No!" Edith cried, as the serpent's tail knocked him over.

The serpent reared back in triumph, jaws opening wide—but before it could bite the fallen unicorn, a flame-bright bolt struck from the sky. Callum's hooves knocked the serpent's head aside. It snapped at him, but the pegasus was already wheeling away. Fast as a falcon, he looped and dove around the snake, making it spin and twist in defense.

Rory pulled her back further as Fenrir joined the fight, fangs bared and eyes seething with hellfire. "I have to help them. Can you hang on?"

She clutched at him, both of them ducking as the serpent's tail lashed over their heads. "Hang onto what?"

To her astonishment, he grinned at her. He seized her in a brief, crushing kiss.

"Me," he said, and shifted.

Now she understood. She scrambled onto his back. She barely had time to grab onto his feathers before he was airborne. The world spun dizzyingly around her head as he dove at the serpent.

His outstretched claws raked through the monster's scales. Its hisses turned into a shriek of pain. Edith clung tight with her knees as Rory barrel-rolled away, avoiding its counterattack.

Massive fangs clashed shut inches from her head, but she wasn't afraid. She was with her mate.

As long as they were together, nothing could stop them.

The serpent jerked and flinched. Whenever it turned to face one of the shifters, another would dart in, taking advantage of its distraction. But they were all so small, compared to the horned monstrosity. Even Rory's fierce talons were just inflicting flesh wounds. How could they hope to kill it?

Then Joe arrived.

Shining blue-black scales crashed against the monster's duller coils. The horned serpent screeched as the sea dragon wrapped around it.

Joe's webbed, taloned feet grappled with his foe, pinning it down under his greater weight. His massive jaws closed over the back of the serpent's neck with a very final-sounding *crunch*.

With a last thrashing spasm, the monster went still.

The sea dragon released the creature, backing away. Joe shimmered, shrinking back into human form. He suddenly seemed *very* small.

"*Bleugh.*" Joe spat out black ichor, swiping the back of his hand across his mouth. "Definitely could have used some chili."

CHAPTER 36

*E*dith slid off his back, though she kept one hand on his furred shoulder. "Is it dead?"

I think so, he sent back telepathically, since he couldn't speak out loud in griffin form. **But it could be a trick. Stay back for a moment.**

He cautiously approached the fallen serpent, careful to keep his own body between it and his mate. He stared into the glassy crimson eyes, watching for any sign of life.

While he was still crouching in readiness, Fenrir trotted past him. Before Rory could call him back, the hellhound sniffed the forked tongue lolling out of the serpent's slack mouth.

Then he cocked a leg, and peed on it.

Edith choked. *"Fenrir!"*

The hellhound sat back on his haunches. **Is dead.**

"Good," Callum said. He was staring straight up. "Now what do we do about that?"

Rory followed his gaze. In the excitement of the fight with the… whatever it had been, he'd almost forgotten about the *other* creature.

Dark storm clouds churned above their heads, completely hiding the sun. The only light was the dull, hellish glow from the approaching wildfire. Burning embers swirled through the smoky darkness, carried by the rising wind.

"It's all right," Rory said, feeling the tension from the rest of the squad. "When the horned serpent was possessing me, I could sense something of its thoughts too. It went after me because it wanted to use our combined strength to kill that thing."

"But weren't they working together?" Blaise asked.

"No." He smiled at his mate. "You were right, Edith. When you came across the hare, the serpent was using its body to try to escape from the blaze. *That*," he pointed up at the gathering storm, "was hunting it. The serpent called it *the guardian*. The *last* guardian, in fact. That's why it turned up in Antler. It was going after the serpent again."

"The bear," Edith said, her eyes widening. "The serpent was in the bear."

"Right. That's what it does. It jumps from body to body. I think it ate minds, somehow. Every time it jumped into a stronger body, it got stronger too."

"Well, after Fenrir's demonstration, I think we can be pretty sure it's not jumping anywhere else." Joe was still in a tense crouch, clearly ready to shift at the slightest threat. "So what's our sparky friend doing here *now*?"

"Come to see that its enemy is really dead, I guess." Rory tipped his head back, deliberately keeping his body language loose and unthreatening as he searched the dense clouds. "Everyone just stay calm. It's not here to hurt us. It's on our side."

Lightning stabbed down.

"Has anyone told *it* that?" Blaise yelled as thunder shook the ground.

He'd shifted on reflex, covering both Edith and himself with his wings. The lightning hadn't struck *that* close, but white-hot afterimages of the jagged bolt still danced across his eyes. A towering pine some fifty feet away had become a smoking stump. Burning debris pattered down, setting light to the undergrowth.

Pinpoints of pain lanced through his feathers. He shook the smoldering splinters free, wincing. To his relief, Joe had shifted too. His armored coils protected the rest of the squad.

Stop! he roared at the unseen creature, with the full force of the alpha voice.

Electricity arced ominously through the black, boiling clouds. He hadn't really expected it to work—his power relied on natural dominance, and his opponent was even more powerful than himself.

But not more powerful than all of them.

He reached out mentally to his squad. *Everyone, lend me your strength. If Wystan's right and it is a shifter, we should be able to communicate telepathically. Let's see if we can get through to it.*

One by one, their minds linked with his. Wystan, gleaming and constant as the North Star. Joe, like sunlight on the surface of the sea, bright dazzle over dangerous depths. Callum, dark and silent, close to his back as his own shadow. Fenrir, all wordless emotion and fierce, snarling loyalty. Blaise's frozen fire.

Lastly, he reached for Edith. Their souls closed together like interlinked hands, completing the circle. Her bright courage steadied him. Together, they united the disparate strengths of the squad into a single powerful voice, focused on the threatening storm.

WE ARE NOT YOUR ENEMIES. They spoke together as one mind, one will. *BUT IF YOU DO NOT STOP, WE WILL STOP YOU.*

The clouds recoiled from the force of their shout. Through the shredding veils, a vast shape loomed over them, wings blocking out the sky. For a moment, a pair of blank white eyes stared down at them like twin moons, cold and remote.

The great wings swept round. Rory dug his claws into the ground, nearly bowled over by the thunderclap of displaced air as the creature flapped away. Flames leaped up in its wake, fanned by its wing beats. He sheltered Edith again from a surge of storm-tossed debris.

One burning branch fell on the dead serpent's tail. The corpse went up as though soaked in oil, spewing out thick plumes of acrid smoke.

Rory grabbed Edith, throwing her onto his back. *Wystan, with me —Callum, take Joe and Blaise! Fenrir, go, go!*

Fenrir phased out just as flame swept through where he'd been standing. Rory launched himself into the air, snatching Wystan up in his talons. Callum followed, wing beats labored as he struggled to gain height with his greater burden.

Fire engulfed the forest. He cupped his wings to catch the rising heat, soaring safely out of reach of the licking flames. Trees lit up like matches, the fire leaping from branch to branch in the blink of an eye.

Edith tugged on his feathers. "Rory. Look."

She wasn't staring down at the spreading devastation. From her posture, he could tell that her attention was fixed on something behind them. He banked, circling.

Trailing tattered veils of cloud, a vast shape soared away from the raging wildfire. It had a condor's broad wings and a heavy, hooked beak. Odd, angular patterns marked the storm-grey feathers like tribal tattoos, seething with electric white light.

"I know what it is," Edith whispered. Her voice shook with awe. "It's a Thunderbird."

CHAPTER 37

"*I* don't care if it's the motherloving Easter Bunny!" Rory had never seen Buck so furious. "You go after that monster and kill it! Right now!"

"Chief, it's long gone." Rory kept his own voice calm. "There was no way Callum and I could keep up with it while carrying everyone else."

Buck's fists were clenched so hard, Rory could see them shaking at his side. "Then you should have ditched the others. You took it on by yourself before."

Rory shook his head. "If I try to fight it without support, I'll just get myself killed. It's stronger than me. I'm pretty sure it was holding back the previous times I've faced it. On some level, it didn't really want to hurt me."

"Well it damn well wants to hurt other people," Buck snarled. "It's *killed* people."

"I know," Rory said grimly. "And I promise we'll work out a way to stop it. But right now, we have to stop this fire, before *it* claims any lives. It's going to take all of us to get it under control."

For a moment, Rory thought Buck might actually hit him. He braced himself, lifting his chin and meeting the chief's eyes steadily.

With a muttered curse, Buck lowered his fist, turning away. He clapped his hands together, attracting the attention of the rest of the crew.

"Listen up, boys and girls!" Buck jumped up into a fallen trunk, where they could all see him. "Situation's changed up top, and our lives are about to get a whole lot more interesting."

Tanner frowned, looking around at the crew as they gathered around Buck. "Where's Seth?"

"Didn't make it," Buck said curtly. "And if we're all not going to go the same way, we're going to have to move fast. So pay attention."

Every eye fixed on him...except for Edith's. She appeared to be totally focused on the pebble between her palms.

Buck scowled at her. "Am I boring you, Edith?"

"No, chief." Edith didn't raise her head. "I can either pay attention, or I can look at you and get distracted by every twitch of your face. I'm autistic."

Buck hesitated fractionally. Then he grunted.

"Fair enough," he said. "Okay, crew. Here's what we're going to do..."

"We have reached a new low," Blaise announced out of the darkness. "This is *awful*."

"I didn't think anything could be worse than the brisket." Joe's voice drifted mournfully from further down the line. "I was mistaken. I just put peanut butter all over my so-called chicken noodles. I thought it was going to be hot sauce."

"Did it improve the flavor?" Wystan asked hopefully, from somewhere over to Edith's right.

"Not even slightly. Fenrir, what have you got over there?"

Frog. Muffled crunching sounds emanated from the hellhound's direction. *Not sharing.*

Rory was a solid warmth against her side. His shoulder brushed against hers as he heaved a sigh.

She wrinkled her nose at him. "Don't tell me you'd actually prefer a raw frog."

"No." It was so dark, even sitting right next to him she could barely make out the curve of his smile. "I was just thinking about the time you brought us all beans. Remember that?"

There was a moment of reverent silence, as though the entire squad was gazing at some sacred, shining vision.

Blaise let out a low moan. "I would kill for some beans right now."

Edith didn't disagree. Abandoning the last of her rubbery, chemical-infused ration, she leaned against Rory instead. Even sweaty and covered in mud, he *still* managed to smell good.

He stroked stray tendrils of hair back from her face, tucking them behind her ear. His voice dropped to a deep, gentle rumble, pitched for her alone. "Okay?"

"You're the one who had a giant snake inside his skin earlier today." She nestled into the hollow of his shoulder. "And then worked fourteen hours straight cutting line. Are *you* okay?"

He chuckled ruefully. "I'm about ready to faceplant in the dirt. But at least we stopped the fire from getting to the town."

His satisfaction glowed in her heart, echoing her own. She smiled, then had to fight back a yawn. "Still got a lot to mop up."

His lips brushed the top of her head. "Other ground crews are coming in. Together, we'll get it contained. Buck's going to make sure we stay on this one to the end."

"In case the Thunderbird comes back?" She felt him nod. "Do you think it will?"

He was silent for a moment, gazing up at the smoke-shrouded stars. "I don't know. I don't think so. But I don't really have a clue what it wants. I don't understand why it set fire to the forest when its enemy was already dead."

She found his hand in the dark. "We're going to have to face it again sometime, aren't we."

He let out a long sigh. "I don't want to hurt it. But Buck's right. We can't let it hurt people."

She squeezed his fingers warningly. "Just as long as you don't get any silly ideas about going after it alone."

He bent his head to kiss her. "Never," he murmured against her lips. "I know where my strength lies."

His mouth tasted of smoke. Despite her exhaustion, fire lit in her blood. She curved her hands around the back of his neck, drawing him down deeper.

Wystan cleared his throat. "We *are* all keeping alert for spot fires, aren't we—*ow!* Who threw that?"

"Sorry," Blaise said, sounding not at all sorry. "Just clearing debris off the line. Didn't know you were over there. And there's no need for everyone to keep watch. I'll yell if I sense anything flaring up."

Rory's radio buzzed. He drew back from her at last, untangling himself enough to unhook it from his belt. She overheard him exchange a few quiet words with Buck.

"Good news, squad," Rory announced, clicking the radio off again. "Our relief shift has arrived. Another crew is hiking up to take over for the night. Buck says to make scratch camp and get some sleep."

"Oh, thank the tides." Joe paused, his voice turning dismayed. "Wait, scratch camp? Here?"

"We're going to pick back up at dawn. We have to stay in the area." Rory got up, pulling her to her own feet. "Fenrir, can you find us a good spot?"

Yes. Pack follow. Will lead to soft grass, good hunting. Fenrir's red eyes glowed in the night like beacons. *Many frogs.*

"Camping under the stars," Joe said gloomily. "Yay. If I'd been you, Edith, I would have stayed up in that fire lookout tower. At least you had a bed up there. And beans."

"And a bath," Edith said, grinning. "Well, a bucket, at least. Of cold water."

"A *bucket*." Joe made a pained sound. "Of *cold water*. Stop tormenting us by speaking of such unimaginable luxuries. I might cry."

Rory's low laugh rumbled through her chest. His arm tightened around her shoulders.

"Hope you aren't regretting your life choices," he murmured into her ear.

She was filthier than she'd ever thought it was possible to be. Every inch of her skin was black with soot. She was so tired she could have happily curled up right there on the bare earth and slept for a week. Her feet hurt, her lips were cracked, and the self-heating ready-to-eat meal *had* been utterly disgusting.

She snuggled closer to her mate. "Not in the slightest."

EPILOGUE

The roar of the helicopter vibrated his bones. His griffin yowled disconsolately in his mind, tail lashing at the tooth-rattling din.

Sorry, Rory said silently to his animal. *We can't always fly ourselves.*

He glanced around, checking on the rest of his squad. Most of them had strained, faraway expressions as they coped with their own agitated beasts. A shifter's wild nature generally didn't mix well with man-made forms of air transport.

Edith looked positively relaxed by comparison. She had her big headphones on, completely covering her ears, as she usually did when they travelled. She rocked in time with her music, hands fluttering gently.

Over the past few months, he'd learned to read the infinite subtleties of her ever-dancing hands. She was excited and on edge, but not distressed.

Of course, he didn't need her hands to tell him that. The mate bond glowed in his soul, sparkling like a diamond in the sun. He reached out to her, just because he could.

She didn't look round, but her head tilted. Her soul interwove through his. The private intimacy of that union never failed to take his breath away.

The intoxicating closeness of her soul reminded him of *other* forms of closeness that they'd shared recently. They'd had a whole three days of leave in between assignments. They'd scarcely left their bed the entire time. Three glorious days and nights treasuring her body, worshipping his mate...

He shifted position in his seat, surreptitiously tugging his turn out jacket lower.

Edith's bemused laughter rippled in his mind. *Even after three entire days? Haven't you had enough yet?*

"Of you?" he breathed back. He let the effect she had on him fill his heart. "Never."

She caught her lip between her teeth, cheeks pinking delightfully as his desire rippled down the mate bond. She tried to give him a stern look, which was completely belied by the way her own body was responding.

Stop that, she said, not entirely convincingly. *We're working.*

His own grin widened, but he desisted. They *were* working. Though maybe if they weren't too tired after their shift, they could find some secluded glade...

Wystan, who was sitting opposite them, cast him a faintly pained look. Rory shrugged at him, mouthing *sorry*. He didn't want to cause the unicorn shifter discomfort, but it wasn't *his* fault he had such a sexy mate.

Blaise let out a low whistle. She had her forehead pressed to the small window, hands cupped against the glass. "Wow. Will you look at that."

Rory leaned past Edith, peering out himself.

On second thought, they probably weren't going to be finding a nice private glade anytime soon.

As far as the eye could see, the land burned. Vast swathes of the Californian forest were actively ablaze, fire crowning the trees. Ugly, barren lines like rough roads cut through the once-pristine wilderness, from bulldozers desperately trying to halt the advance. Even as he watched, a tendril of fire probed at a trench, finding just enough uncleared fuel to snake across to the other side.

"Big," was Callum's only comment.

"Big is an understatement," Wystan said, looking pale. "The word 'apocalyptic' springs to mind."

"That's why we're here." Rory said, sitting back again. "At least we have plenty of help. There are hundreds of crews battling this thing. We just have to deal with our little bit."

"The hottest bit," Joe said. "Why couldn't we deal with the bit near a beach? Or at least near a nice town well-stocked with bars and admiring ladies?"

"I'll make sure to pass on your preferences to Buck." Rory grabbed hold of a strap as the helicopter lurched. "Looks like we're here. Let's go, team."

The helicopter hovered, not quite touching down. Along with the rest of the crew, they scrambled to grab their gear and jump down to the ground. Their transport didn't wait around, immediately lifting back into the sky to go and get the next crew.

"All right boys and girls!" Buck called as the helicopter thudded away. "Welcome to the Harley Fire, spike camp 15B. This is the biggest assignment most of you've seen yet, so stay tight and don't get lost. I'm going to go see what's what. Try not to break any limbs or start any fights or seduce anyone's girl for five whole minutes, *Joe*. Sit. Stay."

"She wasn't someone's girl, she was a grown-ass woman who was delightfully clear about what she wanted," Joe muttered as Buck stalked away. "That guy was just a possessive douchebro. And it only happened *one time*."

"So far," Wystan murmured.

Rory abruptly felt Edith tense. Her hands flurried. She clamped them to her sides, forcibly stilling them in a way he hadn't seen her do for months.

"Edith?" he asked, concerned. "What's wrong?"

She was staring across the wide, bulldozer-razed clearing. Another crew was lounging on the fresh-cut stumps, backpacks piled at their feet, clearly waiting for their own Superintendent to come back from the command meeting.

"You remember my previous crew? The one that fired me?" She jerked her chin, face pale under her freckles. "That's them."

At her side, Fenrir growled. *Courage, Stone Bitch. Have pack of your own, now. Show them your teeth.*

The other crew had noticed them as well. From their equipment, they were Type 2 hand crew, not hotshots—not qualified to run chainsaws or work the hottest part of the fire. A few of the men straightened. There was suddenly a lot more flexing going on.

Blaise rolled her eyes. *"Boys."*

A big, burly man wandered over. From the markings on the helmet tucked under his arm, he was a squad boss too. Clearly recognizing Rory as his counterpart, he gave him a cautious but not unfriendly nod.

"Hotshots, huh?" he said with respect. He offered his hand. "I guess we'll be following you today."

Edith had sidled out of sight behind him. Rory clasped the other man's hand firmly, looking him straight in the eye.

"We'll clear the way for you," he said. "Hope you can keep up."

"Oh, my squad are good. Strong men, real men, one and all." His gaze flicked over Rory's crew t-shirt. "Hey, Thunder Mountain! You're out of Montana, right?"

"That's right."

"We're from there too." The man hesitated. "Say…you guys hiring?"

"Not mid-season," Rory said. "Maybe next year. Why?"

"Always wanted to be a hotshot." The man glanced back at his own crew, his voice dropping. He tapped his wallet pocket meaningfully. "If there's anything I can do to, you know, get you to put in a good word for me with your chief…you get my drift?"

"You can put in an application like anyone else," Rory said coolly. "But I have to warn you, we only take the best."

Deliberately, he moved to one side, turning.

244

"Edith," he said in a loud voice that carried across the clearing. "You're on saw today."

Since it was a big, multi-crew assignment, they'd all labeled their helmets. *STONE* stood out stark and clear as she raised her head proudly.

"Sure thing, Rory," she said, without so much as a glance at her old boss or crew. "I'll go sort out the gear."

The other man's jaw had dropped. "E-Edith?" he stuttered. "Edith Stone?"

She gave him a cheery, dismissive wave. Her fingers rippled with silent laughter as she strode off, hips swinging.

Her old boss stared after her, eyes round with shock. "That—that was Edith Stone. You, uh...you *do* know what she is, right?"

"Yes." Rory settled his own helmet onto his head. "The best fire-fighter on my squad."

"His *face*," Blaise said yet again. She giggled, clinking water bottles with Edith as if making a toast. "Oh man. I wish I'd been in time to get a picture. That was epic."

Edith grinned. "Was he *very* jealous?"

"Sick as a dog," Blaise assured her. "Uh, no offence, Fenrir."

The hellhound, who was flopped in the shade with his tongue hanging out, waved his tail in a lazy wag.

"*And* we left them in the dust," Wystan said with deep satisfaction. He shaded his eyes, looking back down the hill. "They're still a good half mile back, by my reckoning."

Callum shrugged. "Only human."

"Hey!" Edith tossed a twig at him in playful mock-outrage. "What do you think *I* am?"

Callum's mouth curled up fractionally. "One of us."

They all looked up as Rory's shadow fell over them. He clipped his radio back to his belt, frowning.

"Break time's over, team," he said. "That was Buck. Control needs us to split here. There are two teams already working east and west over here. We're going to go reinforce one of them, and Tanner will take B and C squads to help the other."

"So which way are we going?" Blaise asked.

"Up to us. Tanner says he doesn't mind, so the choice is ours." Rory rubbed the back of his neck, scanning the dry, scrubby forest around them. "Anyone got a preference?"

Edith shook her head along with the others. Or, she realized, most of the others. Joe, who'd been splashing water over his head to cool down, had gone still. He stared intently down into his cupped palm.

"Joe?" she asked. "Something up?"

He jerked as though she'd startled him. "No. Nothing. West. We should go west."

Blaise huffed, shaking her head. "Of course you want the path that goes downhill."

"Yeah." Joe flicked water from his hand, his customary grin reappearing. "You know me. Anything for an easy life."

"West it is then." Rory shouldered his Pulaski. "Let's go."

They fell into line, hiking through the bone-dry undergrowth. Dust puffed up under Edith's boots. Her legs fell into easy, enjoyable rhythm, following Rory.

In no more than five miles, they heard saws working ahead. The ever-present smoke grew thicker. Ominous crackles undercut the roar of the chainsaws. Orange light flickered through the trees.

A full crew was already working on extending a fireline, racing the oncoming fire. The woman at the front looked up as they approached, powering down her chainsaw.

"Are we ever glad to see you," she said, pushing her safety helmet up her sweaty forehead. "We need all the help we can get to beat this thing."

Rory smacked palms with her, nodding. "Glad to be here. Where do you want us?"

She pointed. "There's a hellish tangle that way. If you could get through it, I'd be grateful. Which one of you is Animal Rescue?"

They all exchanged puzzled glances.

"Uh, none of us," Rory said, blinking. "Why?"

The woman swore colorfully. "There's a baby deer or something hiding in there. I think it's hurt. None of us have been able to coax it out. I called it in two hours ago. Those incompetent idiots at Control *promised* they were sending someone."

"Well, we might be able to help anyway." Edith could feel from the mate bond that Rory was stifling a grin. "We're pretty good with animals."

The woman swept her hand round in an inviting gesture. "Be my guest. The poor thing has been crying for its mother for hours. It's been breaking all our hearts."

Rory cocked an eyebrow round at them all as the woman rejoined her crew. "Huh. Just as well we came this way. Well, let's see what we can do. Fenrir, you'd better hang back a bit."

The hellhound grumbled, but lay down. The rest of them tagged along at Rory's heels. The 'tangle' that the woman had indicated was a solid wall of brambles with wicked, two-inch thorns. Rory crouched, trying to peer through it.

"Callum?" he asked. "Sense anything?"

Callum's eyebrows drew down. "Yes. But it's...odd."

A soft, plaintive call came from the heart of the thicket.

"Oh, poor thing," Edith exclaimed. "Whatever it is, it's just a baby."

"I think I see how it got in there." Rory pressed even closer to the ground. "None of us are going to be able to fit through, though."

Wystan was already unslinging his medical kit. "If we fire up the saw, we'll terrify it. It could hurt itself even further. Can you call it out, Rory?"

"Only one way to find out." Rory dropped his voice into a soft, gentle purr. *"It's all right, little one. We won't hurt you."*

There was a pause. The strange, chirping call came again, sounding uncertain.

"That's it." Carefully, Rory reached into the brambles. He used the thick sleeve of his protective jacket to hold the cruel thorns back, widening the gap. *"We're friends. We want to help. Come out."*

Brambles rustled. Slowly, tentatively, a white shape emerged.

It wasn't a deer.

"Wystan," Rory said, as they all stared at the trembling baby unicorn. "I think this one's for you."

~

Wystan's story continues in Wildfire Unicorn
- available on Amazon now!

ALSO BY ZOE CHANT

All these books are set in the same world, and feature cameos and cross-over characters.

Fire & Rescue Shifters

Firefighter Dragon

Firefighter Pegasus

Firefighter Griffin

Firefighter Sea Dragon

The Master Shark's Mate

Firefighter Unicorn

Firefighter Phoenix

Fire & Rescue Shifters: Collection 1 (Books 1-3)

Fire & Rescue Shifters: Collection 2 (Books 4-7)

The Sea Dragon's Lion

Coyote in the Sea

First Mission

Fire & Rescue Shifters: Wildfire Crew

Wildfire Griffin

Wildfire Unicorn

Wildfire Sea Dragon

Wildfire Pegasus

Wildfire Hellhound

Wildfire Phoenix

Fae Mates

Tithed to the Fae

I also have many more series set in different worlds! See the complete list at
www.zoechant.com

Made in United States
North Haven, CT
10 August 2022